BLACK SKY EVENT SEI

T.L. PAYNE

Utter Devastation
Black Sky Event Series, Book Two
Copyright © 2025 by T. L. Payne
All rights reserved.

No part of this book may be reproduced in any form or by any electronic or mechanical means, including information storage and retrieval systems, without written permission from the author, except for the use of brief quotations in a book review.

Don't forget to sign up for my spam-free newsletter at www.tlpayne.com to be among the first to know of new releases, giveaways, and special offers.

Created with Vellum

Contents

Preface	v
Prologue	1
1. Arthur Carlisle	7
2. Bee Carlisle	12
3. Willow Carlisle	19
4. Carson Carlisle	25
5. Bee	29
6. Carson	36
7. Knox Selway	40
8. Carson	44
9. Willow	50
10. Arthur	55
11. Carson	60
12. Willow	67
13. Bee	71
14. Willow	77
15. Carson	83
16. Willow	90
17. Carson	95
18. Arthur	100
19. Willow	104
20. Carson	111
21. Willow	117
22. Carson	124
23. Willow	130
24. Carson	136
25. Willow	142
26. Willow	149
27. Willow	158
28. Willow	165
29. Arthur	170
30. Bee	178
31. Carson	184
32. Carson	191

33. Carson	195
34. Carson	201
35. Bee	206
36. Willow	210
37. Carson	218
38. Bee	223
39. Carson	230
40. Willow	236
41. Willow	243
42. Willow	249
43. Willow	254
44. Bee	260
45. Willow	266
46. Willow	272
47. Willow	279
48. Carson	286
Also by T. L. Payne	293
About the Author	297

Preface

Real real towns, cities, and institutions are used in this novel. However, the author has taken occasional liberties for the story's sake, and versions within these pages are purely fictional.

Thank you in advance for understanding an author's creative license.

Prologue

This is the journal of Miguel Salazar.
If you're reading this, don't bother returning it. I'm dead.

✷ Journal Entry ✷

Tuesday, September 16

I suppose I should introduce myself—for whoever finds this after I'm gone.

My name is Miguel Salazar. I was born in Dodge City, Kansas, the son of immigrants who came to this country on green cards, working in the local slaughterhouses until they earned their citizenship. They are good, kind people. Honest. Hardworking. They deserved a better son than me. They taught me right and did their best to keep me in school. Before joining my crew, I was a straight-A student. I loved to read and had even written a book of my own, but in my neighborhood, book smarts got you nowhere. If you wanted to survive, you joined a gang.

My lawyer says they will transfer me to the "Castle on the Cumberland" on Friday to change into my scarlet-red death row uniform and wait to be executed. Kentucky State Penitentiary in Eddyville, Kentucky, will be where I die for my sins.

I'm not looking forward to the solitude of death row as much as I thought I would. It allows me too much time to think. I wish they'd just do it—right out there on the courthouse square—a firing squad would be appropriate. Don't you think? Would their family want to watch it? I've thought a lot about my last words to them—even though I told them already before my sentencing.

I'm sorry for what I did. Every time I close my eyes, I see their faces.

✷ Journal Entry ✷

Wednesday, September 17

Father Johnson told me to keep a daily journal to count my blessings and record my prayers. I thought it was stupid. What blessings? He said it would help keep my mind occupied and help me see the ways the Lord was still at work in my life. I don't think God listens to the prayers of men like me. Why would he? My only prayer now is for a quick death. The trial is over, and the sentence is final. They gave me the death penalty. I won't fight it. I deserve to die for what I did.

✷ Journal Entry ✷

Utter Devastation

Friday, September 19

I'm watching the sky explode. The colors! I don't know what took down the electric grid, but whatever it was, it left behind something beautiful. It feels odd. I should be dead. Maybe I should've been dead a long time ago. I thought today would be the day.

The bus was moving too fast when the sky lit up like Judgment Day. At first, it just looked like another summer storm rolling over the hills. But the sky turned this eerie shade of molten gold like the sun had cracked open and was bleeding fire across the clouds. Then the flickering started. Every light. Every engine. Every radio. Just gone.

I remember the guard up front, Harris, cursing as the traffic ahead suddenly stopped. The tires skidded as he tried to correct the skid, but the road had other plans. We were dead metal rolling. The bus tipped, flipped, and crumpled like an empty soda can. The screaming, the grinding of metal against asphalt, the sickening crunch of bone and glass—it all blended into one endless sound that felt like it was tearing my skull open.

When I came to, the bus was sideways in a ditch just outside a place called Caneyville. Maybe a few hundred people lived here before today. Maybe less. The windshield was shattered. The emergency lights flickered once and died. Most guards were slumped over in their seats, red pooling beneath them, steam rising from the cooling engine. A couple were still alive, moaning, but they wouldn't be for long.

And the prisoners? The ones that could walk were already gone, scattering into the woods and the back roads like roaches in the light. Some took off toward the town, looking for anything they could take. A few of them—the bad ones—lingered, looking at the wounded guards like scavengers watching something still twitching.

That's when I made the first choice. Not to run. Not to follow. I grabbed the first thing I could—a shattered piece of metal from the wreckage—and held it tight, my breath coming fast and shallow. I wasn't going to be a part of whatever came next. But I wasn't ready to stop it either.

Not yet.

✸ Journal Entry ✸

Saturday, September 20

It's been less than twenty-four hours since the lights went out, and Caneyville's not a town anymore. It's a carcass.

I walked the length of it at dawn, hoping I was wrong. Hoping the people here had found a way to fight back. But all I saw was proof that the worst of us had won. The gas station was a wreck, its windows busted in, shelves toppled, and blood smeared on the tile floor like someone had been dragged out kicking. One of the old men from the bus—Smitty, a small-time dealer—was still loitering around outside, stuffing his face with beef jerky. His eyes were wild and unfocused, like he'd already given up pretending to be anything other than a predator.

He saw me, smirked, and said, "Ain't no rules anymore, Ghost. Shouldn't waste time playin' a good guy."

I didn't answer. I just kept walking.

Farther up the road, I found a house with its front door wide open. Inside, the furniture was overturned, drawers ripped out, stuffing spilling from couch cushions. A family had lived here once. The pictures on the walls were still hanging, crooked, frozen in time, showing birthdays, vacations, and Christmas mornings. But the house was empty now. The kind of empty that didn't just mean "left in a hurry." Something bad had happened here.

I found them in the backyard. An older man and a woman, their faces slack, throats slit. They'd fought. The blood on the old man's hands told me that. But one against eleven wasn't much of a fight. I felt something heavy in my chest then. A weight that settled deep. I was looking at what I should have been. Just another body in the dirt. I wasn't supposed to be here. But then I heard it—a sound coming from the church down the road. A hymn, barely there, but enough.

That's how I found the survivors.

There are sixteen of us now. Twelve adults, four kids.

They're huddled in the church basement, whispering prayers that remain unanswered. The food won't last long. The water even less. And the others—the ones still out there? They've grown bored and started to hunt.

Q, or Quinnell Ramsland, the gang leader who got popped for trafficking underage girls, has taken over the old motel on the edge of town. I saw his people moving supplies there today, faces painted in streaks of soot and blood.

Daryl "The Butcher" has made a den out of the town clinic. I don't know what he's doing in there, but I saw a man go in and never come out. And Jon Hagen… I don't know where he is. That's what scares me most.

I have a guard's shotgun, which I took from his body before the wreck cooled. Four shells left. I can fight to protect the church. I can try. But it won't be enough.

✷ Journal Entry ✷

Sunday, September 21

It's day three since the lights went out and hell rained down on Caneyville, Kentucky. We're still on our own.

I lost two today. Dale and Adam.

We were heading toward the post office, looking for supplies, when we heard the screams. Adam ran ahead. He shouldn't have. By the time I caught up, Q's crew had him on his knees, hands bound, Q standing over him like he was an offering. I tried to stop them. I raised the gun. Shouted. Demanded. They smiled at me. Q nodded, and then they slit Adam's throat right in front of me. Dale tried to run. He didn't make it twenty feet before the bullets mowed him down. I should have fired. I should have killed them all.

But I didn't. I pulled back. I ran. Then I found the others and told them to stay put. Now, it's past sunset, and I'm writing this in the church attic while Q's crew are lighting torches down on Main Street, partying like they own the town—because they do.

I can't save these people. I never should have tried.

Tomorrow, I'm going to walk away.

Tomorrow, they'll be on their own.

ONE

Arthur Carlisle

Carlisle Residence
   Lakewood Heights
   Dallas, Texas
   Day Three

Three days had passed since the most devastating solar superstorm in modern history struck, plunging the world into chaos. The sound of glass shattering still made Arthur Carlisle flinch. He moved carefully in the darkness, his fingers brushing over the coffee table before reaching the window. He pulled back a corner of the heavy moving blanket that covered it just far enough to peek out. On the street outside, a small group of young people carried armloads of shoe boxes, electronics, and alcohol down the street. They weren't running. At this point, they didn't appear at all concerned about getting caught looting from the shopping center at the end of Arthur's block.

Behind him, Arthur heard a flick and spun around to see a tiny flame reflecting in the eyes of his wife, Katherine. He lunged forward, snatching it from her hand just as the spark flared to life.

With a sharp pinch, he extinguished it between his fingers before she could light the candle sitting on the coffee table. They couldn't risk it. Not again. "We need to keep a low profile, remember?"

The night before had been a lesson. A group of young people had come knocking on their door—asking for help, or so they'd claimed. Katherine, ever the teacher, had moved to let them in before Arthur could stop her. His seventy-five-year-old knees had slowed him down, but by the time he had reached her, her hand was already on the handle of the glass storm door. Arthur barely managed to stop her in time. When she hesitated, the leader of the group—a pockmark-faced teenager with cold eyes—had tried to yank open the door. Arthur had brandished his shotgun, forcing them to back away.

They laughed as they left.

Not angry. Not afraid. Laughing.

Arthur should have known something was off from the start. He should have warned Katherine about them after what he saw on the first day of the blackout at the middle school when he'd gone to pick her up. There, in the school's pickup line, he'd spotted that same girl—the one with half her head shaved, wearing a black jacket in ninety-degree weather, the one with the strange symbol on her backpack. Arthur had recognized it at once because he'd spent hours scrubbing the same symbol off his garage door months earlier. He had dismissed it back then as some random act of vandalism. Now, he knew better.

"I'm sorry, sweetheart. We can't light the candles. I'm just trying to keep us safe," he said.

He understood how difficult this was for her. Just three days ago, their lives had been normal. He had spent his mornings tinkering with his 1967 Chevy Impala SS, getting it ready for the Lone Star Nationals at the Texas Motor Speedway at the end of the month. Katherine had been teaching and planning where she wanted to spend Christmas break. They'd argued about where to go, back when arguments still felt important. Arthur had wanted to visit Carson in Colorado and then maybe go to D.C. to see Willow. Katherine had wanted a beach vacation—a cruise, sand, sun, and fruity drinks with umbrellas. Arthur had hated the idea.

The worst solar superstorm in modern history had made the choice for them. Now, huddled inside their Old East Dallas home in the dark, they tried to avoid attracting the attention of the crowds of people coming and going from the shopping center. Their once quiet Lakewood Heights neighborhood, filled with a mix of new builds and gracefully aging homes, had become unrecognizable by the foot traffic going through it.

Katherine reappeared a moment later with a can of tuna and a sleeve of crackers in hand. She set them on the coffee table next to the candle, then reached down to open one. The metal lid peeled back with a soft pop, releasing the sharp, briny scent of fish into the air.

"You should eat."

Arthur turned toward her but didn't move. "We should conserve. We don't know how long it will have to last."

Katherine huffed. "But we have all that stuff Carson left us. You said it was enough for seven days. Enough for Carson to arrive here."

Arthur glanced back toward the heavy window covering, still parted from when he had peeked outside. He gripped the fabric and pulled it shut. Carson should have arrived by now. Boulder, Colorado, was only a twelve-hour drive. Something had delayed him. "We need to be prepared for a longer wait."

Katherine exhaled sharply and moved around the coffee table to stand beside him. "But we have the groceries we got after the lights went out."

They had only got those because of Carson. When Carson's first emergency text had come through, Arthur had gone straight to the seven-day emergency pack in the guest room. Inside, he'd found several pages of instructions telling him what to do to survive until his son could make it to Dallas. One of those emergency procedures Carson had outlined—after filling the bathtub full of water—was to take the thousand dollars of cash he'd left in the envelope and rush to the grocery at the end of the block to buy food before it was all gone.

Buy as much shelf-stable food as the cash will purchase. Focus on canned meats like tuna, salmon, and canned chicken. Grab peanut butter, protein bars, nuts and seeds, dried fruits, hard cheeses. Avoid things that require cooking.

Arthur hadn't hesitated.

He had taken the envelope of cash Carson had left and, after picking up Katherine from school, stopped at a neighborhood grocery and bought shelf-stable food.

"Yes, but like I said, we don't know how long it will have to last."

He'd inventoried everything right away and hidden most of it in places around the house and garage that he hoped no one would look—if those kids forced themselves inside. He and Katherine had bought another four weeks of food but weren't able to grab enough bottled water. Fortunately, what was in the bathtub, along with the forty gallons in the water heater, would last the two of them for another three weeks if they didn't do laundry or use more than a gallon a day each.

There wasn't enough to flush the toilet, so Arthur had rigged up a five-gallon bucket in the garage for them to use as a makeshift potty. He had lined the rim with leftover foam pipe insulation and layered the inside with sand from an old bag in the shed. Each time they used it, they added another scoop of sand and a little kitty litter he kept for oil spills. It helped with the smell.

Katherine moved sideways and sat on the sofa. "Do you really think it will take them that long to get the lights back on?"

Arthur exhaled slowly. He didn't want to upset her, but she needed to know the truth. He lowered himself onto the sofa beside her and took her hand in his. "Carson said it could take months."

Katherine flinched as if he'd struck her. "That can't be right. I can't accept that."

"Whether you accept it or not, that's reality, dear."

She didn't respond right away. Instead, she just sat there, staring at the can of tuna. It was open, and now they had to eat it. He didn't want to ration food like they were in some kind of war zone. But the what-ifs concerned him.

Finally, she whispered, "What happens if Carson doesn't come?"

Arthur tightened his jaw, turned from the window, and met her gaze. "Carson *will* come. If he said he would, nothing will stop him," he said with certainty. His son was resourceful. Smart. Prepared. Arthur wished he'd asked Carson more questions and pressed him on what came next. Surely, Carson didn't intend to stay in Dallas while it collapsed around them. Then he recalled the group text Carson had sent warning them of the solar superstorm.

... *Mom, stay put. I'm coming to you.*

Carson adored his mother. He'd want to protect and care for her in this crisis. Would he leave him and Katherine to go to her, or did he have another plan that involved them all? But if he didn't get here soon, leaving might not be an option.

Outside, the sound of shattered glass echoed down the street. Arthur's stomach clenched. They weren't the only ones trying to survive this. And some people weren't just waiting for things to go back to normal. They were ready to tear it all down.

Arthur glanced toward the door. All the doors were reinforced with steel brackets and boards, according to Carson's instructions. He said they would hold. No one could kick the door in to gain entry, but all it would take to break through the two-by-four lumber across the window would be a hammer or a saw. A determined person could eventually get inside.

Arthur ran a hand through his thinning, silver hair.

Then...

Then he'd have to stop them.

TWO

Bee Carlisle

Carlisle Residence
Wild Plum Lake
Highland, Arkansas
Day Three

"Stay with me, Ezra! Stay with me!" Bee Carlisle's own voice echoed in her head as she gripped Ezra's hand. His blood was warm and sticky between her fingers. The chaotic scene back at her home on Wild Plum Lake replayed over and over in her mind —the moment Audree's ex had burst through the window, the flash of the gun, the way Ezra had staggered back, his face twisting in shock and pain in unison with Audree's gut-wrenching screams as Jimmy ripped her baby from her arms.

Now, Bee sat rigid in the back seat of her neighbors' minivan. Her nerves were frayed to the breaking point on the ten-minute drive to the emergency room. Ezra's head lolled against the window, his breath shallow, his hand pressed to his shoulder where blood bloomed across his shirt. Behind them, Audree rocked back

Utter Devastation

and forth, clutching her baby's blanket to her chest, her breath coming in sharp, ragged gasps.

"Almost there," Mark gritted out as he took the turn onto the highway. His wife, Gretchen, was in the passenger seat.

Audree let out a wail and buried her face in the soft fabric of the blanket. "He has my baby," she sobbed. "I should have fought harder! I should have gone after him—"

Bee turned in her seat and placed a firm hand on Audree's thigh. "We'll get him back, Audree. As soon as Ezra's at the hospital, Mark will take you straight to the police station. They'll get Josiah back to you."

Audree's tear-filled eyes lifted to meet Bee's, full of fear. "What if he hurts him before they get there? Josiah's not his kid. Mark has just done this to punish me."

Gretchen twisted in her seat to face them. "He won't," she said, her voice steady and certain. "Then he'd have no hold over you."

Bee wanted to believe her. But as the hospital's emergency sign came into view, the only thing she knew for sure was that none of them would rest until that baby was safe.

Cars clogged the emergency room drop-off lane, leaving no room to maneuver. The small parking lot was full; some vehicles were even double-parked, blocking others in.

"There's nowhere to park," Gretchen said as they pulled in.

Bee reached for the door handle. "Just stop here—I'll run in and get help."

"No. I'll carry him!" Mark shoved the van into Park.

Bee reached out for Ezra's hand. "Hang on, Ezra. We're at the hospital. They'll take care of you."

Mark yanked open the back passenger door and had Ezra out in one swift motion. Bee rushed to his side, gripping Ezra's hand as they hurried toward the entrance. The automatic doors remained closed as they approached. A handful of ashen-faced people loitered just inside. One of them pushed the doors open manually and stepped aside as Mark and Bee rushed in. Dim emergency lights cast shadows over the waiting room, the hum of a struggling backup generator the only sound beneath the murmur of anxious voices.

"We need help here!" Mark's voice boomed through the crowded space.

Silence. No response.

Bee's pulse pounded in her ears as she scanned the room. The reception desk sat empty, its computer screens dark. A few chairs lay on their side, abandoned in haste. No nurses, no doctors—only rows of tense faces, eyes darting between them and the hallway beyond, as if waiting for someone to emerge.

Mark cursed under his breath and adjusted Ezra's weight. "Enough of this!" He veered toward a side door. Bee was right beside him, moving through into a dimly lit hallway.

"Can we get some help here?" Bee shouted. "Nurse! Doctor!"

A door burst open at the end of the corridor, and a woman in scrubs sprinted toward them. "What happened?" she demanded, already signaling for help.

"Gunshot wound to the chest," Mark said.

The nurse spun around, shouting for assistance this time. Within seconds, a gurney appeared. Wheels rattled against the linoleum. Hands reached out, taking Ezra from Mark and Bee, whisking him down the hallway behind a set of double doors.

Bee exhaled sharply and turned to Mark. "I've got this. You get Audree to the police."

Mark gave a firm nod and took off through the waiting room doors, disappearing into the night. Bee pivoted, her heart still pounding as she followed the medical staff into the trauma room. The fluorescent lights overhead glared down, making the sterile white walls feel almost suffocating.

"What's his name?" one of the nurses asked.

"Ezra. Ezra Turner," Bee replied.

The nurses moved with seamless coordination. One sliced

through Ezra's blood-soaked shirt with trauma shears, while another prepared IV fluids and pain medication.

"Open your eyes, Ezra. Stay awake," a third nurse said as she set up the cardiac monitor and attached sticky leads to his clammy skin.

One of the nurses glanced at the door. "Where's the doc?" she called over her shoulder.

"Coming," another answered as she snapped on a pair of gloves.

Ezra groaned, his head shifting. His eyes fluttered open, glassy and unfocused.

"Stay with us, Ezra," one of the nurses said, adjusting his oxygen mask.

Bee's fingers curled into fists at her sides. They had to keep him alive long enough to get him out of there. From what she knew, White River Medical was only a Level III trauma center. Under normal circumstances, they'd focus on stopping the bleeding, starting fluids, and keeping him stable before transferring him to Little Rock for surgery.

But these weren't normal circumstances.

Outside the window, the hospital's backup generator rumbled steadily, the deep mechanical hum filling the silence. A few weeks ago, she might not have given it a second thought. But now it was the only thing keeping this place running.

Three days.

It had only been three days since the world had gone dark. Three days since the coronal mass ejection had slammed into Earth's magnetosphere, frying transformers, overloading power stations, and plunging entire regions into chaos. Bee replayed her last conversation with Carson, his voice steady as he reassured her about the predicted solar storms.

"Northeast Arkansas won't be affected, Mom," he had said with absolute certainty. He'd been wrong. Carson was a space weather prediction scientist. If he had foreseen the severity, he would have warned her. An image of the seven-day bag he'd left in her closet flashed through her mind. She'd forgotten all about it until then.

A sharp pang twisted in her gut. *Carson and Willow.* Her children—one in Boulder, the other in Washington, DC. She hadn't heard a word from them since everything went dark. No texts or calls. No way to know if they were safe. There had been no warning. No time to prepare. One moment, everything was normal—airports bustling, traffic humming, life moving as usual. Then the next, the power grid failed, and the world plunged into darkness. No electricity. No phone service. No internet.

Bee pressed her back against the wall near the trauma room door in an effort to stay out of their way. The erratic beeping of the monitor punctuated the tense atmosphere as they worked to stabilize Ezra. And he wasn't the only one fighting to survive. Bee glanced at the nurses, their faces tight with exhaustion. How much longer could they keep going like this? How many patients would die because help was out of reach?

The door burst open, and a doctor strode in. His scrubs were wrinkled and spotted with blood and who knows what else. Bee's gaze dropped to the name badge clipped to his shirt. *Dr. Mitchell.* She stared at the name tag a moment longer. *Mitchell.* It stirred something. Then it clicked—his wife. She'd met her once at a fundraiser for the library, years ago. Polished, soft-spoken, the type who always sent thank-you cards and brought lemon bars to school events. She'd briefly mentioned her husband was a doctor. Small world. Smaller, now.

He spared Bee a fleeting glance before assessing Ezra. "What've we got?" he asked, snapping on gloves as he moved to the bedside.

"Gunshot wound to the left infraclavicular region," the nurse reported. "Possible vascular involvement. BP's seventy over forty and dropping—heart rate's pushing one hundred and forty." She tightened the IV line. "We've started two large bores running fluids."

Bee stared at the doors, her pulse still hammering in her ears. She pressed a fist to her mouth and steadied her breathing, trying not to think about the way Ezra's body had gone still as the doctor barked orders over the shrill beeping of the monitors.

Dr. Mitchell swore under his breath. "He needs blood. Get O-negative until we can type him. We need to get a central line in, now!"

One of the nurses darted out the door while another moved to insert a fresh IV into Ezra's other arm.

Bee edged forward. "Can you do surgery here?"

Dr. Mitchell gave her a tight look, his hands already pressing against Ezra's wound, assessing the damage. "No. We'll stabilize him, but he really needs a trauma surgeon in Little Rock."

Bee's stomach twisted. "How soon can he be transported?"

"That's the problem." He shot a glance at the nurse, who was adjusting the oxygen flow. "Any update from Little Rock?"

"No, sir. We still can't communicate with them."

The doctor shifted his gaze to Bee. "The hospital's landlines are down, and cell service is out, too. EMS tried using shortwave radios, but even those aren't working. MedFlight is grounded. Without power at regional airports and with fuel running low, helicopters aren't able to fly. Even if we could get Ezra to Little Rock by ambulance, the roads are all jammed, and there is no guarantee the trauma center there won't be overwhelmed."

Bee's pulse spiked.

"We'll do everything we can to keep him stable until we can get him out of here."

Ezra groaned, his fingers twitching as his eyelids fluttered. Bee stepped closer, reaching for his hand. His skin was clammy and cold.

"I'm here, Ezra," she murmured.

His lips parted, but no words came. His breathing hitched. The monitors beeped a warning.

"Dammit!" Dr. Mitchell said. "He's crashing!"

The room exploded into motion. The doctor shouted orders, his hands moving faster as the heart monitor's rhythm grew erratic. Bee's stomach dropped.

"Charge the paddles," someone called.

Bee backed against the wall, her breath locked in her throat. The last thing she saw before someone pushed her back out into the hallway was the doctor pressing the defibrillator to Ezra's chest.

Then the doors slammed shut, leaving her outside. Waiting. Helpless.

THREE

Willow Carlisle

Rosewick Crossing Apartments
La Plata, Maryland
Day Three

"How is he doing?" retired Colonel Byron Guynn asked from the doorway to the bedroom.

Willow Carlisle rose from the chair beside the bed and crossed the dark room. "He's sleeping. I think he's having nightmares, though." She stepped around the older man into the small hall outside her bedroom and closed the door behind her.

"He's been through a lot in the last three days. Nightmares are to be expected."

She still didn't know all the details of Knox's journey since the solar superstorms struck Earth. Somewhere along the way, he'd gotten caught in the crossfire of someone else's gunfight. Now, after emergency surgery, he lay on her bed, recovering from a gunshot wound to his left biceps. A blood transfusion would have hastened the process. However, due to the overwhelming volume of emergent cases, the hospital had run out of blood products.

Colonel Guynn turned and led Willow into the living room. She moved to the sliding glass doors that led to her second-story balcony, where hours earlier they'd barricaded the door with supplies scavenged from the home improvement store across the street from her apartment complex. They'd avoided trouble there but hadn't been so fortunate at the pawn shop.

After trading Guynn's gold watch and her diamond stud earrings for a shotgun and thirteen shells, they'd encountered a small group of men loitering outside the shop, intent on taking the weapons and ammo from them. Willow shuddered at the memory. It had all happened so fast. One minute, the dude was lunging for the shopping bag containing the shotgun shells. The next, he was reaching for his knife. The image was seared into her brain, along with the moment the bullet from her pistol struck him. She could still see the look on his face as he dropped to the ground, clutching his chest. She'd killed a man, and that fact never left her thoughts.

"You should get some sleep," Guynn urged.

Willow turned to face him. She wasn't sure where she'd be if he hadn't agreed to give her a ride home. It still amazed her that she'd asked a stranger for a ride, but she was mentally and physically exhausted. Getting out of Washington DC had been harrowing, to say the least. Chaos struck after the solar storms hit—starting with the fire at her office building. After she and a fellow journalist assisted the injured to the hospital, she'd struck out for home on foot due to the total gridlock of the city streets. It was a horrific experience, with looting and violence everywhere.

"I can't sleep, Colonel. My mind won't shut off." She moved to the sofa and lowered herself onto the cushion. "In the military, did you ever have to kill anyone?"

He hesitated for a moment.

"Yes. Lots of the enemy," Guynn said. "It was my job."

Willow swallowed hard. Shooting someone hadn't been in her employment description. She was an investigative journalist, not a soldier or police officer. Yet, she'd had to take a life to save herself and Guynn.

"How'd you deal with it?" she asked.

"Honestly?"

She nodded.

"I drank for ten years, destroying two marriages and losing the respect of my children."

"I'm sorry."

"Me, too." Guynn leaned forward, resting his elbows on his knees, his gaze steady on Willow. "But you don't have to go down that path. And you shouldn't."

Willow's throat tightened. "Then what do I do?"

He let out a slow breath. "First, you accept the truth—you did what you had to do. You survived. That doesn't make you a bad person."

"It doesn't feel that simple."

"It's not," he admitted. "But you can't let it eat you alive. You don't dwell on the moment you pulled the trigger. You focus on why you did it and who you saved. What you still have to fight for."

She nodded, absorbing his words. She was glad it had been the other guy and not Guynn. He was a good man, and the world was short of those types of people.

"And you talk about it," he continued. "Not necessarily with me, but with someone you trust. Don't bottle it up, don't try to outrun it. It'll catch you every time."

Willow let out a shaky breath. "And if it already feels like it's catching up?"

He gave her a long, knowing look. "Then you meet it head-on. You acknowledge what happened, but you don't let it define you. You keep moving forward, one step at a time."

She exhaled, her hands relaxing just a little. "Did it ever get easier for you?"

Guynn's lips pressed into a thin line. "No. But I got better at carrying it." He sat down beside her and placed his hand on her shoulder. "You will, too." He stood. "I'll make you some chamomile tea. That should help relax you."

"I can get it," she said, standing.

"How about you grab the tea, and I'll light the propane stove?"

She smiled. "Deal. Are you having some?"

"I'm having strong black coffee. Black as death."

Willow raised an eyebrow. "You won't sleep if you drink that."

"That's the idea."

"You're going to stay up all night? Is that necessary?"

He removed the rod from the tracks of the sliding door and slid it open. Raised voices drifted in.

"Yep. I think it's prudent," Guynn said as he stepped out onto the balcony.

Willow grabbed two mugs from the cabinet and then retrieved a tea bag from the container. On her way to the balcony, she picked up the canister of instant coffee, unsure how much it took to make a mug of "black as death" Joe. Upon joining Guynn, Willow was accosted by the smell of smoke. "Where is that coming from?"

"Down the block. I'm not sure what's burning."

She wrinkled her nose. "Smells like tires."

"Those too," Guynn said, taking the mug from her and scooping four large scoops of coffee into it.

After the water was boiling, Guynn poured it into Willow's cup and then filled his own. They stood on the balcony, watching the chaos play out across the road. People were fist fighting in the parking lot outside the home improvement store. Willow turned her back to the scene, having witnessed enough violence for a lifetime, and took a seat in a chair at the tiny bistro table Knox had helped pick out. Guynn lowered himself into the one across from her and stared up at the vividly colored night sky. Neither spoke, each lost in their own thoughts as they drank their beverages.

Minutes passed, and Guynn had drained his mug. "I think I need one more."

He rose, and while he made his way to the kitchen for more water, Willow stood and glanced in the direction of the fire. Below her, in the complex's parking lot, she heard hushed voices. She shifted her gaze but didn't see anyone. She moved to the opposite end of the balcony and leaned over the railing.

"Hey!" she shouted when she spotted the two men and one woman. "Get away from that truck!" She dropped her hand to her waist, ready to pull her pistol from its holster, only to find it wasn't there. For a moment, she panicked, unable to recall what she'd done with the firearm after firing at the man at the pawn shop. And then she recalled Guynn taking it from her trembling hands. *He must still have it.* "Get away from the vehicle!" she shouted once more before moving toward the open sliding door to go out to confront them.

Guynn stopped her as she crossed the living room. "Don't worry about the Suburban." He gestured to a pile of parts in the corner of the living room.

She hadn't noticed them there before. "What's that?"

"The battery, alternator, starter, spark plugs, and wires. Our transport's not going anywhere without those."

"When did you do that?"

"When we first got back here before unloading the vehicle. You were up here checking on Knox."

Willow smiled. "Smart. That sounds like something Knox would have done."

"It's got a kill switch installed under the dash to prevent theft, but a determined person might be able to feel around and find it. So, I disabled it." The lines on his forehead deepened. "My main concern is making a quick getaway, but that's already difficult with Knox and his condition." He stepped back out onto the balcony and leaned over the rail.

Willow followed and stood by his side. "They're gone."

"For now."

She stared down at the Suburban. "What about the gas? Can't they steal that?"

He reached into his pocket and retrieved his keys. "It's got a locking gas cap. I put that on there just before coming to DC. I suppose they could puncture a hole in the fuel tank, but there wasn't much in there to start with. I was going to scavenge for more in the morning."

"We should have grabbed fuel cans while we were at the home improvement store," Willow said.

"I've got two in the back. I stole them from the bed of a truck in the hospital parking lot."

"You did? How did I not see that?"

"You were in the recovery room with Knox."

Willow smiled. "How much fuel will we need to reach your friend's place in Missouri?"

"We're not going to Missouri."

Willow's heart sank. "We're not?"

"No." He turned and filled the kettle with the water he'd retrieved from the kitchen and lit the stove again. "We're all heading to Arkansas. I think a girl needs her mother at a time like this."

FOUR

Carson Carlisle

Commerce City, Colorado
Day Four

The sun had just cleared the horizon when Carson and Julie crested a small hill on 56th Ave East. The steady hum of their tires rolling over cracked asphalt was the only sound between them. Sophie, secured in her carrier, let out a soft chirp, her tiny claws scratching against the plastic carrier. Carson shifted on his bike seat and scanned the horizon. What he saw made his stomach clench.

Julie's face paled as she pulled up beside him. "Jesus…"

The scene ahead was a wasteland of charred devastation. A fire had burned hot and fast, fueled by dry brush, leaving nothing but blackened earth and the skeletal remains of homes, businesses, and lives that had vanished in the inferno. The ground around them had turned to ash, and the once-thriving terrain was now an endless graveyard of devastation. Thin tendrils of steam curled from where embers still smoldered beneath the surface.

Carson inhaled and immediately regretted it—the acrid stench clung to his throat; it was like breathing in death itself. He leaned over the handlebars of his bike, his gut roiling from the sight. He had expected destruction—he had seen enough of it already. But this? It was worse than anything he had imagined.

Julie swallowed hard beside him. "All those people. If only we—"

"Don't," Carson snapped, shaking his head. He couldn't afford to think about that.

A gust of wind kicked up a cloud of ash, making Julie cough as she pulled her scarf over her nose and mouth. "Should we keep going this way?" she asked.

Carson hesitated. The road ahead was dangerous, but going south now would leave them too close to Denver—and potential trouble. They had no choice.

"We stick to the route," he said. "But we stay sharp. No stopping, no talking to anyone. Just keep moving." Carson clenched his jaw and forced his eyes forward. Ahead, the smoke still billowed on the horizon, a thick, toxic haze that blurred the edges of the sun. The pavement beneath them was cracked and crumbling, heat still rising from the scorched earth.

Julie rode alongside him. "What if the fire kicks back up?"

Her concerns were valid. If the fire had spread just a little farther ... if the wind had shifted in the wrong direction—if anything had gone differently—they'd be trapped. He swallowed hard. *Keep moving.* That was all that mattered now. Julie shot him a glance, waiting for his lead. He forced himself to focus. "Then we find another way," he said, his voice steadier than he felt.

No further words were necessary.

Carson and Julie were quiet as they continued east, but soon, the thickening smoke forced them to turn south just before East 470 Highway. Hacking and coughing, Carson led the way. As they rode through the ruined neighborhood, he heard something. *Survivors?* Without a word, Carson veered off the road onto a side street, weaving around burned-out cars and debris.

"What are you doing? Julie asked, catching up with him.

"Didn't you hear that?"

"What?"

"A kid."

Julie raised an eyebrow. "A child?"

"A small child is crying."

"I didn't hear it."

"I did." Carson turned toward the sound.

Carson didn't think anyone could have survived the wildfire, but he was sure he'd heard a voice. He slammed the brakes on his bike, his pulse hammering.

"Listen," he whispered.

Julie stopped beside him, holding her breath. A cry. Faint but unmistakable.

"I hear it," she said, pointing east. "Over there."

Without hesitation, they raced down the scorched street through debris. The sound came again—a child's wail, raw with fear.

"Look!" Julie pointed toward the only house left standing amid the destruction. A lone survivor in a sea of ruin.

Sitting on the curb out front was a small child, no more than five or six. Barefoot. Dust-streaked. Crying. Carson and Julie skidded to a stop, but the moment the girl saw them, she jumped up and bolted for the front door. Julie dropped her bike and held up her hands.

"Hey, sweetie, it's okay! We won't hurt you."

The girl hesitated, gripping the doorknob with tiny, trembling fingers.

Julie took a slow step forward. "We're here to help. Is your mommy or daddy home?"

Wide, tear-filled eyes met hers. "No."

"Who's watching you? Grandma?"

"No."

Julie knelt beside her. "My name's Julie, and this is Carson. What's yours?"

"Raelynn," she sniffled.

As Julie spoke to the child, Carson scanned the charred neighborhood, his mind racing. How had this house been spared when everything around was nothing but ashes? How had this child survived? Had anyone inside survived?

Julie stepped closer. "Are you here alone?"

Raelynn shook her head. "No."

Julie glanced back at Carson. "Who's with you then?"

"Henry."

Julie softened. "Can we talk to Henry?"

Raelynn's brow furrowed. "He can't talk."

Julie exchanged a look with Carson.

"Why not?"

"He's a baby," Raelynn said as if they should know that fact.

"It's just you and your baby brother here?"

She nodded.

"Where's your mommy and daddy?"

"At work."

"They left you here without a babysitter?"

"No. Addison was watching us, but she left to get help during the fire." Raelynn's lower lip trembled. "She said to wait here, and she'd come right back, but she never did. I waited and waited."

Julie ran a hand over Raelynn's tangled hair. "Can we come in and check on your baby brother?"

Nodding, Raelynn took her hand and turned toward the door.

FIVE

Bee

White River Medical Center
Cherokee Village, Arkansas
Day Four

While Bee waited outside the door to Ezra's trauma room, listening to the medical staff attempt to save his life, Rex, the liquor store owner, appeared at her side. She glanced up, tears staining her cheeks.

"How is he?" Rex asked.

"Fighting for his life."

"I saw you guys pull in and rushed over right after Mark tore out of the parking lot. What happened?" He nodded at the blood on her hands and blouse.

"An intruder shot Ezra," Bee said, shifting her gaze back to the door, willing it to open and for the doc to emerge with good news.

"Anyone else injured?"

Bee wasn't in the mood to play twenty questions. She pivoted toward him and gave him the short version of the story.

"Jimmy Smatter shot Ezra?"

"And then he took his girlfriend's baby and fled."

Rex exhaled sharply, running a hand over his close-cropped hair. "Jimmy Smatter. That kid used to be a straight-A student, back when his world was stable—before his mom got hooked on meth and overdosed."

Bee had no sympathy for a man like Jimmy. It didn't matter who he used to be in the past. Now, he was a violent criminal.

Rex shifted his weight. "Can I get you anything, Bee? I've got food and water in my RV."

"No." Bee barely registered the offer. Her nails dug into her palms, frustration coiling tight inside her.

"Let's find you a seat, Bee," Rex said, placing his arm around her shoulders. "I'll go get you something stronger to calm your nerves."

Her heart ached as he led her toward the waiting room. "I feel like I'm drowning, Rex. Ezra, baby Josiah, my kids."

Hours had passed while Ezra fought for his life down the hall, and as morning dawned, all Bee could do was wait. She slumped against the hard plastic chair, exhaustion pressing down on her like a lead balloon. Families packed the hospital waiting room, huddling together and murmuring prayers. Others stared at the walls, lost in their own private grief. The generators kept the hospital running, but the air circulation was weak, and it was stifling inside. She hadn't slept. Every time she closed her eyes, she saw Ezra bleeding out on her guest room floor. Heard Audree's screams. Felt the cold, gnawing fear that her world was unraveling.

She rubbed her face, blinking against the blurriness creeping into her vision. Her hands trembled as she fisted them in her lap. Carson, Willow, and Knox—where were they? Were they safe? Did they have food? Water? She couldn't stop picturing their faces, and the not knowing was tearing her apart. She was nearly ready to

Utter Devastation

crack from the worry when the double doors swung open. Dr. Mitchell strode out, looking as exhausted as she felt. Bee shot to her feet, her stomach twisting into knots. Rex, who'd been pacing the floors, came to her side.

"He's stable," the doctor said, and just like that, her knees buckled. Rex grabbed her arm and steadied her.

Bee let out a shaky breath and pressed a hand to her chest. "He's alive?"

The doctor nodded. "Yes. We got him through surgery, but he's weak. He won't wake for several more hours. You should go home and get some rest."

Home? The word had lost its meaning. Where was home now? It was a crime scene. She wasn't sure she'd ever feel safe there again. But she nodded anyway. "Thank you." She turned away, feeling hollow. Relief should have filled her, but it was tangled with the weight of everything else. Ezra had survived, yet the world was still crumbling around her.

Rex led her to the entrance. "C'mon," he said. "I'll take you home."

Bee followed him outside into the early morning chill. The sky was streaked with the first rays of dawn, but the town was eerily quiet. No hum of traffic, no streetlights. Just silence. They walked next door to Rex's liquor store, where his cousin stood watch with a rifle slung over his shoulder.

"How's Ezra?" he asked.

"Stable," Rex replied. "I need to borrow your truck to take Ms. Bee home."

He gave Rex a quick nod, handing over a set of keys.

Rex led Bee to an old pickup parked behind the store. She climbed in, exhaling as she leaned her head back against the seat. A moment later, the truck rumbled to life, and they pulled away from the hospital.

"You okay?" Rex asked.

She didn't answer right away. "I don't know."

Rex glanced over at her. "Things are gonna get worse, Bee. This is just the start."

She turned her head, watching him in the dim light. "How much worse?"

Rex returned his gaze to the road. "The store shelves are already bare. When the generators fail, the wastewater treatment plant will stop working. Sewage will back up into people's homes. Water's already stopped flowing. Won't be long before folks get sick from drinking whatever they can find. The hospital's already over capacity. There won't be enough doctors or nurses to treat everyone."

She knew he wasn't exaggerating, and Bee shivered at the thought. "Carson showed me how to filter water from the lake behind my house." The memory of the bag he'd left in her closet surfaced. At least she'd have clean water. But what about her neighbors? What about their kids? Bee rubbed her hands together, trying to shake off the chill that had nothing to do with the morning air. "I can't stop thinking about Audree and Josiah," she admitted. "It's been hours since Mark took her to the police station. They should be home by now, safe … and Jimmy should be behind bars."

Rex made a low sound in his throat, neither agreement nor disagreement. "Yeah … should be."

Bee caught the edge in his voice. "What?"

Rex exhaled, his grip tightening on the wheel. "I don't like banking on 'should be.' That kid's a cockroach. You think he won't find a way to wiggle out of this?"

Bee frowned, her stomach knotting. She wanted to believe Jimmy was locked away, and Audree and her baby were finally free of him. But doubt slithered into her mind, coiling tight. She shook her head and focused on the immediate crisis. "Even if they're safe for now … what about the rest of us? What happens when people start running out of food?"

Rex's expression darkened. "They'll do whatever it takes to get more."

Bee swallowed.

"I've been thinking a lot about that. If we don't get ahead of this, we're screwed."

She turned toward him. "What do you mean?"

"My neighborhood is closing ranks. We're fortifying. People are already getting desperate, and it won't be long before they start going door to door, looking for anything they can take."

Bee stared at him. "You're talking about turning people away?"

"We have to. No one has enough to feed an army of starving strangers. We take care of our own, or we won't survive either."

"You make it sound so ... heartless."

"It's not heartless," Rex said. "It's survival. We're not talking about handing out an extra can of beans here and there. We're talking about the floodgates opening. You give to one, you give to all. And then what? You're standing in your own house with an empty pantry while they're walking away with your last meal?"

Bee thought about Bob, her nosy neighbor, and how he'd watched her when she fed her neighbors spaghetti that first day. He'd seen her generosity and what she was willing to share. Would he try to turn people against her if she didn't do things his way? She glanced out the window at the darkened town, the otherworldly glow of the auroras waning in the early morning light. She wanted to believe people would come together—help each other. But fear made people do terrible things. "Isn't there something else we can do?" she asked quietly. "Some way to help, rather than just shutting people out?"

Rex sighed. "No one survives this alone. But that doesn't mean we open our doors to just anyone. A group only works if everyone contributes. If you don't have food, you need a skill. Something to offer. Otherwise, you're just another mouth to feed."

Bee didn't respond right away. She didn't want to accept that, but she couldn't deny the logic. She exhaled, staring out the roadway as he turned down a side street. "I get it, Rex," she said finally. "But what happens when someone you know—someone you like—shows up starving? When they have kids crying for food?"

Rex didn't answer her.

Bee pressed her lips together, the image of hungry children flashing through her mind. The thought made her stomach twist. "Are you ready to tell them no?"

"You will, or you won't survive," he said bluntly.

The truck turned onto her street, but she barely registered the movement. Her thoughts were spiraling—about food, water, and the choices no one should ever have to make.

Then she saw them. Red and blue lights flashed at the end of the block, bouncing off houses. Squad cars formed a barrier across the road. Several officers stood in a tight circle near the entrance of a house, their faces tense.

Rex cursed under his breath and pulled over to the curb.

"That's Audree's house!" Bee's pulse kicked into overdrive. She reached for the door handle.

Rex grabbed her wrist before she could jump out. "Wait."

Bee yanked free. "I have to see what's going on."

"Okay." He exhaled sharply. "I'm heading back to the liquor store. I'll check on Ezra while I'm there. When he wakes up, I'll send someone to let you know and give you a ride to see him."

Bee hesitated, guilt gnawing at her. She still felt responsible for what had happened to him. Ezra wouldn't have gotten shot if she hadn't dragged him into this mess. "When he wakes," she said, "let him know I'll come take care of him until he's mended."

Rex said something under his breath about stubborn women but didn't argue. Instead, he nodded and put the truck into gear. "I'll tell him."

She climbed out of the truck, slamming the door behind her, and hurried toward the flashing lights. As she got closer, she spotted Mark standing near the porch, speaking in low, clipped tones to another officer. Gretchen was there too, arms crossed, her face unreadable. Audree stood off to the side, clutching baby Josiah. She looked haggard, her face streaked with dried tears. Bee's heart dropped. She rushed toward them, but before she could reach Audree, Mark intercepted her.

"Bee, you need to stay back."

"What happened?" she demanded, her voice tight. "Is Jimmy—"

Mark's jaw clenched. "Gone."

Bee blinked. "What do you mean, gone?"

SWAT officers still surrounded the house, rifles lowered but ready.

Mark ran a hand through his hair, his expression grim. "He was here. Barricaded himself inside with the baby. For hours, SWAT thought he might've hurt Josiah because they didn't hear a sound coming from the house. But then, right before SWAT breached the door, they picked up Josiah's cries."

"And Jimmy?"

Mark shook his head. "By the time they got in, he was already gone."

Bee felt the blood drain from her face. "You mean he escaped?"

"Yeah. Slipped out before they even got here, they said."

Bee's legs felt unsteady beneath her. She turned to Audree, who pressed a trembling kiss to her baby's forehead.

"He could still be nearby," Bee murmured.

Mark's face darkened. "That's what we're afraid of."

Bee scanned the street, searching between houses. Jimmy was still out there—more dangerous than ever.

SIX

Carson

High Prairie Estates
   Denver, Colorado
   Day Four

Raelynn led Carson and Julie inside her home. The second they entered, the smell hit them. The air was thick with spoiled food and dirty diapers. From down the hall, the whimper of an infant carried toward them. Raelynn led them to a small bedroom and pushed open the door. Carson gagged. The room was a disaster. An infant, no more than two or three months old, lay in his crib, his face red from crying, his diaper overflowing. Piles of soiled diapers littered the floor.

"Oh, sweetheart…" Julie rushed over and scooped up the baby.

Carson stepped carefully over the mess, glancing around. "Where are his diapers?"

Raelynn's voice was small. "He's out."

Julie grabbed the last wipe from a box and turned to Carson. "You have any safety pins in that bag of yours?"

"A couple." Carson dropped his pack and removed his sewing

kit. He had two large and several small safety pins. The smaller ones were useful for DIY fishing hooks, securing improvised bandages, temporary fixes for torn clothing, removing splinters, and if he were Knox, his sister's boyfriend, he could even use them to pick a lock. "Here," he said, handing them to her.

In just a couple of minutes, Julie had the child cleaned up and secured a makeshift diaper on him from scraps of a thin baby blanket. Yet, having a clean diaper didn't stop the baby from crying.

"He's probably hungry," Raelynn said.

"Does he have a bottle we can give him?"

"It's empty."

Julie swaddled the child in another blanket and nodded toward the door. "We should check to see if they have formula."

"Henry doesn't eat formula. Only Mommy's milk," Raelynn said. "She keeps it in the freezer."

"It will have defrosted. Everything inside will be rancid," Carson said.

How had Raelynn and her brother survived? The smoke from the wildfire alone would have been deadly, not to mention the suffocating heat it would have produced. He'd never know the answer. Right then, the biggest issue was the kids' well-being. How were they going to care for them, and how were they supposed to locate their parents in all this chaos?

"We have to feed him something," Julie said.

Carson glanced around the kitchen. On the counter, he saw a jar of peanut butter and another of jelly. He picked one up and then another. They were both empty. It looked as if Raelynn had been surviving on them. He tried the pantry, hoping they kept formula there as a backup. It was stocked with the usual dry goods children enjoyed, like macaroni and cheese, and on the top shelf, he found a box of Pop-Tarts, but nothing an infant could eat. He removed one of the Pop-Tarts from its box. "Are you hungry, Raelynn?" he asked as he ripped open the package.

She nodded, a smile crossing her face.

Carson handed her the pastry and turned to Julie. "There's nothing in there for Henry."

"Let me see," Julie said, pushing him out of the way. She reached in and removed a can of evaporated milk. She handed it to Carson and then grabbed a bottle of Karo syrup.

"What are you going to make with that?"

"Emergency formula. People on social media were posting the recipe when there was a formula shortage during COVID-19," Julie said. "Hold him while I make his bottle."

He stared down at the infant and then looked up at Julie.

She shot him a look. "What? Take him," she demanded.

Carson stiffened. "Not sure that's a good idea. I've never held a baby, and he's so small. I could … crush him or something."

"Don't be silly. Hold your arms out."

He did, and Julie placed the infant in his arms.

"Support his head," she said, nudging his elbow up.

He rocked the crying child as Julie made the bottle. He didn't understand how such a loud noise could come from such a small body.

Julie moved to his side, holding the bottle. "You want to do it?"

Carson shook his head. "I might hurt him."

Julie laughed and took the baby from him. The second the nipple touched Henry's lips, the wailing stopped.

The silence was glorious.

"How long will that milk last him?" Carson asked.

"About twenty-four hours. We have to find more before then." There was desperation in her voice.

And now, they were responsible for two children. Carson swallowed. It was one thing to look out for himself and Julie. But an infant and a five-year-old? In a world that was unraveling by the minute? This was a whole different level of survival. Carson searched the house for anything that could lead them to the children's family—an address book, a phone number.

Nothing.

Utter Devastation

His gaze landed on a row of hooks by the door leading to the garage. On it were two sets of keys. Hope flickered in his chest. He snatched them up and ran outside. There, he studied the two vehicles parked in the drive. He immediately dismissed the Tesla for many reasons, but the ability to charge its battery was chief among them. He doubted it would run after being exposed to such heat. Carson wiped the sweat from his brow and peered at the Toyota RAV4. A layer of ash and soot dulled its silver paint, but otherwise, it looked intact. No shattered windows. No melted tires. Frame intact. But looks could be deceiving. He scanned the surrounding wreckage. The fire had licked at the edges of the driveway, coming within feet of the vehicle.

"Think it'll run?" Julie asked from the doorway of the house.

Carson exhaled sharply. "Only one way to find out."

SEVEN

Knox Selway

Rosewick Crossing Apartments
La Plata, Maryland
Day Four

Sunlight streamed in through the blinds in Willow's bedroom as Knox drifted between sleep and consciousness, his body weightless and heavy all at once. His left arm burned, the ache persistent and dull, but it was the fatigue that dragged him under again and again. It had been years since he'd felt this weak—or maybe he never had. His body was betraying him, demanding rest when he had none to give. He had to stay awake. He had to move. The bed beneath him was soft, like sinking into a bog. The warmth of the blanket wrapped around him felt suffocating, but every time he wiggled out from under it, a shiver wracked his body. He swallowed, his mouth as dry as sand. He needed water. They had to leave.

The thought hit him like a jolt of electricity, a spike of urgency cutting through the haze in his mind. They were wasting time. Carson had warned him about this. The cities would empty soon, sending a human flood across the countryside searching for food, water, and safety. There was none. He knew how fast the system collapsed. The just-in-time supply model had resulted in empty grocery store shelves days ago. By now, genuine desperation had begun. Knox ran a hand over his face, fingers catching in his greasy hair. He hated feeling like dead weight. His limbs were sluggish, his thoughts foggy. Sleep clawed at him, dragging him back under, but he fought it. He had to convince Willow. They had to go before…

A sound stirred him—light, careful footsteps. *Willow's?*

She stroked his shoulder, her fingers warm against his clammy skin. "Knox," she murmured. "It's time for your antibiotic, and you need to drink something."

He forced his eyelids open, squinting against the dim light. Her face hovered above him, concern etched into every line.

Willow helped him sit up, fluffing the pillows and arranging them behind him. She lowered herself onto the bed next to him and put the water glass to his lips. Knox took a sip and then another. "Open your mouth," she said.

He complied, and she placed a pill on his tongue. "What is that?" he asked after swallowing.

"Antibiotics. How's your pain?"

"Manageable."

"Good. They were out of pain meds."

"I feel weak as a kitten."

"You lost a lot of blood. The hospital was out of that, too. Doc said it'd take a while for you to regain your strength. Do you have any shortness of breath?"

"Not really. Just tired."

"The nurse said you'd need to take an iron supplement for a while to help build your red blood cells back up. I have some in the bathroom." She rose and disappeared, returning a moment later with a bottle in one hand and an iron pill in another. "Here. These are a low dosage. You'll need to take them three times a day. The nurse said you'd absorb them better spread out through the day."

"That much?"

"Would you rather I feed you liver and onions?"

Knox smiled. "I like liver, especially when your mom makes it."

"Gross. Take the iron. I'm fresh out of liver."

After he took them, she adjusted his pillows, and he lay back. She pulled the blanket up to his chest and kissed him on the lips.

"We need to go," he rasped.

Willow sighed. "Knox, we're not going anywhere until you're stronger. You can barely sit up. How are you going to make it to Arkansas like this?"

"We can't wait," he insisted, though even talking made him dizzy. "You don't understand. Every hour we sit here, more people hit the roads. And they aren't going to be friendly."

She shook her head. "No. You need rest."

Knox cursed under his breath. He couldn't fight her on it right now—at least not feeling this way.

"I love you, Knox. Sleep now."

He let her settle him back down, feigning compliance.

"Don't worry about a thing," she said on her way toward the door.

That wasn't going to happen.

As soon as she left the room, he clenched his jaw and forced himself upright. His head spun, and a black haze crept into the edges of his vision. He gritted his teeth, waiting for it to pass. *I can't lie here while the world burns around us.* Slowly, he inched his legs over the side of the bed. His bare feet hit the floor, cool and solid beneath him. He braced himself, pushing up onto his shaking legs. Every muscle trembled with effort. His vision blurred, and for a second, he swayed.

Move.

Eventually, he did. One foot. Then the other. He reached the

Utter Devastation

door, gripping the frame for support. His heart pounded as he pulled it open and stepped into the hallway. He spotted Guynn in the living room, in deep conversation with Willow.

Knox took a breath, forcing himself to straighten. "I need to talk to you," he said, his voice hoarse but firm.

Willow stomped across the floor, her eyes widening in alarm. "What the hell are you doing? You need to be in bed!"

He shook his head and gripped the doorframe tighter. "No, Willow. Listen to me!" He turned his gaze to Guynn. "We can't wait until I'm better. We have to go now."

Guynn's gaze was sharp and assessing.

"I know you've seen it, sir. You know what happens when a system collapses. The flood of refugees, the chaos, the violence. It's coming."

Guynn exhaled slowly. "I saw it in Iraq. Syria. The fall of regimes, the mass migrations—people desperate for food, water, safety. But those places had an army to keep the crowds contained." He met Willow's eyes. "We don't have that here. Once people start moving, nothing will stop them. And there's nowhere for them to go. No aid camps, no safe zones. Just hungry, terrified people looking for whatever they can take."

Willow folded her arms. "And you think we'll be safer on the road with him like this?"

Knox nodded. "Safer than here. We need to stay ahead of them. If we wait until I'm fully healed, we won't have a chance."

Willow let out a breath, rubbing her temples. She glanced at Guynn. "You agree with him?"

"I do."

Willow closed her eyes for a second before throwing her hands up. "Fine. Let's load up, then."

Knox sagged against the doorframe, relief washing over him. He had won. Now, he just had to survive the trip.

EIGHT

Carson

High Prairie Estates
  Denver, Colorado
  Day Four

Carson hit the key fob. Nothing happened. It failed to unlock the driver's door. He inserted the key and then slid inside.

Julie leaned against the open door. "Well? Moment of truth."

Carson pressed the push-to-start button.

Still nothing.

He let out a frustrated breath. "Figures."

"Battery?" Julie asked.

He nodded. A dead battery wasn't surprising. Even without direct flame, the intense heat from the fire could have drained it or damaged the wiring. Either way, they weren't going anywhere without a jump. He returned to the house and entered the garage, hoping to find a portable battery charger. Instead, there was an additional vehicle—a 2013 Tacoma pickup truck. Carson moved to the driver's door and tried the door handle. Unlocked. A tiny relief. He slid inside and found the key to it in the cup holder.

Utter Devastation

Julie appeared outside the truck, holding the baby.

Carson smiled at her, inserted the key in the ignition, and turned it. The truck immediately roared to life.

Yes!

She let out a loud whoop. "Hell, yes! We've got wheels."

Raelynn stood in the doorway. "That's my daddy's truck. He doesn't let anyone drive it."

"We're just going to borrow it to go find you and your brother some food."

"That's okay, right?" Julie asked her.

"I guess so."

Carson glanced down to check the fuel gauge. It was just over a quarter full. Enough to get them farther down the road. They might find a gas can and siphon some from an abandoned vehicle. He tried the headlights and both blinkers. All of them worked. He hoped that meant the wiring was still in one piece. Carson climbed out of the truck and examined the tires. He popped the hood and checked the battery cables and engine. He wasn't a mechanic—cars had been his dad's and Willow's thing. Carson had been more interested in science and technology. Later, when he was older, they'd connected over other stuff, like golf. Carson lowered the hood and turned to face Julie. "If you'll gather some of the children's things, I'll push the cars in the drive out of the way and back this out."

"What about the bikes?" Julie asked.

The truck was faster and safer. But if they ran out of gas or had to abandon it, bikes were easier to maneuver. However, he wasn't sure how they'd managed with the kids. He exhaled sharply. "We take them. I'll put them in the bed. If we run into a roadblock, we might need them."

Julie turned to go and then stopped and gestured to the rear seats of the extended cab truck. "Will their car seats fit back there?"

Car seats? Kids were a lot of work. Carson rounded the front of the truck, opened the rear driver's side door, and peered inside. "Yeah, I think so. We may need to move the front seats forward to accommodate them."

As Julie slipped into the children's rooms to pack their bags, Carson set to work manually raising the overhead garage door and using the Tacoma to push the Toyota down the driveway. It rolled across the street and wedged itself against the curb out of the way. Carson then loaded his and Julie's bikes and backpacks into the bed of the pickup. He had to break the rear driver's side window of the Tesla to get the door open and remove the children's car seats. Julie appeared at the truck with the kids just as he placed the infant's seat in the back. He had to push the driver's seat forward to make room for Raelynn's feet.

"That's going to be uncomfortable for you," she said.

"I'll be fine."

"Where is Sophie going to ride?" Julie asked, rounding the front of the truck with Henry in her arms.

Carson stepped back and scrunched his face. "In your lap?"

She threw her head back and chuckled. "How about I drive then?"

Carson considered it for a moment. He'd ridden with Julie—once. She drove like the devil was chasing her. He glanced down at Raelynn, who was climbing into her booster seat. Maybe with precious cargo on board, she'd ease off the gas pedal.

"I'll take you up on that."

"Really? I was kidding. I don't want to drive."

Carson threw his hands in the air. "Why did you say that then?"

"Because."

"I will never figure women out."

"You're not supposed to figure us out." She chuckled. "Here, hold the baby. You strapped his seat incorrectly."

"I didn't strap it in at all."

"He's under two years old. His seat has to be rear-facing."

Carson stared back at her. "You got a kid somewhere I don't know about?"

"Me?"

"Yeah. How do you know how to craft a diaper out of a blanket, make infant formula from canned milk, or which way an infant car seat faces?"

Julie was quiet as she buckled the baby into the seat. She stepped back and walked to the driver's side. "I dated a guy with a kid once. We almost got married," she said as she buckled Raelynn's seat belt.

Carson joined her at the driver's door. "I didn't know that about you."

She snickered. "There's a lot you don't know about me, Carson Carlisle."

Carson returned to Raelynn's house to retrieve Sophie. As he neared her carrier on the floor by the refrigerator, his stomach dropped—the door was ajar.

No. No, no, no.

"Sophie?" His voice cracked as he scanned the room. He crouched, peering under the table and behind the couch. She wasn't there. Panic surged through him. Deitra would never forgive him if he lost her cat. Carson bolted through the house, calling her name. "Sophie! Sophie, where are you?" He threw open closet doors, checked under the bed, behind the curtains. Silence. His breath came faster as he shoved open the back door. The yard was still, littered with broken branches and debris. How was he supposed to find one small cat in the middle of all this destruction?

He ran to the side gate and shoved it open, stepping into what had once been the neighborhood. Now, it was almost unrecognizable—collapsed homes, scattered belongings, cars flipped like discarded toys. His throat tightened. "Sophie!" he shouted into the wreckage. His voice sounded small against the weight of devastation around him.

The garage door creaked open, and Julie stepped out, wiping her hands on her jeans. She frowned. "Did she get out?"

"The carrier door was open." He lowered himself to the ground, searching beneath the Tesla in the driveway. No cat.

Raelynn stepped out of the garage. "Sophie's in my mommy's bathroom closet."

Carson frowned. "What's she doing in there?"

"Last time I saw her, she was playing with Daddy's ties."

Relief crashed over him as he sprinted back inside. He flung open the closet door, and there she was—hunched in the shadows, wide green eyes blinking up at him. The moment she saw him, she slinked forward, meowing, her soft fur brushing against his leg. Carson scooped her up and pressed his face into her warm fur. "You almost got left behind, girl," he said, scratching between her ears. "Your mommy would've had my hide ... if she's still alive."

After carrying her through the house to the kitchen, he placed her back into the carrier—this time double-checking the latch. He glanced over and noticed a small white notepad and pen attached to the fridge with a magnet. He hesitated, then pulled the pen free and scribbled a quick note in sharp, decisive letters. If Raelynn and Henry's parents made it home, at least they'd know where to start. Four days. That's how long it had been. The odds were slim, but maybe someone would come. Otherwise, Carson wasn't sure who would care for them long term.

After handing Sophie to Julie, Carson climbed in behind the steering wheel and adjusted the mirrors. He glanced over at Julie in the passenger seat next to him. "Ready?"

Her hands were folded over the top of the carrier. "More than ready."

For the first time in days, they weren't moving forward on two wheels. It meant that in a little over three hours, they'd arrive at Julie's family's ranch, and their journey together would end. A pang of sadness struck him. He pushed it aside. He couldn't afford to get distracted. Too many lives were depending upon him now.

"Let's go," he said.

And with that, he pulled out onto the road, leaving behind the scorched remains.

NINE

Willow

Rosewick Crossing Apartments
La Plata, Maryland
Day Four

Willow worked quickly, sorting their remaining food into boxes while keeping an ear on the conversation happening at the small dining table. Knox sat across from Guynn, a map spread between them. His face was pale, his movements sluggish, but his voice was steady and determined.

"We could take I-40 through Tennessee," Knox said.

"We need to avoid big cities." Guynn traced a line with his finger. "Nashville, Louisville—too many people and too much chaos."

Knox nodded. "Agreed."

Guynn jabbed a finger at a point on the map. "If we go west through Kentucky instead of south through Tennessee, we can stop in Owensboro. I have a cousin there. If his place is still standing, we could resupply, maybe rest for a night."

Willow glanced over. Knox rubbed his temple, his brow

furrowed. She knew he hated how weak he was, how much his body still demanded rest, but he wasn't wrong about leaving. They had to stay ahead of the wave of desperation creeping out of the cities. She closed the last food box and slid it across the counter. "If we have a safe place in Kentucky, that's the route we take."

With the plan settled, Willow holstered her pistol and headed outside with a box of their supplies in her hands. She stood guard on the sidewalk while Guynn worked to repair the Suburban. The night before, he'd removed key engine components as a precaution against car thieves. Now, he had to reinstall them before they could leave. The apartment complex was quiet, but even in broad daylight, every noise made her pulse spike.

Within the hour, they were loaded up and rolling out. Knox sat in the back seat behind Guynn, his hand resting on his wound as if holding himself together. Willow sat in the front passenger seat with her pistol in her lap, her gaze sweeping the street. The town of La Plata looked mostly normal, but she knew better. A few people walked along the sidewalk, carrying bags and moving with purpose, but the tension was there—tightness in their movements and nervous energy. Just past the Starbucks, the sharp flicker of blue lights cut through the midday haze, forcing them to slow. A line of vehicles stretched ahead, idling under the watchful eyes of highway patrol officers.

"Shit," Knox said, his fingers tightening on his thigh.

Guynn exhaled through his nose. "Stay calm."

As they inched along, Knox leaned forward, reaching for the shotgun, but his body faltered, a tremor of weakness stealing his strength. His jaw tightened, frustration flashing across his face. "Willow, take this jacket," he muttered.

Without hesitation, Willow grabbed Guynn's rain jacket from him and draped it over the shotgun where it rested between her and Guynn. It looked like nothing more than another piece of clothing. Concealed, but still within reach. Willow shifted in her seat, sliding her pistol under her thigh. No sudden moves. No reason to draw attention. Up ahead, an officer waved them forward. The moment of truth had arrived. When it was their turn, a state trooper motioned for them to roll down the window. The man was young, sweaty, and pale with exhaustion, but his grip on his rifle was firm.

"Need to see IDs," he said, glancing at the back hatch area of the Suburban. "Anyone else in the vehicle?"

"No," Guynn answered as he handed over their identification.

The trooper barely looked at them before nodding. "Pop the back."

Willow clenched her teeth as Guynn got out and opened the rear hatch. Another trooper peered inside, moving aside a tarp that covered their supplies.

"What's going on?" Knox asked in a calm voice.

The trooper sighed. "Looking for escaped inmates. Some got loose from the county jail two nights ago. Now they're armed and dangerous."

The officer shut the hatch and waved them forward. "You can go, but Route 301 south is closed. You'll need to take Port Tobacco Road."

Guynn nodded. "Understood."

They turned onto the winding two-lane road, passing Murphy's store, where the hand-painted sign boasted **LIVE BAIT & COLD BEER** in bold letters. Past the town's historic, one-room schoolhouse and the reconstructed courthouse, the land opened up into rolling hills. The Port Tobacco River shimmered in the sunlight. Driving through the countryside, the homes that lined the route appeared untouched by the chaos just a few miles away. Willow could almost forget that the solar apocalypse had occurred. But it had.

Willow kept an eye on the farmhouses as they passed. Most were intact. Peaceful. Normal. But as they rolled past one, a large, dark stain on the walkway near the steps caught her eye.

"Is that blood?" she muttered under her breath.

She leaned forward instinctively, her breath catching. The

wrongness of the scene pressed against her like a weight, as if she were standing at the edge of something irreversible. Then, she caught movement as a figure darted into the tree line beside the house. Her pulse spiked. She just got a look, but it was enough—a tall man with a gaunt face. A faded orange jumpsuit clung to his wiry frame, the sleeves ripped off, exposing sinewy arms streaked with red. His eyes were cold and calculating as he stared back at her. A chill slid down her spine. He looked predatory. Like a man who had already decided what he would do next.

Willow's gaze flitted toward the pistol in her lap, and when she returned her gaze to the man, he was gone, swallowed by the trees. Her fingers tightened around the gun as she contemplated what she should do. Should they go back and inform the troopers? By the time they got there, the prisoner would be long gone. Should they turn around and pursue him?

"What is it?" Knox asked, his voice edged with concern.

Willow hesitated, watching the spot where the man had disappeared. Every part of her wanted to stop and help whoever had lived in that house. But there was no one to call. No backup was coming. There were no sirens in the distance. She swallowed hard and shook her head. "I just saw one of those escapees. I think he did something to the homeowners back there."

Knox exhaled sharply but didn't say anything.

What was there to say? Normally, they would have picked up the phone and dialed 911. Given a description. Sent officers racing to the scene. Maybe saved a life. Now, there was nothing. Nothing but the knowledge that a killer was loose, and all she could do was keep driving and hope someone stopped him before he hurt more people.

Hope.

That word felt so useless now.

When they reached Route 301 again, the bridge to Virginia stretched before them, spanning the Potomac. Beyond it lay miles of uncertainty—towns, highways, and back roads winding toward

Virginia, Kentucky, and finally, Arkansas. Would they find the world beyond Maryland in better shape than the ruins of DC and the unraveling streets of La Plata? She hoped so, for their sakes. Knox was still weak, Guynn was pushing past his sixties, and fatigue clung to Willow like a second skin. She prayed for an uneventful journey to her mother's place, but deep down, she knew better.

That kind of luck didn't exist anymore.

TEN

Arthur

Carlisle Residence
  Lakewood Heights
  Dallas, Texas
  Day Four

The night had been restless. Every small noise outside had kept Arthur on edge—shuffling footsteps, distant voices, and the occasional crash of something breaking. Sleep had come in short, unsatisfying bursts, and by the time the first hints of daylight crept through the edges of the heavy blankets covering the windows, he had already been awake for an hour. The air inside the house had grown stale. Without power, the central air was useless, and though at that time of morning it wasn't blistering hot yet, the early September humidity was thick enough to make everything feel damp.

Arthur padded through the house, careful not to disturb Katherine, who was still curled up on the couch where she'd fallen asleep sometime in the early morning hours. His knees ached as he stepped into the garage, easing the door closed behind him. He flicked on a flashlight and headed for the makeshift toilet in the far corner of the garage.

After he finished, he crossed the garage, flicked off the flashlight, and placed it back on the shelf by the door. He turned the knob and eased it open. Immediately, he heard voices. A spike of panic shot through him.

Katherine!

She'd promised not to open that damn door again.

Arthur moved as quickly as his body allowed, stepping through the doorway into the dim living room just in time to see two neighbors, Chevy and Liza, standing just inside the threshold. His gut clenched. The Champmoreaus lived a few houses down—a younger couple, maybe in their late thirties. Good people. Arthur had never been close with them, but they were polite; the kind of neighbors you waved at when checking the mail or chatted with at the grocery store. Now, Chevy's face was unshaven. His dark brown eyes were sunken, his shirt wrinkled and soaked with sweat. Liza clutched his arm, her fingers white-knuckled.

Arthur's pulse steadied. At least his wife hadn't opened the door to strangers—again. But it didn't mean this was safe.

Katherine, oblivious to the rising tension in Arthur's chest, was already setting two plastic cups of water on the coffee table in front of them, along with a can of sardines and a small pack of crackers.

Arthur ground his teeth. She was violating the first rule of survival. Carson would be far from pleased. He swallowed back his frustration and forced himself to stay calm. "Good morning," he said, easing himself into his recliner but not leaning back.

Chevy sat across from him.

"How are things looking out there?" Arthur figured he'd take advantage of the situation at least to gather some much-needed information.

Chevy shook his head. "Real bad."

Arthur already knew that. He wanted details.

Liza, seated next to her husband, was shaking. "We've been out

Utter Devastation

the last couple of days, trying to find food," she said, casting a glance at the spread on the coffee table before her. "The first night saw most of the stores empty. The shopping center up the road? It's a total wreck. Everything worth having is gone. People stripped it clean."

Arthur had figured as much. He'd seen them carrying stuff away in armloads.

Chevy leaned forward and scooped a sardine from the can with his cracker. "We saw fights breaking out," he said, his mouth full. "People beating the hell out of each other for whatever's left. There were bodies in the streets. Not just injured people—dead people."

Arthur's stomach tightened. That hadn't taken long.

Katherine gasped and brought her hand up to cover her throat.

"Any sign of the police?" Arthur kept his face neutral. He needed facts, not emotion.

Chevy took another cracker and shook his head. "First night, we heard sirens. But not since then. Our neighbor across the street —Gary, you know him?"

Arthur nodded. He knew him—didn't care much for the guy. He let his dog do its business on their lawn every morning.

"Someone went into his backyard in the middle of the night and stole his generator. They took the fuel, too."

That's why all the noise stopped. Arthur figured it had just run out of gas.

Liza nodded grimly, halting her sardine-covered cracker inches from her mouth. "He rode his bike to the police station to report it. Said there was only a receptionist there. Only maybe five officers had shown up to work. They told him they weren't taking theft reports. All available officers were handling 'immediate threats to life only.'"

It didn't surprise Arthur.

Liza swallowed her food and then took a long drink. "On his way back, he stopped by the fire station. Said there was only an old, retired fireman there. The rest of the department had been out fighting fires since the blackout. But without water pressure…"

Arthur finished for her. "They can't put them out."

Liza wiped crumbs from her lap. "Entire neighborhoods are burning."

Arthur leaned back in his chair, absorbing the information. And then Chevy said something that made his stomach turn cold.

"The man at the fire station told him to watch out for the kids."

Arthur's spine straightened. "We had some show up at our door already."

"Not just the ones knocking on doors. Not just the small groups." Chevy met Arthur's eyes before taking another cracker. "She said they're running in packs of fifty or more."

The room went silent.

Katherine paled. "What are we supposed to do against a mob like that?"

"Stay inside. Stay quiet," Arthur said. That's what Carson had instructed them to do.

Chevy exhaled slowly, shaking his head. "But I don't think that'll be enough when they start going door to door."

Katherine's breath caught. "Door to door?"

Arthur's fingers tightened around the armrest. "I don't think they'll come this way." He wanted to believe that. Their neighborhood was older, filled with retirees and young families—not the kind of place that would draw a mob's attention. But even as he said it, he knew it was more wishful thinking than certainty.

Liza nodded grimly. "The firehouse guy said they'd already hit an apartment complex about half a mile from here. Broke in, dragged people out, beat them, and took whatever they wanted. The cops showed up but were outnumbered. There was nothing they could do."

Katherine pressed a hand to her mouth. "There has to be a way to stop them. Why don't they call in the National Guard? The Rangers?"

Chevy shook his head as he took the last of the sardines. "Too busy. There are four million people in Dallas alone. We're on our own." With the sardines and crackers gone, he stood and opened the door for Liza. "Thank you for the food and water. Good luck." They stepped out onto the porch.

Arthur locked the door behind them, replacing the boards that were supposed to barricade the door against intruders. He stared at it for a moment. Would it hold up under a mob? Peering through the peephole, he didn't think it would.

Katherine turned to him, eyes wide. "What are we going to do, Artie?"

Arthur's shoulders were tense. There was only one answer. "First, we don't open the door and let people inside." He paused. "Even people we know."

"You mean to turn people away?" Katherine's face twisted. "I can't do that."

Arthur exhaled sharply. Outside, under the North Texas sun, another distant gunshot rang out. He turned toward the window but didn't bother checking. It didn't matter where it had come from. The city was crumbling.

"Then be prepared to have everything we have taken from us and end up like the folks at that apartment complex."

Katherine's mouth snapped shut. She swallowed hard, looking away. "How did it come to this?" she asked, her voice cracking.

"The sun spat on us. And now we've got a hell of a problem." Arthur wiped a hand across the back of his neck, sweat slicking his palm. He was struggling after three nights of little sleep, but there was still so much left to do.

He stood in the dim light filtering through the heavy curtains, eyeing the front door and its reinforcement. The steel brackets and lumber braces were solid—for now. But if a mob really wanted in, they'd find a way.

ELEVEN

Carson

High Prairie Estates
Denver, Colorado
Day Four

As they pulled away from Raelynn's home, Carson glanced into the Tacoma's rearview mirror. Raelynn placed a pacifier in her infant brother's mouth, her small hands careful, like she'd been doing it all her life. The baby's soft sucking noises filled the silence. Carson returned his gaze to the road, focusing on the cracked pavement ahead as they neared the on-ramp for Interstate 70. First things first—find baby formula, diapers, and supplies for Henry. But after that? "So," he said, his voice low. "Long-term plan. What are we going to do with them?"

Julie shifted in the passenger seat, clutching Sophie's carrier. She didn't answer right away.

Carson didn't push it. He let the road stretch between them, the hum of tires against asphalt filling the space where words should have been.

Julie folded her arms, her eyes sharp. "I haven't had time to think about it."

"I have," he admitted. "And I don't like any of the options."

"Me neither."

Carson tapped his fingers against the steering wheel. "Keeping them with us isn't realistic, Julie. You know that, right?"

"I know." She glanced back at Raelynn and sighed.

They drove in silence for another mile.

Finally, Carson spoke. "Marco's unit isn't setting up safe zones yet. They're too busy running supply lines and keeping people from tearing each other apart."

Julie's expression darkened. "So, the military isn't an option."

"Not right now." Carson clenched his jaw. "And we can't just take them home and wait for their parents to arrive."

"Good. We agree on something."

Carson rubbed his forehead and stifled a yawn. "That leaves us with two choices. We either take them to the fire station or—"

"You want to leave them there and hope for the best," Julie finished.

Neither of them liked that option.

Julie sighed, adjusting her ponytail. "We don't even know if there's a 'safe' anymore."

"But maybe there is."

"What do you mean?"

Carson hesitated, then said, "A police station."

Julie blinked. "You want to leave them at a police station?"

"Think about it," Carson said. "Disaster training is standard for copy. They have weapons, supplies, and generators. If any law enforcement is still holding out, they'll be there, protecting their communities."

"You want to go into Denver to find a police station? I don't think we'd even make it that far without finding trouble."

"No, not in Denver. One of the small towns we'll be going through here soon."

"That's assuming there are still cops left."

"There are." Carson's voice was firm. "They're not the military—they don't get orders from the Pentagon. I'm talking about the ones who stayed behind to protect their towns and their families. If there's a working government left, they'll be holding things together at the local level."

"And if they're not?"

"Then we move on. We find another option."

Julie turned, looking at him. "You really think a police station is the best place for them?"

Carson's hands tightened on the wheel. "I don't know. But it's the best shot we've got."

Julie glanced back at Raelynn, watching the little girl stroke her brother's tiny fingers. "What if they don't want to stay?"

Carson's throat tightened. He didn't know how to respond. The reality settled between them. There were no perfect answers. No guarantees. Just the best of a terrible set of choices.

"All right. We'll check a police station first. But if they won't take them—"

Carson nodded. "Then we keep moving."

Julie closed her eyes briefly, then turned her gaze back to the road. "I just hope we're making the right call."

Carson didn't answer. He just kept driving. Because hope wasn't a strategy, and right now, a strategy was all they had left.

"There!" Julie pointed through the windshield a few miles down the road. "There's a Wally World."

Carson stared at the massive blue and yellow sign in the distance. Another big box store?

The last one had almost killed them. Julie had been attacked. Circumstances had forced him to kill a man—his first, but unfortunately not his last. And less than twelve hours ago, back at Earl's garage, he'd only just survived a shootout with a gang that wouldn't have thought twice about slaughtering them all. His body still ached from the close call, the bruises and scrapes he hadn't had time to tend. The sound of bullets ricocheting off the cars of the barricade still lingered in his memory, like a ghost that wouldn't leave. He exhaled sharply, dragging a hand down his face.

Carson glanced into the rearview mirror where Raelynn rested with her head against the window, the baby snug in his car seat. "Are you sure about this?"

"No, but what choice do we have? The baby needs food, Carson."

He let that settle. Of course, they had no choice. Survival was about what you could live with, not what you wanted. He veered off the main road, pulling behind a crumbling tire shop. "Stay here," he said, killing the engine.

Julie reached for his arm before he could get out. "No heroics, Carson. Get in, grab what we need, and get out."

Carson smirked despite himself. "Since when have I been a hero?"

Julie let out a quiet breath that might have been a laugh, but there was no humor in it. Only exhaustion.

"I'll be careful." Carson squeezed her hand, then slipped out of the truck and eased the door closed. He moved swiftly, staying low as he navigated the wreckage of the parking lot. Rifle at the ready, he swept the scene. No gunfire. No movement. That didn't mean it was safe—only that the danger hadn't shown itself yet.

The automatic doors of the Walmart had been shattered, leaving jagged glass scattered like ice on the pavement. He placed his feet with care, ears straining for any sign of life inside. Then he saw them—three men in military fatigues, rifles slung across their chests, standing just beyond the entrance. They were too clean to be scavengers. Too disciplined. Carson tucked his Glock into his holster and pulled the tail of his shirt down to conceal it. The presence of the military could be favorable—or very bad. It all depended on who was calling the shots. He took a slow step forward, raising his hands just enough to show he wasn't a threat.

The soldiers reacted instantly, rifles up, fingers hovering over triggers.

"Hold it right there!" one of them barked.

Carson froze. "Not looking for trouble," he said evenly. "Just need supplies. Got kids with me. A baby."

The soldier who'd spoken—a young guy with sharp eyes and an uneasy stance—studied him for a moment. The tension in the air felt like the precursor to a gunfight.

Then one of the soldiers took a step forward. He tilted his head, eyes narrowing.

"Carson?"

Carson's body tensed. The voice was familiar, but it took a second to place it. When the man stepped into the light, the past slammed into Carson like a truck.

Marco Diaz?

They'd played pickleball together before life had boiled down to nothing but survival and hard choices. Marco had been a solid guy—quick with a joke. Seeing him now, in this dead world, felt like grasping onto the last frayed thread of something long gone.

"Shit, Marco?"

Marco gave a tired smirk. "Hell, man. I thought you'd be holed up in your bunker by now."

Carson shook his head. "Wildfire took it. Been moving east since it all went sideways."

"Sideways is an understatement. Buckley locked down fast. Too fast."

Carson glanced at the other soldiers, who still held their rifles at the ready but didn't look eager to fire. "Is Buckley still operational?"

"Not really. We've received orders to link up with FEMA and the National Guard to restore the peace, secure resources, and help with the recovery. But you know what that means, right?"

Carson shook his head.

Marco's voice was tight. "It means we're supposed to leave our families behind. They expect us to follow directives, keep the peace, and help rebuild ... but my wife and kid? They're still back home. No power, food, or protection." His jaw flexed. "They expect us to hold the damn country together while our own families fend for themselves."

Carson didn't know what to say about that, but he understood the conflict raging in Marco's eyes. "What are you doing here?" Carson asked, keeping his voice low.

Marco huffed out a humorless laugh. "Getting food and supplies to see our families through while we're gone." He glanced at the other soldiers. "We're not leaving them to starve."

Carson studied him. "I understand. So, what's next?"

"We're heading south, man. Fort Carson. That's where we're supposed to regroup." He hesitated. "If it's still there."

Carson nodded, taking that in.

Marco gestured toward the piled supplies. "We can spare some formula and diapers. Not much, but it'll help."

"I appreciate it."

Marco motioned for him to follow. Much of the store had been ransacked, but the soldiers had secured a decent stockpile of essentials—meds, baby supplies, and canned goods. Near the pharmacy, crates of medical supplies were stacked in neat piles. Carson grabbed what they needed—baby formula, diapers, a pack of wipes, and some bottled water. Not much, but enough for the next couple of days.

As he turned to leave, Marco stopped him. "Listen," he said. "You need to get as far from here as possible. Fast. Denver's getting worse. And Buckley and the other bases? They're not gonna hold."

Carson's stomach clenched. "What do you mean?"

Marco's expression darkened. "Things are unraveling fast. FEMA's already overwhelmed. The Guards stretched thin. If Fort Carson pulls out, it won't just be a locked-down base—it'll be abandoned."

Carson's mind raced.

Marco sighed. "Just don't stick around to see what happens."

"I hear you. Thanks for the heads-up."

Marco clapped him on the shoulder. "Take care of yourself, Carson."

"You, too."

Back at the truck, Julie was behind the wheel. When Carson slid into the passenger seat beside her, she looked at the supplies in his lap, then back at him. "Any trouble?"

He hesitated. "Nope."

Julie studied him for a moment, then nodded. She didn't ask for details. Maybe she didn't want them. He glanced in the rearview mirror. Both the kids were still asleep—for now, at least.

"Let's go," he said.

Julie started the engine, and they pulled away from the Walmart, leaving behind the airmen who still had a mission—no matter the cost to their families.

TWELVE

Willow

Glory Days Antique Store
 Newburg, Maryland
 Day Four

Willow yawned as the road stretched ahead. An antique store came into view, its weathered sign swinging in the breeze.

"I stopped here on my way up." Knox smirked but didn't look at her. "Yeah. I had to slap a tourniquet on my arm before I could browse the fine selection of rusty farm implements."

Willow turned sharply toward him, the last traces of fatigue fading. "This is where it happened?"

"Just up the road from here," he said, turning to face his window.

She knew not to push or ask too many questions. He'd open up to her about it all when he was ready, not a moment before.

Willow exhaled and forced a smirk. "You know, while you were sleeping, I went shopping in one, too." She lifted her hands, making exaggerated air quotes around shopping, but the joke didn't land quite the same. Not now.

"I'm almost afraid to ask."

Willow's smirk widened. "The antique store in La Plata. It had some useful stuff—manual-powered tools, a kerosene lantern, a hand-crank coffee grinder, a cast-iron Dutch oven, and a portable over-the-coals cooking grate."

"Sounds like you were actually listening when Carson talked about this stuff."

Willow's expression sobered. "He was right to be concerned, wasn't he?"

"Yeah. And now we'll have to listen to him say 'I told you so' for the next year."

Willow fell quiet. Her fingers traced the edge of her seat, turning it over in her mind. Finally, she asked, "Do you think he'll make it to Mom's?"

"Carson? Of course. Your brother can handle himself. Besides, he's got an arsenal of weapons and a solid plan to get away from populated areas as soon as possible."

Willow let out a breath, but she was far from relieved. "I still don't know why he doesn't just stay put at his mountain retreat. He has everything he needs to survive for years there."

"Because he has a strong sense of obligation to make sure his family survives as well."

"I don't like the idea of him going into Dallas." She chewed on that for a moment. "Lord knows how he'll get Dad to leave and travel to Mom's, not to mention convince Katherine."

Knox's lips pressed into a thin line. "Yeah, I don't know how he'll do it either—or how he expects all that to play out. Your mom's not going to be thrilled to see your dad and his new wife on her doorstep."

Willow let out a humorless chuckle. "That's putting it mildly." The thought of her parents in the same space again, especially under circumstances this dire, was almost laughable. Almost.

"Carson will find a way," Knox said after a long pause. "He always does."

Utter Devastation

Willow nodded, but the worry didn't fade from her eyes.

They rode in silence for a while, the boxes of supplies rattling in the back. The weight of everything—not just the world collapsing around them, but the personal storms ahead—pressed down on them all. Some battles were inevitable. And sometimes the hardest ones weren't against strangers.

A few minutes later, Knox nodded toward the liquor store on the left side of the road. "That's where it happened."

Willow followed his gaze, gripping her pistol a little tighter as she lifted it from her lap, just in case. The place looked like a war zone with empty boxes and shattered bottles all over the parking lot, glinting in the midday sun like jagged teeth. The windows had been blown out, and the exterior was pockmarked with bullet holes. There were no bodies. She exhaled, scanning for any sign of life, but the place seemed abandoned now.

Up ahead, the truck stop told a different story. There, a handful of figures loitered in the lot, their postures tense, tracking the passing vehicle with hungry eyes. The colonel must've seen it, too, because he stomped the gas pedal, and the Suburban surged forward past the truck stop before anyone had a chance to make a move.

Knox let out a slow breath. "Good call."

Guynn didn't take his eyes off the road. "I may be old, but I know a bad hand when I see one. Not looking to gamble today."

Willow twisted in her seat, watching the figures shrink in the distance. No one followed.

Up ahead, no smoke rose from the towers at the power generation plant. Its skeletal silhouette stood cold and lifeless against the sky. The sight sent a hollow pang through Willow's chest. No power. No recovery. She rubbed her temples. Surviving without electricity was going to be harder than most people realized. Society had taken power for granted—flipping a switch, charging a phone, stocking a fridge without worrying if the food would rot by morning. That was all over now. Some places would repair their grids faster than others. There had to be towns, maybe entire cities, that had backup transformers, replacement parts, and the know-how to piece things back together.

But what about the places that didn't?

Would people flee to the cities that got the lights back on? Would the last remaining bastions of electricity turn into over-crowded refugee centers? Or would those towns barricade themselves against the flood of desperate outsiders? Willow's mind conjured images of packed roads leading to the faint glow of a city on the horizon—refugees scrambling for a chance at normalcy, only to be turned away at gunpoint. She turned to Knox. "Do you think people will start migrating to places that get the power back first?"

He was quiet for a moment before answering. "Yeah. People go where the food and safety are. Doesn't mean the locals will welcome them."

Guynn let out a dry chuckle from the driver's seat. "They won't. Those places will close their borders faster than you can say 'state of emergency.' The people who have power won't want to share it. And the ones who don't?" He shook his head. "They'll take it by force if they have to."

Willow swallowed hard, her gaze drifting back to the dead power plant. The world wasn't just in the dark. It was about to become a battlefield.

THIRTEEN

Bee

Wild Plum Lake Estates
Highland, Arkansas
Day Four

Hours stretched as Bee stood outside Audree's house, waiting for the police to finish their search for Jimmy. The tension on the street felt suffocating. Flashing lights cast eerie shapes against the houses, making everything look distorted and unfamiliar. Bee was trying to come up with a plan to keep Audree and Josiah safe.

She strode toward Sheriff Ray Dunlap, who stood behind his patrol SUV, speaking in low tones with the SWAT team leader. Bee knew him well enough from the Stag Lodge over the years. He was in his late fifties, stocky with a permanent sunburn across the bridge of his nose from years of working in the Arkansas heat. His uniform was rumpled, and the deep lines on his face made him look older than he probably was. He wasn't a bad man, just an overworked one, trying to hold things together as everything unraveled.

Bee lingered a few steps away, arms crossed, listening.

"Roadblocks are set up on the highway," the SWAT leader, a tall man with sharp features and graying hair, was saying. "We've got units stationed at key intersections. He's on foot and could be anywhere by now."

Sheriff Dunlap exhaled heavily. "He's a slippery little SOB. There's a reason he's managed to stay out of serious trouble all these years. Knows how to disappear."

The SWAT leader frowned. "Well, he's not Houdini. We'll find him."

"Yeah, but will we find him before he does something worse?" the sheriff said. "We need more men."

The SWAT leader gave him a look. "We don't have more men."

Bee's frustration flared. *You don't have more men. You don't have enough supplies. You don't have control.* And that meant people like Jimmy could do whatever the hell they wanted. That was all Bee needed to hear. She strode forward, not bothering to mask her irritation.

"Sheriff."

Dunlap turned, his expression weary. "Bee."

She didn't waste time. "What are you going to do to keep Audree and the baby safe?"

"Find Jimmy."

Bee's fingers curled into fists. "What if he finds Audree before you find him?"

"Jimmy? He's halfway to Little Rock by now. He won't show his face in this town again."

Bee let out a sharp laugh, devoid of humor. "So, you're just going to do nothing to protect his victims?"

The sheriff sighed, rubbing a hand over his jaw. "We're stretched thin, Bee. We'll do our best to run patrols through the neighborhood, but you know how it is."

Bee's frustration boiled over. "We tried locking doors, Sheriff. That didn't stop Jimmy from breaking in, stealing the baby, and putting a bullet in Ezra. He's dangerous, and he's still out there."

"We're doing everything we can," he said, his voice tight.

Not good enough.

Bee pivoted away, scanning the small crowd gathered nearby. Bob and a few others stood in a loose huddle, watching the conversation unfold. Their expressions ranged from concern to outright impatience. She didn't hesitate. She marched up to them, her voice clear and steady. "What can we do to secure our neighborhood? We can't just sit back and hope the cops will protect us."

Bob's face lit up. "About time," he said, crossing his arms. "We need to lock this place down. I've been saying it for days. If we don't get a system in place, we're gonna have trouble."

"What do you suggest?" She didn't like how much he was enjoying this, but she kept her expression neutral.

Bob turned to the others. "We block the entrances. Post armed men at night. Make sure no one comes in."

A murmur ran through the group. Some nodded, while others shifted uneasily.

"No exceptions," Bob continued. "No letting in strangers, no bleeding hearts handing out supplies. We protect our own."

Bee's stomach tightened. So, that was the price.

A man near the back frowned. "You're talking about armed men walking the streets? That's a little extreme, Bob."

"We have children in this neighborhood," one woman added.

Bob scoffed. "Exactly. They're the ones that need protection. You think people won't get desperate? You think the store shelves are gonna magically fill back up? The hungry mobs are coming, and we'll be the only ones with food and security. We prepare now, or we suffer later."

"And what about people who live here but left to find supplies or check on family?" Bee folded her arms. Are you saying we turn them away, too?"

Bob gave a one-shouldered shrug. "That's the cost of security. If we start making exceptions, we lose control."

Her stomach twisted. That would mean she couldn't leave to

check on Ezra. Carson and Willow also couldn't join the community. How could she be expected to turn away her own children? How could anyone else?

Tension rippled through the group. Some were eager, nodding along with Bob's hardline stance. Others looked uneasy, clearly torn between wanting security and fearing what strict control could mean for them in the long run.

Bee took a step forward, her jaw set. "We do need security," she admitted, meeting Bob's smug expression with an unwavering stare. "But we're not turning this place into a dictatorship."

"Dictatorship?" he scoffed. "I'm trying to keep us alive."

"I know," Bee said. "And you're not wrong about the danger. But people should be able to come home. If we lock the doors on our own, we're no better than the ones we're trying to protect ourselves from."

"So, what's your plan?" someone called.

Bee exhaled. *Think. This has to work!*

"Immediate family only," she said firmly. "If they've got a connection to someone in the neighborhood, they can come in. But no strangers. No drifters." Rex's words ran through her mind. "We're not taking in people just because they knock on the door."

Bob's face twisted. "That's a mistake. That's a lot of family members, and we don't know them."

"Maybe," she shot back. "But it's the only way this works. We're not abandoning our own. And I'll bet most of you aren't ready to turn away your own kids, siblings, or spouses just because they weren't home when things fell apart."

That hit a nerve. People murmured, some nodding in agreement.

Bee turned to Mark. "Start a list of people willing to patrol. If they've got a gun, they're on the front line. If they don't, we'll figure something else out for them."

He nodded, pulling a notepad from his back pocket. Several

men stepped forward. Hunting was a way of life here, and most had at least a rifle.

Bob shook his head, muttering under his breath.

Bee ignored him and turned to Gretchen. "We'll also need to support those standing guard. They can't be out there on an empty stomach. Start organizing meals for them—small rations from all of us. It doesn't have to be much. But everyone contributes something."

The shift in the crowd was subtle, but Bee saw it. People exchanged hesitant looks. Some whispered, others frowned.

"We don't have enough to spare," a woman spoke up. "I've got maybe two days' worth of food left for my family."

"My water's almost gone," someone else added.

The unease spread like wildfire. They weren't just preparing for trouble; they were already there. Bee's stomach knotted. She'd assumed most of them were like her—hanging on, but with at least a small cushion of supplies. But if they were already running dry...

"We'll think of something," she said, forcing confidence into her voice. But for the first time, she wasn't sure how they were going to make it. Bee stood before the gathered crowd, her mind racing. They had made progress—security measures were in place, and patrols were being organized—but food and water were an even bigger concern. She had to act fast. "The lake," she said finally. "It's our best chance for water."

A few neighbors nodded. They all knew the lake was their primary water source, but no one had taken the lead on making it usable.

Bee turned to a few men standing near the back. "I need people to start gathering containers—buckets, coolers, anything that will hold water. We're going to filter it."

An older man named Hank frowned. "Filter it with what?"

Bee hesitated, then forced herself to push past her doubt. "Carson left me an emergency bag with water filters. We can make it safe to drink."

Hank nodded, but his expression was still doubtful. "You sure about that? Lake water? What about all the lawn chemicals that have run off into it?"

Bee hesitated, recalling the different filter options Carson had given her. She wasn't sure if they'd remove lawn chemicals. She met Hank's doubtful gaze. "I can't promise it's perfect, but I do know this—if we don't drink, we won't make it long enough to worry about what's in that water." She met his gaze. "The filters I have will get rid of bacteria and parasites. As for the chemicals? If we can't find a better source, we'll have to take our chances. Dehydration will kill us a hell of a lot faster than whatever's in that lake."

The others murmured in agreement. That settled it.

She turned to another group, which included Mark. "I need a few people to start fishing. They stocked the lake just before the lights went out. It's the best shot we have at fresh food."

"We'll get what we can," Mark said, gesturing to the men around him. "Let's go."

Bob, standing with his usual scowl, crossed his arms. "How long do you think that'll last, Bee? That lake's got fish now, sure. But it won't if everyone starts pulling them out every day."

"We'll deal with that later," she said firmly. "Right now, people need to eat."

FOURTEEN

Willow

James Madison Parkway
Newburg, Maryland
Day Four

The waters of the Potomac stretched out beneath them as the Suburban crossed the bridge into Virginia. The boundary line between Maryland and Virginia felt more than just geographical—it was another step into the unknown, leaving behind the last scraps of normalcy.

Knox shifted in his seat and gestured downstream. "That's where I got the Vespa."

Willow arched a brow.

"It was a sweet ride."

"Where'd you find it?" Guynn asked.

Knox smirked. "Met a woman at a gas station near Fort…" He trailed off, seemingly lost in thought.

"Fort AP Hill," Guynn supplied with a grunt.

"It's Fort Walker now," Knox said, nodding.

"Still can't believe they renamed that place."

Willow glanced at him in the rearview mirror. "You don't like the name change?"

Guynn let out a low chuckle, shaking his head. "Oh, I don't give a damn what they call a base. But I can guarantee you that renaming military bases didn't change racism one iota. Waste of time and money. Should've put that effort into fixing the damn grid instead."

"Maybe they'll rename it again when the power's back on." Knox smirked. You can put in a request."

"Yeah, I'll get right on that." He chuckled. "Anyway, continue your story about the girl and the Vespa."

"I met Elise near Fort AP Hill—at a gas station after I wrecked my truck in a police chase."

Willow's eyes widened. "A police chase?"

"It wasn't my fault. An ICE detainee on the run jacked my ride."

Willow was shocked at all that he'd gone through on his way to Maryland.

"These guys were harassing Elise and…"

"And you played hero?" Willow asked, though she didn't need to. She knew Knox.

"She was alone and needed help. I escorted her to her boyfriend's bar. He gave me the Vespa as a thank you."

After a few minutes, Guynn cleared his throat. "So," he said, glancing into the rearview mirror. "What'd you think of the Vespa?"

"It was a sweet ride for a scooter," Knox said. "Wish I could have kept it—or returned it to Elise and Dan."

Guynn chuckled. "I spent decades in the military, and I've driven just about every vehicle you can think of—tanks, Humvees, deuce and a halfs—but the most fun I've had on wheels was in Italy, zipping around like some European café racer on a damn Vespa."

"Please tell me there are pictures," Willow joked.

"No pictures, but there's a story."

"Let me guess. It involves an Italian woman."

"Well, yes, it does." Guynn sighed wistfully. "I was serving in Germany and was on leave. I rented a Vespa to see the sights—the proper way—the way the Italians do it. Classic-style scooters have a history that is just as long and winding as the Amalfi Coast. Did you know 'Vespa' means 'wasp' in Italian?"

Knox raised an eyebrow. "Like … the bug?"

"Exactly. Because of the way it buzzes along and the shape—headlight, mirrors, handlebars—they sort of look like an insect. Italians have a flair for naming things, you know."

Willow smiled, imagining it. "So, what, you just zipped around Rome on a scooter?"

"Rome? No. Florence, Tuscany, the rolling countryside. There's something about the sound of a Vespa in Italy. That, the church bells, and the espresso machines—those sounds take me right back."

"Sounds nice," Willow said. Those places were on her to-visit list, but she was always so busy. Now, she wondered if she'd ever have that opportunity again.

Guynn's voice softened. "I remember sitting outside a little café in a back alley, just watching people live their lives. You learn a lot about a country by how it drinks its coffee. Italians? They don't take it to go. They stand at the counter, toss back an espresso, and take a moment to exist before they carry on. La dolce vita, they call it. The sweet life."

"Sounds like you miss it."

Guynn sighed. "I miss a lot of things, Willow."

Silence fell again, but this time, it was reflective.

"I regret leaving that Vespa behind," Knox said. "It was a cool ride."

"Yeah, but I bet it didn't handle off-roading too well." Guynn chuckled.

Knox smirked. "Oh, I had it airborne at least once. Damn thing could move when I needed it to."

Willow shook her head. "I don't even want to know."

After a long pause, he asked, "I wonder how the rest of the country's doing?"

"Hopefully better than here," Guynn said.

Knox dragged a hand through his hair. "My mom and sister are in Florida. I just hope the blackout hasn't reached that far."

Willow glanced at him in the mirror. "What do you think she'd do?"

"She's tough." He exhaled, his fingers tapping against his knee. "But she's alone. If things are as bad down there as they were in Virginia and Maryland, I don't know how she's holding up."

Guynn frowned. "What about you, Willow? You said your brother was in Boulder. What about your dad?"

"Dallas." She stared out the window.

"Probably faring better than most," Knox said. "If the outage didn't reach that far south, he might be okay. But the north and central parts of the country? Without power, without food distribution…" He shook his head. "We haven't seen a single sign of a government response—no FEMA, no National Guard. Right now, the country's on its own."

Guynn's fingers tapped the wheel thoughtfully. "We rely on supply chains, power grids, and Amazon deliveries. Rip that away, and people lose their damn minds."

"Yeah. I saw enough of that firsthand," Knox said.

They grew quiet again, the road stretching endlessly ahead.

Knox shifted, staring out the window at the passing trees.

"Colonel, you never finished telling us about the woman you met in Italy," Willow said.

"Ludovica." He said her name like a memory he hadn't dusted off in years. "She was beautiful … and very married."

Knox let out a low whistle. "That sounds like a deadly combination."

Utter Devastation

"Oh, it nearly was," Guynn admitted. "I didn't know she was married, of course—not until her husband burst through the door of their home and chased me into the street in my underwear."

Willow doubled over, laughing so hard she could barely breathe. Knox chuckled too, but his faded quickly, exhaustion catching up to him.

"Go ahead, get it out of your system."

Willow wiped a tear from the corner of her eye. "I just—you, Colonel? Running through the streets of Italy in your underwear?"

"I had two choices—get my ass beat by an angry Italian or make a run for it. I figured I liked my face the way it was."

Knox shook his head. "I take it you never saw Ludovica again?"

"Oh, I saw her once more—at a café a few days later. She winked at me and whispered, 'Mi dispiace' as she walked by with her husband."

"What's that mean?" Willow asked, still catching her breath.

Guynn sighed. "'I'm sorry.'"

Knox smirked. "Damn. She played you."

"Son, I let myself be played." He glanced down at the instrument panel. Willow followed his gaze, her eyes landing on the gas gauge. There was just under a quarter tank of fuel left. They wouldn't make it much farther without stopping. No telling when they'd find another station with working pumps.

Knox leaned forward. "We're gonna need gas soon."

Guynn nodded, scanning the road ahead. Up ahead, Willow spotted a small gas station. She pointed. "Look. There's a convenience store with fuel pumps." The Suburban slowed. Willow's eyes narrowed as she took in the place. She sat forward, peering through the windshield.

"It looks open. I saw someone go inside," Knox said.

"Let's cross our fingers they have a generator to pump fuel," Guynn said.

The Suburban idled beside the pumps as the midday sun baked

the cracked pavement. The gas station looked worn down but functional, the faint hum of a generator somewhere in the distance giving them hope. A man in his fifties stood near the door, eyeing their vehicle.

"I'll be right back," Guynn said as he cut the engine and unbuckled his seatbelt. "Gonna see if they'll sell us some fuel."

Willow glanced toward the store, watching as Guynn stepped out, adjusting his stance like a man always prepared for trouble. The door swung shut behind him as he disappeared inside. Willow glanced back at Knox. "I need to find a restroom," she said, already reaching for the door handle.

Knox gave her a look. "You sure that's a good idea? You should wait for the colonel. I'd escort you, but you might have to carry me back."

"What, you think I can't handle peeing by myself?"

Knox huffed but didn't argue.

Willow climbed out and spotted a sign on the side of the building indicating a public restroom. She headed in that direction, moving quickly. Then she heard it. A sharp, muffled cry.

She froze mid-step.

Near the shadowed side of the building, a man had a woman pinned against the wall. His fingers were twisted into her hair, yanking her head back as she struggled. Near her feet was a child —no older than six, sobbing.

Willow's blood went cold.

FIFTEEN

Carson

Interstate 70
Aurora, Colorado
Day Four

The steady hum of the Tacoma's engine was the only sound in the cab as Carson drove east on Interstate 70 into the sun. Julie sat beside him, staring out the window, lost in thought. She hadn't said much since they left Walmart. The encounter with Marco and his team still lingered in the air between them—what the soldiers had given them in supplies paled in comparison to what they had learned. Things were unraveling quickly.

Carson ran a hand through his hair. He had always known the world had changed, but hearing Marco talk about FEMA's failures, the military's stretched-thin resources, and the growing unrest in Denver showed him the true extent of the CME's impact.

Raelynn whispered something to the baby in the back seat, her small voice soothing against the tense silence in the cab. At least one of them was confident.

Then Carson saw it. Up ahead, the highway was blocked. At

first, it looked like another wreck—a pile-up of burned-out cars, something he could maneuver around. But as they got closer, his gut clenched. Scattered across the scorched landscape lay the twisted carcasses of fallen aircraft. Some had disintegrated on impact, their fuselages split open like crushed soda cans, jagged metal still curled and warped from the heat. Others had gouged deep trenches into the earth, their final, desperate skid marks still visible before they erupted into fireballs. Smoke no longer poured from the wreckage. The air reeked of burnt fuel, scorched rubber, and the unmistakable scent of decayed flesh. Carson inhaled sharply and regretted it—the acrid stench clung to his throat, bitter and toxic, like breathing in death itself. He gripped the steering wheel hard, his gut roiling from the sight. He had already seen so much destruction. But this? It was worse than anything he had imagined.

Julie swallowed hard beside him. "All those people."

"If only we—"

"Don't," Julie snapped, shaking her head. "Don't think like that."

But it was already too late. His mind conjured the image of Deitra—his girlfriend, strapped into her seat, oblivious to what was coming, maybe chatting with the flight attendant, maybe staring out the window, watching the world go dark before the plane lost power and plummeted from the sky. A choked sound tore from his throat. His stomach lurched. He just managed to fling the door open and stumble out before his stomach heaved, emptying its contents onto the pavement.

Julie was there in an instant, kneeling beside him, her hand firm on his back. "Carson…"

He spat bile and wiped his mouth with the back of his hand, his breath ragged. "I should have warned them," he rasped. "I knew, Julie. I saw the early data. I could've—"

"Stop!" she barked. "We can't think like that. Besides, you tried—I did nothing while you risked your career to confront lead-

Utter Devastation

ership about the flawed data—the AI models that ignored the warning signs. And me? I should have done more. I should have —" She paused and drew in a breath, glancing around. "We have to keep moving forward. What-ifs won't bring Deitra back. They won't help your sister or your dad or your mom to survive this. The only thing that matters now is what we do next."

Carson's throat burned, his chest aching with the weight of her words. He took in the scene ahead. A plane had crashed on the highway. The twisted wreckage of a commercial airliner lay sprawled across the road, its metal carcass torn open, its insides spilling onto the pavement. The tail jutted into the sky at an unnatural angle, blackened from fire. The remains of one wing lay in a million pieces across the median like a bomb had gone off midflight. A jagged tear through the cockpit exposed twisted metal and shattered glass.

There were no signs of life.

Julie exhaled, pressing a hand to her mouth. "Damn."

Carson felt cold, even as sweat slicked his palms. His girlfriend Deitra had been on a plane from Dallas to Denver. His lungs locked up. His thoughts swirled. Panic seized his gut. Could this be her plane?

Oh, God!

The air around him suddenly felt too thick, suffocating. He had to know. Had to make sure she wasn't here, injured, suffering, waiting for help that would never come. His legs carried him forward, his body moving on instinct as he stepped into the wreckage, navigating around burned-out luggage, torn seats, and pieces of bodies scattered like debris.

"Carson!" Julie's voice snapped after him.

He felt like he was standing in a long, dark tunnel.

This was his fault. He had caused it all.

He stopped at the torn-open fuselage, his breath coming in ragged gasps. There were still people strapped to their seats, bodies frozen in their last moments of terror. Some were charred beyond recognition, burned down to bone, their hands still gripping the armrests. The force of the impact had thrown others clear of the plane, leaving their bodies broken and lifeless on the pavement.

Carson scanned each face—or what was left of them—his vision blurring. "Deitra!" he screamed into the wind. She wasn't there. But she could be in the next one.

A cracked phone lay in the wreckage, its shattered screen black.

A pink sneaker lay beside it, half-melted. Farther away, sat a teddy bear blackened by fire.

"Damn it!" Carson's chest heaved, his knees threatening to buckle.

This was what he had failed to stop.

"Carson, stop," Julie called out from the truck. "There's no one left." She lowered her voice. "No one made it out, Carson. Look at this."

He did.

At the melted bodies. At the ruins of what was once human.

"There's no way Deitra would have survived even if she were on this plane," Julie said softly. "And there's no way to know if it was hers."

Carson closed his eyes, his hands clenching into fists. He wanted to argue and keep searching, but the truth was right there in front of him. This wasn't just another wreck. It was a graveyard. Where were the fire trucks? Where were the authorities? Did anyone even know this had happened?

Julie called again, her voice tinged with urgency now. "Carson, we need to go. The children can't see this."

His muscles locked up. Then, through the haze of grief and guilt, he heard it. A low, pained moan. Carson's head snapped up. Not from the plane—but nearby.

Julie heard it, too. She turned toward the pile of crushed vehicles near the edge of the wreckage. Her eyes widened. "Someone's alive."

Utter Devastation

The sound came from a crumpled sedan, half-crushed beneath a fallen wing. The windshield was shattered, the metal folded inward, trapping the driver inside.

Carson and Julie rushed over, scanning the wreckage.

The man inside was a ruin of burns, broken bones, and raw wounds, his leg twisted beneath the dashboard. Half of his face had gone, burned beyond recognition, but his eyes—sunken and pained—blinked sluggishly up at them.

Julie exhaled sharply. "Oh ... my."

Carson crouched beside him. "Hey," he said, keeping his voice calm. "We're gonna get you out of here."

"F-figured ... I was d-dead already," he whispered through cracked lips.

Julie grabbed a bottle of water and twisted the cap off. "Can you drink?"

The man nodded weakly, and she tilted the bottle to his lips. He swallowed with painful effort, his body shaking.

Julie pulled Carson a few feet away. "Carson, what are we going to do? He's trapped in there. He needs a doctor."

"I know." The reality of what they were about to do hit him like a gut punch. The man wasn't just injured—he was dying. And moving him would be torture. Carson ran to the Tacoma, yanked open the bed of the truck, and fumbled through tools and supplies. His hand landed on a pry bar. It would have to do.

The wreckage groaned as he wedged the bar into the twisted metal and forced it apart with slow, deliberate effort. Every shift and snap of sheared metal elicited a raw, guttural sound of pain from the man. Julie was kneeling beside him, murmuring something soft and reassuring, but her expression was tight, her jaw clenched, her eyes shining with a helplessness she rarely showed. Carson gritted his teeth and kept working, twisting metal, and attempting to pull him from the wreckage. The man's feeble cries were torture to Carson's ears. He didn't beg them to stop, but every time they moved him even an inch, his broken body trembled, and his lips twisted in agony.

The smell was unbearable. Burned flesh. The sickly scent of cooked hair and seared fabric. Carson had never smelled death before, but this had to be it. Julie turned pale, swallowing convulsively as she worked beside him. At one point, she turned her head and pressed her fist against her mouth, dry-heaving. Carson wasn't sure how he managed himself.

"Don't stop," the man rasped. "Please … just … get me out. I don't want to die here."

Carson exhaled sharply. "Almost there."

Another pull. Another choked groan.

Then—finally—he was free. But he wasn't moving. For a horrible moment, Carson thought they'd killed him. Then his chest rose a millimeter or two.

His eyes fluttered open. "Home," he whispered, his voice so weak Carson barely heard it.

Julie wiped the back of her hand across her mouth. "We have to cover him."

"With what?" Carson's voice came out raspy from holding back emotion.

"Baby blankets."

Carson hesitated. Baby blankets. Henry's.

She was already moving toward the truck, flinging open the door and yanking out every clean blanket she could find in the diaper bag.

As Carson moved in that direction, his gaze flickered toward the back seat. Raelynn was hunched forward, her tiny hands gripping the edge of her booster seat. Her face was pale, her wide eyes shiny with unshed tears. She understood. She knew what was happening. Henry, awakened by the sound of the truck's door, started to wail, his small cries piercing through the suffocating silence. Raelynn's wide, tear-brimmed eyes stayed fixed on the man in the wreckage.

Utter Devastation

"Close your eyes, baby," Julie murmured, brushing a trembling hand over the little girl's hair before turning to run back to the man. She unfolded two soft baby blankets and draped them over him, shielding as much of his ruined flesh as she could.

Meanwhile, Carson scanned the wreckage, searching for anything that could hold the man's weight without tearing his fragile body apart. Amid the twisted metal and scorched earth of the westbound lane, he spotted a large aluminum road sign, partially covered by dirt. It had been ripped from its post in the crash, now dented and blackened by fire. He crouched, gripping the edge of the jagged metal and wrenching it free from the debris. The word "Airport" was the only visible word beneath the soot.

A bitter thought lodged itself in Carson's mind. Some of these people had been on their way home. Now, they were never going to make it.

Julie's sharp inhale snapped him back. "Will that work?" she asked, now standing beside him.

"It has to."

Together, they dragged the sign closer, the scorched metal grating against the pavement. Carson crouched beside what had once been the driver's side door, trying to ignore the stench of the man's charred skin. "Sir." He kept his voice low and steady. "We're going to move you."

The man's eyelids fluttered weakly. His fingers twitched under the blanket. "Do it." His voice was barely a breath.

Carson's gut clenched.

Julie knelt at the man's side. "This is gonna hurt," she warned. "I won't lie to you."

He swallowed, his throat working painfully slow. "Just ... g-get me home. Pl ... ease."

SIXTEEN

Willow

Gas and Go
King George, Virginia
Day Four

Willow had only intended to find a restroom. A simple, forgettable task. Now she stood there in the gas station parking lot, witnessing an assault against a woman and child. The man hadn't noticed her yet. He was too focused on his victims. Willow's pulse pounded in her ears. Her body moved before her mind even had time to process what was happening.

This wasn't happening! Not on her watch!

Willow stepped up the pace, her boots crunching against the gravel, and called out, "Leave them alone!"

The man—tall, scruffy, with a cruel twist to his mouth—turned his head without loosening his grip on the woman's hair. His lips curled into a sneer.

"Or what?" he barked.

Willow took a step closer, her hand hovering over her holster. "I said, leave them alone!"

Utter Devastation

The man's smile widened, his teeth yellowed and jagged. He turned fully toward her now, still holding the woman by the hair, but unconcerned. She heard the footsteps a split second before impact. A force slammed into her from behind and sent her sprawling forward onto the gravel. Pain exploded through her ribs as the air whooshed from her lungs. Her hands scraped against the rough ground, the sting barely registering through the shock. The weight of a man pressed down on her back, pinning her. As she gasped for air, her pistol was stripped from her grasp.

Damn it! Stupid! Stupid!

She forced her muscles to react, channeling everything she'd learned from self-defense training. The moment he shifted his weight, she slammed her elbow back and into his ribs. A sharp grunt erupted above her. She rolled and twisted underneath him, driving her knee into his groin with enough force to make him howl with agony. He rolled away.

The gun clattered to the ground, but before she could reach for it, the second man—the one who had been tormenting the woman—kicked it out of her reach.

Willow narrowly had time to brace herself before the first man came at her again.

She pivoted, dodging his grasp, and threw a quick combination—an elbow strike to his jaw, followed by a brutal knee to his ribs. He stumbled, hopping on one leg, but it wasn't enough to drop him.

The second man laughed. "You got some fight in you. I like that."

Rage burned through her veins. She wasn't fighting for herself. She was fighting for that mother and child.

The first man lunged again, and this time, she was ready.

She feinted left, then drove her fist into his throat with a crushing strike. He staggered back, choking, his hands clutching at his neck. Before he could recover, she followed up with a devastating kick to the side of his knee, which sent him sprawling onto the gravel. She landed a boot to his temple, and then he was out cold.

Willow turned, locking onto the second man again—the one now gripping the woman by the hair. He shoved his victim aside and rolled his shoulders, eyes gleaming with sick excitement.

"Oh, this is gonna be fun."

That was exactly what Willow was thinking.

He charged at her shoulder down. Willow waited until the last possible second. Then she stepped aside, grabbed his arm, and twisted his momentum against him, slamming him face-first into the side of the building. The impact sent a sickening crack through the air.

He stumbled back, dazed, blood dripping down his nose, but still grinning. "That all you got?"

She didn't answer. Instead, she delivered a brutal combination—three rapid strikes to his ribs, a knee to his gut, and a final, crushing kick to his kneecap. He crumpled to the ground, moaning in pain.

Willow pivoted to focus on the woman and child, but they had vanished.

Where did they go?

Before Willow could process the thought, something slammed into her side. The ground rushed up to meet her, hard and unforgiving. The impact knocked the breath from her lungs, leaving her gasping, vision blurring at the edges.

Move!

But her body wouldn't listen. Panic clawed at the edges of Willow's mind. Was she blacking out? No. No, she couldn't. Not now.

Focus! Get up now!

The man's weight crushed her into the pavement and pinned her like a caged animal. She could feel his hot breath against her neck and his grip tightening around her wrist. Fury boiled in her gut.

Not again.

Willow arched her back, twisting, fighting—but a sudden, searing pain exploded through her ribs as he drove fist after fist into her side. Pain. Sharp, raw, and infuriating. A deep, primal growl erupted from her throat as she hooked her leg over his, using his weight against him. His balance shifted—just enough. She rolled hard and fast. The second she was on top, Willow didn't hesitate. She landed a series of palm strikes to his nose.

One. Two. Three.

Cartilage crunched under her hands, and the bastard let out a strangled yell. She tore free, staggering to her feet, her body screaming at her to stop, to breathe. He was still down but not for long. The stunned man now lay on his back with his knees parted.

Wide open.

Willow drove her heel into his groin with every ounce of force she had left. His body jerked as a guttural, choking noise escaped him. He curled inward, rolling to his side, writhing in agony. She spat on him, fury surging through her veins.

Pathetic.

A final kick to the ribs sent him sprawling. Begging. "Okay, okay! Enough!" he wheezed, his hands raised in surrender.

Willow stood over him, chest heaving, hands shaking with adrenaline. She wasn't scared anymore. She was done being hunted. He'd picked the wrong damn woman. "You piece of shit. You think you can beat on a woman." Willow stepped back, breathing hard, fists still clenched. Her pulse thundered in her ears.

A car door creaked open behind her. Knox, unsteady on his feet, stepped out of the Suburban. Behind him, Guynn emerged from the store, surveying the scene with a raised eyebrow.

"I guess you got this handled."

Willow exhaled sharply, rolling her shoulders to shake off the tension. She walked over and picked up her pistol from where it had landed on the pavement.

Knox leaned against the truck's door, his expression dark. "What happened?"

"They were attacking a woman and her kid. I couldn't just stand there."

"You could've gotten yourself killed, Willow!"

She squared her shoulders. "I'm not going to watch a woman and kid get beat up and do nothing."

Knox sighed heavily, glancing at the two men still groaning in the dirt. "Anyway. Nice job!"

SEVENTEEN

Carson

Interstate 70
Aurora, Colorado
Day Four

Carson and Julie braced themselves, positioning their hands beneath the poor man's shoulders and hips.

They counted together.

"One."

"Two."

"Three!"

As soon as they lifted him, he screamed—a high-pitched, wavering cry that would haunt Carson's dreams for the rest of his life. Julie's hands shook as they eased him onto the sign. The injured man's body shook, his jaw clenching.

"Aaaahh... P-pleeease—" he gasped, his voice a ragged whisper. "D-don't stop."

Carson's vision blurred for a second. They had to finish this. Julie bit her lip so hard it bled, but she forced herself to keep moving, gripping the edge of the metal sheet and lifting with all her strength. Carson grabbed the other side. The man let out a choked cry, his head falling back as his body spasmed.

"I'm so sorry," Julie whispered.

Together, they lifted the makeshift stretcher and hastened toward the truck. The man's whimpers weakened to short, wet gasps. They maneuvered the sign onto the truck bed, lowering it with care so the metal didn't shift beneath him. He exhaled sharply, his body going still for a terrifying second. Then, his chest rose—barely.

His pulse hammering, Carson stared down at what was left of the man. "We should cover him with our emergency blankets to keep him warm." He moved to the front of the bed and opened the top pouch in search of two of the metalized plastic sheets meant to prevent or treat hypothermia. He hoped they would act as a windbreaker in the bed of the truck.

Julie hesitated. "Where's the closest hospital?"

Their patient's eyelids fluttered open. "No hospitals," he rasped.

Julie frowned. "Where's home?"

The man's ragged breath hitched, his body trembling beneath the blankets. His charred fingers twitched where they lay limp against his chest. "Wallet … p-pocket," he rasped. His voice was so faint, Carson almost didn't hear it.

Carson's stomach twisted. He glanced at Julie. Her jaw was tight, her face pale beneath the grime and soot. They both knew how much this was going to hurt him. But there was no choice.

Carson took a steadying breath and forced his own hesitation aside. "I'm sorry," he murmured.

The man blinked twice. "Do it."

Carson slid a hand beneath his hip.

The moment Carson shifted his weight, the man went rigid. A violent, full-body tremor wracked his frame, his mouth opening in a silent scream. His burned fingers clawed weakly at the air, but no sound came.

Utter Devastation

Not a whimper.
Not a cry.
Nothing.

Carson's chest ached at the sight. The fire had even stolen his ability to scream. Every instinct in Carson urged him to stop the torment. But the man had asked for this. Carson gritted his teeth and forced himself to continue, gently rolling him just enough to slip his fingers into the back pocket of his tattered, blood-soaked jeans. Carson's fingers closed around the wallet, and he pulled it free before easing the man back down as carefully as he could.

The man's eyes fluttered, his lips parting in a silent sob, his entire body quivering. Julie reached for him and smoothed the blankets over his trembling frame, her voice a gentle murmur of reassurance. Carson stood there with the scorched leather wallet in his hand, horrified by what he had just done.

It felt too heavy in his hands. He was surprised the driver's license inside was still legible. The photo stared back at him—a man who had once been whole, smiling, unscarred. Now, he was dying in the back of the truck.

Carson's voice came out hoarse as he said the name out loud. "Bruce Coriton. 308 Rock Island Avenue, Ramah, Colorado."

He turned and leaned into the cab, fumbling with his Colorado state map, spreading it across the driver's seat. He found Ramah quickly. Thirty miles west of Limon. Not far off their intended route. But for Bruce? It might as well be a lifetime away.

Julie hesitated. "He needs a hospital."

Carson's hands tightened into fists. "The hospitals are in Denver. You saw the streets. Even if we make it there, they'll be overrun with injured people."

Julie exhaled sharply, pressing her fingers against her forehead.

Carson turned toward the truck bed, his gaze drifting to Bruce, then to Raelynn, who was curled in her booster seat, clutching Sophie's carrier like a lifeline.

"He just wants to go home," he said.

Julie closed her eyes for a long moment. Then she nodded and walked toward the passenger side door of the truck.

Carson moved to the rear of the truck, leaning over the bed. "We'll take you home."

Bruce's lips twitched, his eyes fluttering shut. Maybe it was relief. Maybe it was just exhaustion. But he was still alive.

Carson's hand tightened around the door handle, but a feeling prickled at the back of his neck—a presence, a weight. He glanced into the back seat. Raelynn sat still as stone, her wide eyes locked on him. She had seen everything. Carson's chest tightened. *What do I say to her?* Shaking his head, he climbed behind the wheel and started the engine.

He put the truck into gear, and it rumbled beneath them as they pulled away from the wreckage. The metallic taste of adrenaline still clung to his tongue, and his muscles felt like they had been locked in place for hours. He forced himself to glance in the rearview mirror one last time. At the plane wreckage, still smoldering in the distance. At the crushed cars with their silent occupants. At the lives that had ended in fire and terror. His stomach clenched. He should have warned people sooner. Should have done something. And now, Bruce was dying in the bed of his truck, hanging on by a thread, because Carson had decided he wouldn't let another person die alone. The weight of it hit him all at once. His hands trembled against the steering wheel. Beside him, Julie pressed her forehead against the window, her fingers rubbing at her temples as if she could push the memory away.

Neither of them spoke.

The enormity of what they'd just done—the pain they had caused by trying to help—pressed down on them like a crushing weight. They had pulled a man from hell, only to watch him suffer even more. And yet, they had no choice. Carson swallowed hard, his throat tight, his vision swimming for a brief second before he forced himself to focus.

Then, from the backseat came a small, uncertain voice. "What is that back there?"

Julie twisted in her seat. "That, Raelynn..." She hesitated, then softened her tone. "That is a man. He's hurt, and we're going to take him home."

Raelynn's enormous eyes flickered toward the back window, but she didn't press for more.

Julie leaned over the seat and rummaged in the diaper bag, pulling out a worn children's book and pressing it gently into Raelynn's lap. "Here, sweetheart," she murmured. "Read this to your brother."

She stared at the book for a long second, then nodded, opening it with small, careful fingers.

Carson studied Henry, whose tiny chest was rising and falling with deep, peaceful breaths. And Raelynn, her small body hunched over the pages, her lips moving as she read softly. He turned his gaze to Julie, exhaustion pulling at her features as she stared through the windshield at the road ahead. And for the first time, the full weight of responsibility slammed into him. *How the heck did I become responsible for so many fragile lives?* He could barely look after himself. Now?

Now, he had to keep all of them alive, too.

As they pulled away from the wreckage, Carson took one last look at the plane. He still didn't know if Deitra had been on that flight. But he agreed with Julie. No one on the plane had survived the crash. But someone on the ground had, and he wasn't going to fail this man, too.

EIGHTEEN

Arthur

Carlisle Residence
Lakewood Heights
Dallas, Texas
Day Four

The weakest points were the windows. And if those kids came back in numbers, if they had sledgehammers or crowbars, he and Katherine would have seconds—maybe minutes—before they were inside. The answer was clear. He had to make entry as difficult as possible. Arthur ran through his plan again, every detail playing out in his head. Once night fell, he'd use the furniture dolly to move the heavy concrete planters from the back patio around to the front walk. He wouldn't make it look obvious—just enough to narrow the approach so that no one could get a running start at the door. The planters would absorb force from any attempt to break in, slowing down any battering attempts. But that wasn't enough. The windows needed more protection.

Katherine helped as they rearranged the house to turn their sanctuary into a barricade. First, they used the furniture dolly from

Utter Devastation

the garage to move the China hutch against the two front windows. The solid wood frame and glass shelves weren't perfect, but stacking the dishes back inside it added a comforting weight; it would be more difficult to knock over now.

After resting for nearly thirty minutes to recover, Arthur set to work, emptying the fridge of putrid-smelling perishables and moving it forward to block the breakfast nook window. A person wouldn't be able to crawl through it, and trying to move it would be loud enough to alert him and Katherine.

Next, he turned his attention to their bedroom windows. The two bookshelves from Katherine's office were wide enough to cover both the windows but weren't very sturdy without books. He tasked Katherine with replacing the books to keep the weight and make it harder to topple. A casual attempt to get in wouldn't work; someone would have to kick it down or pry it loose.

After that, he focused on the guest bedroom window. Back in her office, Arthur dragged her old desk, a thick one-inch oak with steel legs, out the door and into the hall. He had to stop and catch his breath for several minutes before pulling it into their bedroom. Once he had it up on end, he screwed it into the window frame. The legs braced against the headboard of the bed made it a formidable barrier.

By the time he and Katherine had finished fortifying the house, Arthur's lungs burned, his arms shaking from the exertion.

He climbed the attic steps, the wood creaking under his weight as he grabbed the foldable fire escape ladder and set it by the window in the attic bedroom. He prayed they'd never have to use it. Even with the ladder's one-foot-wide, anti-slip rungs, his aging knees would be a problem, not to mention just climbing out the window onto it. Their last way out. He stared at the instructions written in bold writing. "Attach hooks over the windowsill and pull the release strap to unfurl the ladder." If they got cornered, if the house was compromised, this was their only chance.

As he made his way back down, his knees protested. His chest tightened. The strain of the day had caught up to him. Arthur narrowly made it to his recliner before his legs gave out. His pulse thudded in his ears, his breathing shallow as he pressed his hand against his chest. Katherine appeared in the doorway, frowning.

"Are you okay?"

Arthur nodded as he tried to slow his breathing.

"Do you need your nitroglycerin tablets? Did you even take your heart meds today?"

He hadn't.

He'd been rationing them, just like their food—one every other day to make them last until Carson arrived. Maybe that was flawed thinking. Maybe he'd just shortened his own chances of making it through this. He shook his head, and Katherine disappeared into the bathroom to grab his pills. Arthur closed his eyes, focusing on slowing his heartbeat.

Then Katherine screamed.

Arthur's eyes snapped open. "Katherine!" He pushed himself up, legs trembling, staggering to the bathroom.

Katherine stood frozen, staring up at the tiny window above the bathtub. Spray-painted on the outside was the symbol. The same one he'd scrubbed off their garage door months ago.

The same one as on the girl's backpack at the school.

Arthur's breath caught in his chest as he grabbed Katherine's arm and pulled her away from the window. "Get back," he rasped. He pressed a hand against the bathroom wall to steady himself, still recovering from his near-collapse.

Katherine swallowed hard, her face pale as she gripped the sink. "Arthur, that's—"

"I know." He forced himself to look at it again. The symbol was crude, painted in thick, uneven strokes. Was it a mark of claim? A warning? Or a target? Arthur clenched his jaw. He had scrubbed the first one off the garage door weeks ago, thinking it was just some idiot kid tagging random houses. Then he'd seen it again—on the girl's backpack at the school, just before everything

Utter Devastation

went to hell. Now it was back, and this time, it wasn't random. Someone had put it there deliberately.

Katherine let out a shaky breath. "Do you think they saw me?"

He didn't answer. Honestly, he didn't know. If someone had been close enough to paint the mark, close enough to know they were inside, then maybe they'd been watching for a while. Maybe they'd been waiting. His gut twisted. They weren't ready. He stepped forward, careful to stay out of direct sight of the window, and pulled the shower curtain closed. It wouldn't stop a bullet, but it might make it harder to see inside.

"We can't stay here," Katherine whispered.

"I know that, honey." He'd known it since the looting started; since Carson had told them to wait for him. But he wasn't there yet, and Arthur wasn't sure they had time to wait anymore. His eyes drifted back toward the window. The paint was still wet. Whoever had done this wasn't far away. Arthur agreed. They needed to go—but where? The reality hit him like a weight on his chest. He was in his seventies—too old to carry enough food, water, and supplies to keep them alive outside these walls. They had no backup plan or safe haven. And Carson was coming. If they left, how would he ever find them? Carson was their only hope. He had a plan. He'd know what to do. They just had to hold out long enough for him to get here.

NINETEEN

Willow

Gas and Go
King George, Virginia
Day Four

Willow's body ached. Every movement was a reminder of the brutal fight that had just unfolded in the gas station parking lot. Her ribs throbbed where the bastard had landed his punches. Her knuckles were raw, her wrist sore. But she didn't care. Her gaze flicked to Knox as she helped him ease into the Suburban's back seat. He looked worse. Pale. Unsteady. She climbed into the passenger seat, still running on adrenaline and stubbornness, though her limbs felt heavier with every passing second.

Guynn settled into the driver's seat and turned the key. The engine rumbled to life, grounding them in the only thing that mattered now—getting out of there before more trouble found them.

Willow let out a slow breath, bracing herself against the pain in her ribs.

"You good?" Guynn asked.

"Yeah. Do they have fuel?" She gestured to the fuel pumps.

"They're out of gas," he said, shifting into gear. "Fella inside said to try Port Royal. That's south of—"

The flash of blue lights cut across the windshield.

Willow's pulse spiked. Instinctively, she removed her pistol from its holster and slid it beneath her seat. She didn't know what the laws were in Virginia on concealed carrying a weapon.

A sheriff's department vehicle raced into the parking lot, skidding to a stop directly behind them, blocking their exit. A deputy threw open the door to his cruiser and shouted for them to remain in the vehicle as he strode across the parking lot toward the two men.

Willow's gut twisted as she saw the two men pointing their way, talking fast, smirking like they'd already won.

Guynn exhaled sharply. "Let me handle this."

Willow's hands curled into fists. "But they—"

"He's right, Willow," Knox said from the back seat. "We're strangers here. Those men? They could be the sheriff's cousins, nephews, or drinking buddies. You don't know how deep this goes."

Before she could argue, the deputy stood next to the passenger door, his expression unreadable. Then, without warning, he yanked open Willow's door and reached in for her.

Both Knox and Guynn exploded at once.

"Whoa, whoa—slow down now!" Guynn warned.

"Let's hear both sides," Knox snapped.

In seconds, Willow was hauled out of the truck, spun around, and slammed against the rear bumper. "They attacked me! I was trying to stop that guy from beating his wife and kid!" she protested.

The deputy scoffed. His hands skated roughly over her body, forcing her to spread her legs.

Her breath hitched as his hands moved over her thighs, her ribs, her chest—too rough and too invasive. Not like a cop checking for weapons. Like a man exerting power.

The world blurred, memories crashing back like a tidal wave.

Her ex. Pinning her against the wall. His grip was unrelenting, her fear paralyzing. Willow's muscles tensed, every nerve in her body screaming to fight back. But she forced herself to remain still. He had a badge and a gun. If she fought, this could go from bad to worse in an instant.

Guynn's voice cut through the haze.

"She's not resisting."

"Get your hands off her!" Knox shouted.

The deputy ignored them. "You pulled a gun on those men," he accused, tightening his grip on her wrists.

Willow whipped her head around. "Huh? No, I didn't! He attacked me from behind. My weapon fell—"

"So, you admit you had a gun?"

"Yes, but—"

Guynn took a slow step forward, his hands visible. "She was defending herself. We saw the whole thing."

The deputy tensed, his grip tightening on the cuffs. "She's going to jail."

"Give me a second." Guynn reached back as if going for his wallet.

The deputy instantly stepped back, hand flying to his service weapon. "Hands in the air!"

Willow's breath caught in her throat. This was spiraling out of control fast. She turned her head as Knox threw open the truck door. "No! Stay in the truck. I'm fine!" she shouted.

Knox frowned.

Guynn threw up a hand. "Stand down, Knox. Let me handle this."

"There's nothing to handle," the deputy said. "She's under arrest." He grabbed Willow's wrists.

Guynn's voice sharpened. "Then I assume you've already taken statements from all available witnesses?"

More hesitation.

This time, Guynn's eyes narrowed. "You've interviewed the folks in the gas station, right?"

Another pause.

Guynn tilted his head, pressing just enough. "And the woman with the kid that man was abusing?"

Willow watched the deputy's forehead wrinkle.

Then the sound of another vehicle rumbled over the pavement, tires crunching against loose gravel. A second patrol car pulled into the lot and came to a deliberate, unhurried stop beside the first. The deputy stiffened. His grip on Willow's wrists didn't loosen, but his eyes flicked toward the new arrival.

A tall, broad-shouldered man in a khaki uniform stepped out, his sheriff's badge glinting in the sunlight. He adjusted his belt as he appeared to take in the scene—Willow pinned against the Suburban, the deputy's hand on his gun, the colonel standing stock-still with his hands raised, and Knox halfway out of the vehicle, eyes blazing.

The sheriff's expression darkened. "What the hell's going on here?"

The deputy's hold on Willow tightened for a fraction of a second as if he didn't want to let go. Then he exhaled and stepped back, releasing her. "She assaulted two men," he said quickly. "Pulled a gun on them."

The sheriff's sharp gaze shifted to the two men still lingering near the store, smirking like they had the situation in the bag. Then he turned back to Willow, scanning her face, then Guynn's, then Knox's. His jaw ticked, but his voice remained level.

"Let's start over," the sheriff said. "Who's pressing charges?"

The two men straightened, one rubbing his jaw like it still ached.

"I am," the bigger one said. "She attacked me for no reason."

Willow gaped. "You were beating your wife and kid in the parking lot!"

The man scoffed, shaking his head. "She's my woman. I was just talking to her."

"Talking?" Willow barked a laugh. "You had your hand around her throat!"

The sheriff's eyes narrowed. Slowly, he turned back to the deputy. "Did you interview the woman?"

"She was gone when I arrived on the scene."

"You interview any other witnesses?"

The deputy didn't answer.

"We saw the whole thing, Sheriff," Guynn said. "That man was assaulting a woman. Willow intervened. She never pulled a gun. Just defended herself when he attacked her from behind."

The sheriff's jaw twitched again, but his face remained unreadable. He took a slow breath, then turned back to the two men.

"Where's the woman and kid now?"

The man who had accused Willow shifted from foot to foot. "I dunno. She ran off."

The sheriff's eyes locked on to him. "You mean she left the scene while you were busy complaining about getting your ass kicked by a woman?"

The man's face flushed red. "That ain't—"

"Save it." The sheriff cut him off. His focus flicked to Willow. "You hurt?"

Willow blinked. That was not what she was expecting. "No."

His gaze slid to the deputy, hard and assessing. "You frisk her?"

The deputy squared his shoulders. "Yeah. She had a gun."

"And? You confirm she pulled it on them?"

"She admitted to having one."

"That ain't what I asked."

Silence.

The sheriff exhaled through his nose, the furrow in his brow

Utter Devastation

deepening. Then he turned to Guynn, nodding his cap. "You ex-military?"

"Yes, sir."

He side-stepped the deputy and gestured for Guynn to follow him back to his cruiser. After a long conversation, he and Guynn returned.

The sheriff took a long look at him, then at Knox, then at Willow. Then, finally, he turned back to the deputy. "Let 'em go."

The deputy stiffened. "Sheriff, she—"

"I said let 'em go!"

The deputy's jaw flexed, but he didn't argue further.

The sheriff turned back to Willow. "If I were you, I'd get in that truck and drive south like you got somewhere to be."

Willow didn't need to be told twice. She nodded, rubbing her sore wrists as she moved toward the passenger door. Knox hovered beside her, still tense. Guynn gave the sheriff one last knowing nod before sliding into the driver's seat. As they pulled out of the lot, Willow glanced back through the rearview mirror. The sheriff was still standing there, watching them go. As they hit the road, she let out a slow breath.

Knox turned to Guynn. "That was too easy."

"Nothing about that was easy."

Willow swallowed. "That deputy was pissed. He wanted me locked up."

"Yep," Guynn agreed.

"So, why'd the sheriff let me go?"

Guynn didn't answer at first. Then, finally, he glanced at her. "Because that deputy isn't just some cop," he said. "He's the new mayor's son."

Willow's stomach dropped.

Knox let out a low curse. "And the sheriff?"

Guynn's expression was unreadable. "Let's just say he and the mayor aren't exactly on friendly terms."

Willow felt a chill creep down her spine. So, this wasn't about her. It was about something bigger. The sheriff hadn't let them go because he believed she was innocent. He'd done it because arresting her would've meant giving that deputy—and his daddy—the win.

TWENTY

Carson

Casterman's Feed Store
Ramah, Colorado
Day Four

The drive south had been silent except for the soft breathing of the two children in the back seat. Every few minutes, Carson glanced in the mirror, his stomach twisting. He didn't know if Bruce was even still alive beneath the blankets. Either way, he'd keep his word. He'd take the man home to his family. Julie sat beside him, her knuckles white on the dashboard. She had said little since they pulled away from the crash site.

The town of Ramah came into view—a collection of abandoned cars, broken fences, and lifeless streets.

Julie frowned, her eyes scanning the desolation. "I don't like this place."

Carson nodded, his gut churning. "It's too quiet."

Then, ahead—a figure stepped into the road, raising a hand. Carson slowed the truck and tightened his grip on the wheel. The man was stocky, broad-shouldered, and heavily armed. Two more figures emerged from the shadows of an old feed store, carrying shotguns and rifles.

Julie tensed. "This is bad."

Carson's stomach tightened as the first man grinned.

"Welcome to Ramah."

One of the men ventured close, peering into the truck bed. His face twisted in disgust at Bruce's burned, broken body beneath the emergency blankets. "Shit," he said, recoiling. He turned as another man emerged from the feed store. "You gotta see this, Casterman."

Carson's door jerked open, and before he could react, cold metal jabbed into his ribs. A rough hand clamped onto his arm, yanking him from the truck.

"Take his gun," a man barked at the guy beside him.

Carson scarcely had time to tense before his pistol was slipped from its holster.

"Carson!" Julie's voice rang out, sharp with panic. Her passenger door flew open, and she was hauled out just as violently.

The shouting startled Henry awake, his wails joining Raelynn's, filling the truck with high-pitched cries.

"Shut those damn things up!" snarled the man holding Julie.

He frisked her, then shoved her back into her seat before slamming the door.

Julie twisted in her seat, voice shaking but soothing, trying to calm the children.

As she did, a man in his late fifties approached, his stride slow, confident. Carson's eyes swept over him and sized him up in an instant—an old habit, hardwired from experience. Casterman's worn flannel stretched over broad shoulders, and a gut earned from years of overeating, shoved into faded jeans. A leather belt secured a holstered pistol at his hip. His deep-set eyes flicked over Carson and Julie. His patchy, rust-colored hair was short but unkempt, his wild beard failing to hide the smirk tugging at his mouth. But it wasn't just his size or his stance that made Carson's gut tighten. It

Utter Devastation

was the way he carried himself—with the lazy arrogance of a man who was used to owning a room.

Casterman moved like a king surveying his kingdom, his chin lifted, his body language relaxed, like he wasn't even considering the possibility that Carson or Julie could be a threat to him. But Carson could tell—beneath that smug exterior was something else—a hair-trigger temper lurking just beneath the surface. His fingers twitched occasionally at his sides, not out of nervousness, but out of habit. Clearly, he was used to gripping or controlling something. A man who didn't like being questioned.

Stopping beside the second man, Casterman glanced into the truck bed.

Carson didn't like the look in his eyes.

"Now." Casterman let out a low chuckle. "What the hell am I supposed to do with that?"

The man holding Carson shoved him forward, stopping even with Julie's open truck window. Carson could hear Raelynn sniffling, but Henry had settled down.

"He's one of yours," Carson said evenly. "A Ramah local. Bruce Coriton. We brought him home."

Casterman scoffed. "That so?" He stepped closer, gazing down at the dying man. "And did he tell you he was from here?"

Bruce shifted, groaning. His lips barely moved, his breath coming in shallow gasps.

"Take ... me home," he rasped.

"Home?" Casterman let out a mocking chuckle. "Boy, you don't got no home no more."

Carson was confused. He didn't know their back story, but this didn't sound like the homecoming he'd expected for the man.

"Drag him out of there." Casterman spat.

Carson stepped forward, but someone immediately grabbed his arm again. "We brought him here to get help. You're not taking him!"

"Not taking him?" Casterman's grin widened. "Now, that's

funny, 'cause last I checked, this was my town, and this man's my problem."

The second man beside him hesitated, his grip tightening on his rifle. The tension in the air thickened, and Carson felt every muscle in his body coil. His mind raced. This had probably been a man who was untouchable before the collapse—and now? With no law and no one to challenge him? Now, he was a warlord. Carson had seen men like him before. Men who built kingdoms out of fear. Men who saw power as a means to an end—until that end swallowed them whole. And Casterman? The man was already swimming in it. Carson knew if he made the wrong move, he would be dead. Who knows what they'd do with Julie and the children—or Deitra's poor cat?

Julie stuck her head out the window. "Look, we don't want trouble," she said, her voice measured. "We just—"

Casterman cut her off with a wave of his hand. "No, no," he said, pacing in front of them like a predator playing with its food. "You see, I got a real problem here. You roll into my town, dump some half-dead guy at my feet, and expect me to do what? Say 'thank you'?" He stopped suddenly, his eyes boring into Carson's. "That man was dead the moment he stole from me."

Carson's stomach dropped.

Julie's breath hitched. "What?"

"Ain't that funny?" Casterman chuckled darkly. "Y'all went through all that trouble just to bring me a loose end."

Why did Bruce ask to come home if he knew he had enemies here looking for him? Carson wondered.

Casterman leaned over the side of the truck bed, glaring down at the dying man. "You tell them anything, Corinton? Did you unburden yourself with last words, pleading for forgiveness from that God of yours?"

Bruce's eyes fluttered open just enough to see Casterman standing over him. Pure terror filled them.

Casterman reached out and poked Bruce in the chest.

Bruce let out a painful gasp.

"What did you tell them?" A look of disgust twisted Casterman's features. He wiped his hands on his shirt.

"N-nothing," Bruce choked out.

Casterman sighed and shook his head. "Yeah, why would I believe that?" Then—without hesitation—he pulled his gun and shot Bruce Corinton in the head.

Julie gasped, and the children began crying again.

Carson didn't move or breathe.

Tucking his pistol away like he'd just put down an animal, Casterman smiled. He turned back to Carson and leaned casually on the Tacoma.

"Now, then," he shouted over the cries of the children. "Let's talk about what ole Corinton told you about me and my town."

Carson glanced down at Julie's hand trembling near the crack between her seat and the console, hovering over her weapon, but Carson caught her eye and gave a small shake of his head.

No.

There were too many guns pointed at them, too many eyes watching.

Casterman studied them for a moment, then jerked his chin at his men.

"Take 'em."

Two enforcers stepped forward, grabbing Carson and yanking Julie from the truck.

Julie twisted and tried to pull away. "We have kids in the truck—"

"I don't give a shit." Casterman turned to another man.

"Help me get these two contained and then come back out to get rid of the kids."

Carson thrashed against his captor, rage flaring white-hot. "You touch them, and I swear I'll—"

A fist slammed into his gut, knocking the wind out of him.

"What about the truck?" the man asked.

"Hide it. We'll part it out later."

Julie shrieked, struggling. "Don't hurt them! Please—"

But Casterman was already walking away, laughing.

Carson gritted his teeth, trying to catch his breath as they were dragged toward the feed store. As he stumbled forward, he glanced back and caught sight of the pickup again in time to see a young woman, barely college-aged, at the back door of their truck, with Henry in her arms, carefully lifting Raelynn out of her booster seat.

His pulse hammered. She glanced toward him, just for a second. There was fear in her eyes. She wasn't part of this. She was terrified. Carson prayed he was right. And then Sophie's carrier was in her hands. The cat let out a low, mournful yowl.

Carson's chest tightened as the woman disappeared with the kids between two nearby buildings. "She's protecting them," he said under his breath as one of the enforcers shoved him inside. The people of Ramah watched from behind curtains and half-open doors, their expressions a mix of fear and quiet resignation. Not a single one of them tried to stop what was happening.

Right then, Carson knew they weren't leaving Ramah on their own terms.

TWENTY-ONE

Willow

Gas and Go
King George, Virginia
Day Four

Willow was still steaming over her encounter at the gas station when Guynn pointed the Suburban south toward Port Royal, VA, and crossed the bridge over the Rappahannock River. They didn't dare stop at any of the fueling stations in town after the incident with the deputy.

Knox grew even more quiet as they neared the ICE's Caroline Detention Center. He glanced that way as they passed it. Willow followed his gaze. There was no activity at the facility. "Maybe they emptied it out and bussed them all somewhere else," she said.

"Maybe," Guynn muttered.

Willow didn't want to think about the alternative.

The entrance to Fort A.P. Hill loomed ahead, blocked by a tall chain-link fence topped with razor wire. The gate was manned by weary soldiers in rumpled uniforms who tensed as Guynn pulled the Suburban to a stop.

"Stay put," Guynn said as he opened the door. "This won't take long."

"What are we doing here?" Willow asked.

"These guys will know more about the area than anyone. If there's fuel out there, they'll tell us. Besides, I'd like to find out how the rest of the country is faring."

Willow kept her eyes on the soldiers beyond the gate, who had their rifles at the ready. By the scowls on their faces, she sensed they weren't in the mood for a chat.

"Halt right there. The base is closed!" one of the guards shouted as Guynn approached.

Guynn flashed his retired military ID and gave his rank and name. After a brief exchange, they waved him through the barrier.

Willow exhaled, shifting in her seat, her gaze flicking to Knox. His head lolled back against the seat, jaw tight.

"You okay?" she asked, but Knox didn't answer right away.

"Just tired," he rasped. "It's nothing."

She hoped Guynn was successful at obtaining some fuel. Knox wasn't in any shape to walk if they ran out of gas.

Guynn returned fifteen minutes later, his face grim. "We need to keep moving. The government is fractured. Nothing is working as planned. No one's coming to save us."

"About what we expected, right?" Willow asked. They had expected the government to be overwhelmed under such circumstances.

"Yeah," Guynn said. "I just hoped that, on a base level, they'd be able to pull things together. The guard said everyone's been ordered to Richmond to help maintain peace. Riots and looting are hindering any effort to bring in aid to the residents."

They pulled away from the base, heading southwest toward Bowling Green, Virginia, the gas needle dipping lower with every mile. As they rolled into town, Guynn pulled the Suburban alongside a Ford pickup parked at an odd angle to the curb and climbed out, checking under the truck. He gave Willow a thumbs-up and moved toward the rear of their vehicle. Willow stepped out and watched as he popped the back hatch and retrieved the fuel can.

Suddenly, a man burst from a nearby shop, wild-eyed and clutching a shotgun. "Get away from my truck!" he bellowed.

Guynn only just managed to throw the fuel can back into the Suburban before the man fired a warning shot into the air. They didn't stick around to argue. Willow and Guynn jumped back into their vehicle and sped away.

Knox stirred weakly in the back seat. "Jeez, that was close."

"We're out of options," Guynn said. "We need gas, or we're walking."

They had no choice. They were running on fumes. At Ruther Glen, they had to find fuel. Knox couldn't walk. Ten miles later, the Suburban shuddered and coughed, rolling to a stop just off the road. No one was around in town—the storefronts were either looted or boarded up, and trash and abandoned vehicles were scattered across the road.

Guynn turned to Willow. "We need fuel. Now," he said, grabbing his shotgun. "We go in quietly."

Knox remained slumped in the seat, eyes half-lidded.

"Stay here. Keep watch," Guynn told him, handing him the shotgun.

Once again, he and Willow exited their vehicle. Guynn removed the fuel can, an empty plastic milk jug, a hammer, and a screwdriver from the back, and then Willow followed him as they moved across the abandoned street toward a shuttered bank. Several cars sat in the lot, likely repossessed from the owner, but likely still had some fuel in them. It was worth checking. They headed for a silver pickup and got to work. First, Guynn used his pocketknife to cut a section of a plastic jug.

"What's that for?" Willow asked.

"To catch the gasoline. The can won't fit under the tank."

"Wouldn't it be easier to find a hose somewhere and siphon it out?" Willow asked as Guynn grunted, scooting on his back under the truck.

"These newer vehicles have lockable filler caps. The only way past them is to pry, pick, and break the door open. They also have an anti-siphoning valve in the filler tube to prevent the theft of fuel."

Willow held the gas can as Guynn crawled under the truck with a hammer and screwdriver in his hand. Low, urgent voices broke the silence, snapping Willow to attention. Her pulse slammed into overdrive. "Colonel!" she hissed, her voice low but edged with urgency. She spun, reaching for her weapon.

"Hands up, thieves!" a man barked, his silhouette emerging from the shadows, a rifle trained on her chest.

Three more emerged behind him, their gear mismatched but their weapons steady. Civilians, not law enforcement—but dangerous all the same. The leader, a middle-aged man with a military stance, studied them with sharp, assessing eyes.

"What do you think you're doing?"

Willow swallowed hard and slowly raised her hands.

"Get out from underneath that truck. Keep your hands where we can see them."

Guynn struggled to climb out. One of the men marched over, grabbed hold of one of his legs, and yanked him out. Still on his back on the ground, Guynn looked up at the man. "You served?"

"Army. Two tours in Afghanistan," the man said.

"Thank you for your service," Willow said.

The man shot her a look and turned his attention back to Guynn. "Get up, old man."

Guynn had to use the truck bed to brace himself until he got to his feet. The man shoved him, nearly sending the colonel off his feet.

"Colonel!" Willow shouted.

He caught himself on the bumper, stopping for a moment to catch his breath.

"Colonel?" the fellow veteran asked.

"Colonial Byron Guynn, retired," he replied. Guynn straightened and lifted his hands in a non-threatening gesture. "What unit were you with?"

The younger man hesitated before answering. "1st Infantry."

Guynn nodded approvingly. "You ever get stationed in Germany?"

The veteran's face softened. "Yeah, spent a few years in Grafenwöhr."

This is good, Willow thought. Rapport building was an excellent strategy.

Guynn chuckled. "Ah, good ol' Graf. Beer halls and field exercises. I was there back in the late '90s. You make it to Prague while you were over there?"

"Oh yeah. Prague, Amsterdam, even made it down to Spain for a bit."

"That's the way to do it," Guynn said, nodding. "Hell of a place to be stationed. That was back when things made sense."

The vet sighed, his eyes shifting toward his waiting companions. "Yeah. Now, nothing makes sense anymore." A shadow of uncertainty crossed his face. "You think we'll come back from this?"

Guynn followed his gaze toward the impatient men behind him, their body language stiff and restless. "It won't be the politicians in Washington who fix this," he said. "It'll take strong leaders—real people, outside of D.C.—small-town folks, city folks, neighbors looking out for each other until we can rebuild. You're already doing your part, son. Patrolling the streets and keeping your community safe. That matters."

The veteran straightened at that. Guynn pressed on. "We're good people." He gestured down the street to the Suburban. "The guy in the back of our truck? He's a robotics engineer with NASA. Willow here? Investigative journalist. Rooting out corruption in D.C. before this all went to hell. We're just ordinary folks in an extraordinary situation. But right now, we're in a bind."

The veteran's gaze flicked toward the others, his mouth twisting.

"If you could see your way to help us," Guynn added, voice steady, "I'd be in your debt."

Exhaling, the young veteran nodded. "Well, maybe it wouldn't hurt to let you take a gallon or two. Get you down the road, maybe find a station open with fuel."

One of the other men scoffed. "Yeah, good luck with that."

Guynn reached for his pocket, unrolled the bills, and held them out for the men to see. "I can pay forty dollars. Six bucks a gallon?"

One of the veteran's companions shook his head. "I hear the refineries can't make more until the lights are back on, so this is all there is. That makes this fuel worth three times that."

"What about forty bucks for five gallons? I'll fill my container, and we'll go."

"Not enough," the man said. "Twenty dollars a gallon. You get two and get the hell out of our town." He turned to his companions. "Right, guys?"

Willow gritted her teeth. They needed that fuel. She glanced back at the Suburban. Knox was leaning against the window. His eyes were shut. She was now regretting taking him on this road trip so soon. She should have stood her ground and refused. He wasn't ready. He was still too weak to walk, and she and Guynn couldn't carry him half a block, let alone all the way to Arkansas.

The man's companions shrugged. "We split the cash and what's left of the fuel then."

The other men with him nodded in agreement.

"Deal," Guynn said.

The young veteran leaned in toward Willow. "Cash is worthless. But they don't know that yet," he said, his voice just above a whisper.

As Guyn paid the other men, the young veteran slid under the repoed truck, positioned a plastic jug beneath the fuel tank, and punctured it with the hammer and screwdriver. Gasoline trickled in, filling it steadily—until it overflowed, spilling onto the pavement. Willow poured it into their fuel can and handed it back to him. He filled it once more and then crawled out with the plastic container.

"Appreciate it, son," Guynn said as Willow poured the second gallon into the can.

"Hey, fuel's running down the parking lot," one of his companions shouted.

"Willow!" Knox's voice rang out from the Suburban's open window. He held up a pencil. "Use this to plug the hole!"

Willow sprinted back, grabbed the pencil from Knox, and hurried to the truck.

The young vet squinted at it. "What am I supposed to do with that?"

"Wedge it into the hole, tap it in with a hammer," Knox called back. "It'll hold long enough for you to grab another container and get the rest."

The veteran didn't hesitate. He climbed back under the truck, shoved the pencil into the hole, and hammered it in place. The dripping stopped immediately. Meanwhile, Guynn was already headed back to the Suburban with their fuel can, pouring two gallons of fuel into the tank.

The moment he secured the cap, he shot the vet a nod. The young vet waved and watched them go. Within seconds, the Suburban was back on the road, rolling away from Ruther Glen—one step ahead of trouble but running on borrowed time.

TWENTY-TWO

Carson

Casterman's Feed Store
Ramah, Colorado
Day Four

The feed store was dark and smelled of old grain, damp wood, and something rancid beneath it all—like the sour stench of vomit that had dried and festered in the heat. It was a smell that lingered, clinging to the back of the throat and turning the stomach. A heavy hand shoved Carson toward the doorway, sending him stumbling over the uneven floorboards. He caught himself in time, but before he could straighten, fingers twisted into the back of his shirt and yanked him upright.

"Move," the gruff voice barked.

A further shove between his shoulder blades sent Carson staggering deeper inside. Behind him, Julie's boots scraped the wood as she was dragged forward, her sharp breaths coming fast but steady. She wasn't crying. Wasn't begging. He knew she wouldn't.

A single lantern burned in the far corner. The dim, golden light pooled around the lantern, only slightly pushing back the darkness, leaving the corners of the room swallowed in inky black. Torn sacks of grain spilled their contents onto the floor. The walls were lined with old shelves, half empty of supplies. A table stood near the center of the space and was littered with tools that weren't meant for fixing things. Pliers. A hammer. A rusted knife with dried flecks of something brown along the edge.

Julie was shoved against the opposite wall, her back hitting the wooden slats with a dull thud. Before she could find her footing, one of Casterman's men grabbed her arms and yanked them behind her. She fought hard, twisting and kicking, her breath ragged with effort. One sharp kick connected with a man's shin, making him grunt in pain. He punched her in the ribs, and she went slack.

"Don't hurt her," Carson cried out. "Julie, don't fight them." His voice was hoarse, but he kept it calm.

Julie lifted her chin, but she didn't continue to resist.

Rough hands grabbed Carson's wrists, yanking them together and wrapping a rope around them. The rough fibers cut into his skin with each pass.

"Just kill us already," Julie said, her voice thick with contempt.

The woman laughed—a sharp, jagged sound that grated against Carson's nerves. She was lean but wiry, her body all sharp angles and taut muscle. Her dark hair was short, uneven like she'd done it herself with a hunting knife. A tattoo of a bird ran from her temple to her jawline, twisting when she smirked. Her eyes, cold and calculating, gleamed with amusement, but there was something else there too—enjoyment. She liked this. The power. The fear. The control. She shifted her weight onto one hip, rolling her knuckles as if itching to hit something—or someone.

"You think that's how this works?" she asked, crouching in front of Julie. "You think we just kill people for no reason?"

Julie's jaw clenched, her shoulders stiff.

The woman reached out and tapped Julie's cheek with the back of her knuckles—mocking, teasing.

"No, honey," she whispered. "That's not how Casterman plays this game. He gets results."

Carson's muscles coiled, but the ropes held firm. He wanted nothing more than to slam his fist into that smug expression.

"Alicia is right," Casterman said. "I get results. You're gonna tell me where Corinton hid my dope."

Carson now knew the type of people they were dealing with. He'd heard about the rise in drug rings in the area with ties to the notorious Venezuelan-born gang Tren de Aragua. There had been a federal arrest on charges of drug, gun, and sex trafficking being run out of a Denver apartment complex. Were these people mixed up with them?

Carson didn't answer. Julie didn't either.

The silence stretched.

Casterman sighed, shaking his head like a disappointed teacher. "You know, Corinton was never the sharpest tool in the shed. It was suicidal for him to steal from our boss. Now he's gone, and you two are the only ones with answers. So, why don't you save yourselves a whole lot of pain and just tell me where he stashed it?"

Carson licked the blood from his split lip. "We don't know!"

Casterman struck him across the face. "If you know what's good for you and your little family, you'll tell me—before the boss shows up. Because once he and his crew arrive, you'll wish you were dead."

Alicia leaned around Casterman. "We better have our product in hand before that happens."

"We said we don't know anything about your stupid drugs," Julie barked.

Alicia spun around. Then, without hesitation, she swung. The punch was sharp, cracking against Julie's already bruised face. Julie's head snapped to the side, but she didn't cry out.

Carson lunged against his restraints. "You—!"

A fist crashed into his gut. Pain exploded through his ribs,

Utter Devastation

stealing the air from his lungs. He doubled over, gasping before a second blow landed—this time to his face. His vision blurred. His head snapped back against the wooden wall.

"Stop." Julie's voice wavered, but it was still strong.

Casterman tilted his head. "You want it to stop?"

She glared up at him. "We don't know anything."

Casterman hummed in thought, then turned to Alicia. "What do you think?"

Alicia flexed her fingers, rolling her knuckles. "I think they know something. We should separate them—compare their stories."

Julie's breathing was heavy now, her chest rising and falling with contained fury. The woman's smirk widened. She crouched next to Julie and grabbed a fistful of her hair, jerking her head back. Julie winced but didn't cry out. "You're gonna talk—I promise you that."

Julie spat in her face.

Alicia struck Julie across the face again.

Carson felt his blood ignite. He lunged forward, his whole body thrashing against the restraints. "You bitch! You touch her again, I swear—"

Casterman chuckled, watching like it was all a game. "You see my lady friend here? She enjoys a little persuasion. Me? I like efficiency. So, you tell me what I want to know, and we let you and your pretty girlfriend go."

Carson clenched his jaw. "We don't know anything!"

"Then I guess I let her have her fun."

He turned to leave, but Carson caught something—hesitation. It was a small thing, a flicker in Casterman's expression that told him the man wasn't as confident as he let on. He was desperate for that dope.

Alicia rose and approached Carson. She leaned in close, her breath hot against his skin. "Maybe I'll start with the girl. Or maybe the kids." She smiled. "That would get you talking."

Carson's vision tunneled, his muscles burning as he strained against the ropes. "You lay a finger on them, and I'll make sure you die slow."

She giggled, actually giggled, as she stepped back, dusting her hands off like she'd already finished the job.

"Tell me this," Casterman said. "Tell me why Corinton came back here."

"He said he wanted to go home," Julie said. "He was dying, and we figured he wanted to say goodbye to his family."

"Corinton didn't have a family anymore. He was a drunk and killed them in a car crash three years ago."

Carson wasn't sure whether to believe him or not, but it didn't matter—the man was dead. His motives would remain a mystery, but one thing was clear: Bringing him here had been a mistake. He'd put Julie and the children in danger, and now the weight of that choice settled like a stone in his gut.

A sharp rap sounded at the door, and Casterman moved to answer it. Low, hushed voices followed, too quiet for Carson to make out. Then, without another word, Casterman and the woman turned to leave, the door slamming shut behind them. Muffled voices carried from just beyond the door. Carson stiffened, tilting his head, straining to catch their words.

"I just don't get it. If Corinton took the dope and ran, why the hell would he come back here?" one man muttered.

"Maybe he stashed it somewhere before leaving. Maybe he thought no one would find him here," another voice reasoned.

Alicia scoffed. "Corinton wouldn't be stupid enough to carry it on him. It's still in town. That means they might know where it is."

"We'll tear Corinton's house apart. If he stashed it somewhere, it's still here in town."

"What if it's not?" Alicia said.

"Then we find a way to make these two more cooperative. We keep pressing until they talk," Casterman growled. "Or we use the kids. Everyone breaks eventually."

Utter Devastation

Carson's heart pounded.

Julie looked at him, eyes wide. They were running out of time. Footsteps faded down the hallway, and then it was quiet. Carson and Julie sat in silence, the room thick with the echoes of Casterman's threats.

After what felt like an eternity, Julie exhaled shakily. "He's going to kill us."

"No, he's not."

Julie blinked at him. "How do you know?"

"Because he needs something. If he thought we had the drugs, we'd already be dead."

Julie's jaw clenched, her voice low. "We can't let them hurt the kids."

"We won't."

She shook her head. "Carson, I'm scared."

His chest tightened. Julie never let her guard down. Never showed vulnerability. But here, in this place, tied up, beaten, and surrounded by men who could—and would—kill them at any moment, she was human.

Carson's throat went dry. "Me, too."

She looked up at him as if startled by the admission.

"But that means we're still alive," he added. "And as long as we're breathing, we fight."

Julie nodded, her shoulders squaring despite the bruises blooming on her skin. "Damn right, we do."

An hour later, they heard the footsteps return. Carson stiffened as two men burst into the room. Without a word, one of them strode over, grabbed Julie by the arm, and hoisted her to her feet. She tried to resist, but he was too strong.

"Let go of her!" Carson spat.

They ignored him and shoved Julie through the door.

"Carson!" she cried.

"Julie!" he shouted as the door slammed shut.

TWENTY-THREE

Willow

Central Bank
Ruther Glen, Virginia
Day Four

From Ruther Glen, Virginia, Guynn steered the Suburban east, aiming to connect with Interstate 64 at Hadensville. "Keep your eyes open for another vehicle," he said. "We've got about sixteen miles before we're out again. This thing isn't the most fuel-efficient."

"What're you getting?" Knox asked. "Eight or nine miles per gallon?"

"Around that."

Willow leaned over the console and checked the fuel gauge herself. "We need to find a more fuel-efficient vehicle," she said, already scanning the side roads for options. "Stopping for gasoline in every town is dangerous."

"So is stealing a car," Guynn replied.

"We could trade for one," Knox said.

Utter Devastation

"Trade what? I've already traded away my gold watch for the shotgun and given the last of my cash to those guys back there."

"The Suburban," Willow said.

Guynn said nothing.

"I realize you've lovingly restored it, but we're not going to make it to Arkansas in this gas guzzler," Willow said softly. She knew she was asking a lot. She knew all the hours, blood, sweat, and tears it took to restore such a vehicle. After his business failed, her dad had parted with his classic car collection—even the ones they'd worked on together. It had devastated him.

"I don't mind trading the Suburban," Guynn said, finally. "I just don't think it will be that easy. Who's gonna want to trade for a more fuel-efficient vehicle now?"

"Maybe we sweeten the pot," Knox said, jutting his thumb over his shoulder. "We got some good stuff back there, and we won't be able to take it all with us if we're on foot."

He had a valid point, but Willow didn't like the idea. She'd risked her life to obtain that "stuff," and thinking about either abandoning it or trading it away hurt.

"We need to find a mom-and-pop garage or an old farmer—someone who loves to barter. That's who'll take that kind of deal," Guynn said.

Relief washed over Willow. "After seeing you in action, I have absolute faith you can make a deal."

"I hope we trade for one with a lot of legroom like this baby," Knox said.

Willow pictured his six-foot, three-inch frame wedged into the back of a Toyota Yaris, Honda Fit, or Chevy Spark and chuckled.

The winding two-lane roads rocked Knox to sleep but turned Willow's stomach inside out. She cracked the window open, hoping the rush of cool air would help, but it only made her dizzier.

"You need me to pull over?" Guynn asked as she leaned out, taking deep breaths.

Willow managed a nod, pressing a hand over her mouth, willing herself to hold it together just a little longer. Guynn pulled off onto the entrance of a gravel side road, and Willow bolted from the Suburban and vomited in the roadside ditch. Guynn exited the vehicle and handed her a handkerchief. After she wiped her mouth with it, he handed her a peppermint.

"Thanks," she said, unwrapping it and placing the candy in her mouth.

"It should help with your queasy stomach. I've got motion-sickness pills in my overnight bag. If I'd known you got carsick, I would've had you take one before we left your apartment. It's a better preventative than treatment."

"It makes me too sleepy. Can't afford to not be at the top of my game." Her hand instinctively went to her rib cage. She could have died back there at the gas station if those two men had been armed.

Back on the road, Willow couldn't stop thinking about the fight. She'd let emotion dictate action. *I can't afford to make that mistake again. I could have ended up dead or in jail if that deputy had his way.* She shuddered at the memory of his hands on her body. She vowed right then to be more aware. It didn't mean she would stand by and allow vulnerable people to be hurt, but she'd certainly be smarter about it. She should have gotten the colonel's help.

They made it to Montpelier, VA, before the Suburban shuddered to a stop, out of fuel again. The three of them sat there in silence for several minutes, not ready to face their fate. Finally, Knox spoke. "Just leave me here."

Willow spun around in her seat. Shock and anger spread across her face. "What did you say?"

"Leave me here. You two can make it without me."

"Absolutely not!"

Guynn twisted to face Knox. "Enough of that talk, son. We'll scrounge enough fuel to get us farther down the road until we can find a better car."

"And what if you can't? What then? Are you two going to sit here with me until we all run out of food and water? Are we just going to set up camp right here?"

Willow nodded. "If we have to—until you're strong enough to travel. We should have waited—" She began to rant, but Guynn cut her off.

"This isn't the end. I'll grab the gas can and go up to that farmhouse." He pointed up the road a few hundred feet. "Country folk are kind and generous people. We don't need all this fuss. This is our lot, and we have to buck up and deal with it." He pushed open the driver's door and got out.

Willow was out of the car before he could take another step. "I'll go with you."

"That's not necessary. You stay here and keep an eye on Knox and our supplies."

"You say the folks out here are kind and generous, but I watched the Texas Chainsaw Massacre."

Guynn chuckled. "We're not going to be hunted down one by one by Leatherface and his cannibalistic family."

Knox snorted from the back seat. "Good luck trying to convince her without proof, Colonel. She's got a very vivid imagination."

"You two should take this more seriously. You can't just walk up to a stranger's house without backup." Willow put her hands on her hips and glared at them. "Period."

Guynn shot her a look. "You're right. Let's go." He moved toward the rear of the vehicle. With the fuel can in hand, he and Willow walked up the long gravel drive toward the farmhouse.

"Here, you take my pistol, and I'll take the shotgun," Willow said, unholstering the handgun. "You can conceal it better." Walking up on someone's porch with a weapon in hand was universally frowned upon.

Guynn nodded, and they exchanged weapons. He stuffed the pistol in the back waistband of his pants and headed for the front door, while Willow slipped into the shadows behind an overgrown forsythia bush. Peering out cautiously, she watched as Guynn approached the two-story farmhouse. The house stood alone. White paint peeled from its wooden siding. The dark gray roof was a patchwork of repairs. Beyond the house, the woods pressed in, thick and silent. The surrounding landscape was too quiet, and the absence of birdsong or rustling wildlife created an unnatural hush.

She glanced back at the farmhouse. Its front porch was deceptively inviting, with two rocking chairs arranged on a colorful outdoor rug and surrounded by potted plants. She tensed, scenes from horror movies running through her mind, as Guynn climbed the steps, knocked on the red door, and then stepped to one side.

He waited.

Silence.

He knocked again.

Just as Willow began to wonder if the place was abandoned, a floorboard creaked from inside. A moment later, the door eased open. A frail-looking elderly woman stood in the doorway, wrapped in a thick, tattered shawl, her wiry gray hair pulled into a loose bun. Deep-set wrinkles lined her face, her eyes sharp but sunken—like someone who had weathered too many storms and was still waiting for the next. Her thin lips pressed into a flat line as she took in Guynn. Then, her expression softened.

"Come on inside, now," she said, her voice smoky and low, like someone who had spent a lifetime smoking cigarettes.

Guynn didn't move. He gave a dismissive wave, feigning nonchalance.

"I just need to borrow a little gas, ma'am," he said smoothly. "Car ran out back there." He gestured vaguely in the opposite direction of their actual stop.

The elderly woman narrowed her gaze—just a fraction. For a long moment, she said nothing. Then, she let out a dry chuckle. "Well, if it's gas you need... I might have a little to spare." Her bony fingers curled around the doorframe, tapping against the wood, looking him up and down. "You healthy?"

"Um—yes," Guynn said. "I'm not sick if that's what you mean."

The elderly woman smiled. "Good!" She glanced back over her shoulder. "Virgil, we've got a guest."

TWENTY-FOUR

Carson

Casterman's Feed Store
Ramah, Colorado
Day Four

The silence after they took Julie was worse than the violence. Carson sat slumped against the cold wooden wall. His head pounded, and his breaths were slow and ragged. The feed store had fallen eerily quiet. The distant murmurs of Casterman's men had faded into a heavy stillness that pressed in around him. Julie was gone. He didn't know where they had taken her, and that uncertainty gnawed at his frayed nerves more than the pain searing through his ribs. He could still hear her voice echoing in his mind —sharp, defiant, fighting even as they dragged her away.

The ropes around his wrists burned, the fibers digging deeper into his skin with every small shift of his body. His arms had gone numb hours ago, his shoulders stiff from the unnatural position. He flexed his fingers, trying to get some blood flow back, but even that slight movement sent agony slicing through his nerves.

Think, damn it!

His mind was sluggish, weighed down by exhaustion and injury, but he couldn't afford to slip into that haze. He had to stay alert and ready. They weren't going to kill him—not yet. Casterman still thought he had knowledge to share. Something that made him valuable. For now.

Julie, though?

A fresh wave of anger rolled through him, thick and suffocating. He yanked at the restraints, his muscles screaming in protest, but the ropes held fast. A door creaked somewhere in the distance. Heavy boots scraped against the floor. Then his door opened. Every nerve in his body went taut. Men rushed in, and rough hands clamped onto his shoulders. He was dragged up from the cold, filthy floor. Pain exploded through him, a raw, brutal reminder of how much damage they'd already done. He sucked in a sharp breath, hissing.

"Still breathing," someone said.

"Not for long if he doesn't talk," Alicia said. "He's stubborn. Bleeding all over the damn place, but still not saying a word."

Carson let out a weak chuckle, wincing as his split lip protested. "Yeah... People have told me I don't take direction well."

That earned him another sharp jab to his side, sending fire through his ribs. He clenched his teeth, refusing to give them the satisfaction of hearing him cry out.

They beat him till he was nearly unconscious. Then, Casterman's voice cut through the fog of pain like a knife.

"Get Hannah and the old man in here to stitch him up enough to get him talking."

Carson drifted in and out, his mind flickering between the present and distant memories. He had flashes of Bruce in the car, of pulling him out. Then, their arrival here and the rough hands of Casterman's men dragging him inside. He thought he could hear Julie, but then it sounded like Willow. Weakly, he called his sister's name. Somewhere, children laughed. They were in their backyard in Dallas, playing with their dog, Duke. He was tossing a stick and—he was suddenly aware the door had opened again, and this time, the air shifted—not with the weight of brutality, but something softer. Carson forced one of his swollen eyes open.

The young woman who'd taken the children knelt beside him, her gaze sweeping over his injuries, her lips pressed into a firm line. She was in her early twenties with sun-kissed skin and sharp, intelligent eyes that reminded Carson of Willow at that age before DC jaded her. Her honey-brown hair was pulled into a loose braid over one shoulder, wisps escaping to frame a face that was more accustomed to hard work than vanity. There was something steady about her—no nervous fidgeting, no unnecessary words. She was calmness personified. And that, more than anything, made Carson believe he could trust her. She'd risked herself to take the kids. And now, she was here, tending to him. That meant something.

Behind her, an older man was already setting down a medical bag. His face was weathered. He looked exhausted. The young woman's fingers were gentle as she cleaned blood away from his brow with a piece of gauze. The pain jolted him awake. Instinctively, Carson thrashed against the restraints, his body reacting to the pain before his mind could catch up. "Hold still. We're trying to help you." The man's voice was gruff but steady.

Carson's body slumped. "Julie? Where's Julie?" he whispered through split lips.

"We don't know," the woman said. "Just relax and let us take care of you, and then we'll try to find out."

Carson stopped thrashing, but he was anything but relaxed as the man began probing his wounds.

"You're lucky they didn't crack your skull open," he said.

Carson let out a ragged breath. "Feels like they tried."

"Hold still. This is going to hurt," the older man said, holding a suture kit in his hand. "Hannah, hold his head."

Carson tensed as the needle bit into his skin, fire lancing

through his scalp. He clenched his jaw and forced himself to stay still.

"You a doctor?" he asked through gritted teeth.

"Veterinarian."

Carson blinked. "What?"

Hannah smirked but kept her hands firm on Carson's head. "Grandpa's been treating the people of this town for decades—even after he retired. A lot of folks around here don't trust regular doctors, especially after COVID-19."

Carson let that sink in. "So, instead, they go to the town's animal doctor?"

The doctor snorted. "People are animals. Just softer and more dramatic about it."

Hannah shrugged. "They know him. They trust him. That's more than you can say for a lot of so-called professionals."

Carson grimaced as another stitch tugged at his skin, but his mind was already spinning. This man wasn't just useful for patching wounds—he had influence. He had trust. Maybe, just maybe, that meant he could help them with more than just medical care. His jaw clenched. "Julie. You h-have to help her."

Hannah hesitated. "They took her somewhere else. We don't know where yet."

Guilt twisted in Carson's gut. He squeezed his eyes shut. "The kids?"

"You don't need to worry about them," Doc said evenly, still working the stitches.

Carson's gaze snapped to him. "What do you mean?"

Hannah glanced at the door, lowering her voice. "They're safe. We have people looking out for them."

Carson exhaled, relief and uncertainty warring inside him. "For how long?" His voice cracked. "What if Casterman goes after them to make us talk?"

Hannah's grandfather tightened the thread on the last stitch. "He won't find them."

Carson wanted to believe them. But men like Casterman didn't stop when they were cornered.

Hannah wiped the last of the blood from his face. "We're trying to find a way out. There's a sheriff's substation thirty miles from here in Falcon. If we can get past Casterman's guards, we can reach the Calhan police department to contact them."

Carson focused on her. "How many guards?"

The doctor shook his head. "Enough."

"Why are you still here? Why not leave while you had the chance?"

Hannah hesitated, glancing at her grandfather.

The doctor sighed. "It's not that simple. Casterman and Alicia took over after they did away with the mayor. Things spiraled fast. They control all the routes out of town, the food, and the weapons. The people here are scared, and we all know scared people don't fight back."

Carson frowned. "And you?"

The doctor smirked. "I've lived in this town my whole life. No self-proclaimed warlord is going to tell me what to do."

Hannah spoke up, her voice tight. "They think everything is coming back online. That the government will show up any day now, and they'll be back in business."

"They really believe that?"

The doctor snorted. "They're delusional."

Hannah nodded. "They think once the dust settles, they'll be the ones in power. That they'll control everything."

Carson's mind was spinning. Casterman wasn't just some thug running a town—he was playing the long game. He thought he was setting himself up as a king in the ashes of the old world.

Hannah's voice softened. "If we're going to stop him, we have to be smart. If you want to live, you need to work with us."

"Then help me find Julie."

She hesitated. "We will." Then, leaning in close, she slipped a scalpel into his bandaged hand, the cool metal pressing against his palm. Before Carson could thank her, the door banged open. Casterman strolled in, a satisfied smirk curling his lips.

"Okay, Doc. That's enough charity for one day." He tilted his head toward the door. "Out!"

Hannah hesitated. The doctor locked eyes with Carson. Something unspoken passed between them. *Hold on.* Then, with quiet obedience, they left. Casterman stepped closer, boots crunching on the dirty floor. Alicia trailed behind with her arms crossed, watching him like a cat with a mouse.

"Now, unless you'd like the undertaker to be your next visitor…" Casterman crouched in front of Carson. "…you better tell me where Corinton hid my package."

Carson forced himself to meet his gaze. "For the hundredth time. I don't know," he rasped. "Maybe you shouldn't have killed him. He might've come back here to return it."

Casterman leaned in, voice low and deadly. "Or he gave it to you and your girlfriend." He whirled around and headed toward the door. "Maybe Alicia has her more willing to talk now."

"Stop this!" Carson yelled as the door slammed shut.

TWENTY-FIVE

Willow

State Route 610
Montpelier, Virginia
Day Four

The screen door to the old farmhouse creaked open, and an elderly man—Virgil, the woman had called him—stepped onto the porch. He leaned on a metal walker, moving slowly and deliberately, as if every motion required careful thought.

"Who do we have here, Miriam?" he asked with a toothless grin. Wisps of white hair clung to his spotted scalp. His weathered face was a map of deep-set wrinkles, his eyes sharp and clouded with age. A faded plaid flannel shirt hung on his thin frame, tucked into a pair of well-worn denim overalls.

Guynn stepped forward, shaking his hand and then exchanging a few quiet words.

Willow squinted, straining to hear. The words were muffled, just out of reach. Virgil nodded once, then gestured toward the barn with a gnarled, calloused hand.

Nodding, Guynn turned back toward her. "Willow."

Utter Devastation

She stiffened.

His tone was even, calm—but there was something behind it. Something that made her pulse flicker.

"It's fine, Willow. Come on up."

She hesitated, her gut twisting with suspicion. The way the colonel held himself—too relaxed, too composed—didn't sit right. Still, she moved. Cautiously, with the shotgun at her side. Each step up the rickety wooden stairs felt too loud in the suffocating quiet.

Virgil watched her, his expression unreadable.

"They're offering a trade," Guynn explained once she was close. "Five gallons of gas for some work."

Willow's eyes flicked between them, trying to read between the lines.

"Ain't got the strength I used to," Virgil admitted. "Plenty to do around here, but not enough hands to do it."

Willow's jaw tightened.

Miriam moved toward the steps. She smiled—just a little too sweetly. "Come on, then," she said, motioning them forward. "Let's head out to the barn and get to it."

Willow drew in a sharp breath. Work? Fine. But why did it have to be the barn?

Guynn nodded, grabbing the fuel can, and they followed the couple toward the half-collapsed barn. Miriam walked slowly, her cardigan sweater draped tightly around her shoulders. Virgil shuffled beside her, hunched over his walker, the bright yellow tennis balls dragging through the dirt. They didn't speak much—just glanced at each other as if exchanging some unspoken message.

Willow's gut twisted. This was how horror movies started. The seemingly harmless elderly couple ... the isolated farmhouse ... the false sense of hospitality. And now they were leading them into the barn—the perfect place for an ambush. The wooden structure leaned with age. Its once-red paint was now faded to a washed-out rust color, the roof sagging in places. The doors hung slightly ajar, their hinges rusted and streaked with time. The barn stood at the edge of the property, where the tree line had crept closer than it should have—a wall of dark, tangled branches curling over the roof like fingers reaching for prey.

Her finger itched toward the trigger guard of the shotgun she held pointed down at the ground in her right hand. Instead, she swallowed her instinctive fear and kept moving. Guynn walked ahead, as calm as ever. Willow stayed two steps behind, watching. Listening. Waiting. Virgil and Miriam led them inside past an ancient-looking tractor, old farm equipment, household furniture, and bags of clothing to a room at the back of the barn. Miriam pulled open a cracked wooden door, and Willow's blood ran cold. Her gasp echoed through the space. The elderly couple just stared at her.

Virgil groaned. "Lord have mercy, child, you about gave me a heart attack."

Guynn ran a hand over his face. "Sheesh, Willow."

She blinked, breathing hard, looking between them. "…You weren't trying to push him into a secret underground dungeon?" she asked, half-teasing.

Miriam's mouth fell open.

Guynn let out a long sigh. "She's watched too many horror movies."

The elderly couple exchanged a look, and then they burst into laughter. Deep, belly-shaking laughter. Miriam wiped a tear from her eye, shaking her head. "Oh, honey, you got quite the imagination."

"Too many horror movies?" Virgil wheezed. "She's watched the whole damn catalog."

Willow exhaled, pressing a hand to her forehead. "Okay, well … can you blame me? That was incredibly suspicious." She'd misjudged them, but the elderly couple had turned out to be exactly what Guynn had hoped for—good country folk willing to barter.

"We have to go back to our vehicle and let our friend know

we'll be a while," Willow said, shifting uneasily. She was still suspicious, even if the elderly couple seemed harmless enough.

Miriam pursed her lips. "Bring him back with you. Three can get things done faster than two."

"He's injured," Willow countered, glancing toward Guynn.

Virgil, still gripping his walker, grunted. "Then he can watch from the porch with me."

"I don't think he can walk that far, sir," Willow said. She wasn't about to haul Knox uphill in his condition.

Something unspoken passed between Miriam and Virgil, and then Miriam let out a sigh. "Well, why didn't you just say so? No need to make the poor boy suffer." She turned and motioned for them to follow. "C'mon, I'll show you where the gas is. You can drive your vehicle up instead."

Willow and Guynn exchanged a wary glance before falling into step behind her.

Miriam led them around the back of the barn, where an old, three-hundred-gallon gravity-fed fuel tank sat on a rusted steel stand. The metal looked aged, but the spigot and hose attached were well-maintained and free of corrosion. "Still got a little left in here. Virgil put a fuel stabilizer in it a while back. We mostly use it for the lawnmower now."

Guynn ran a hand along the side of the tank, inspecting it. "You don't mind us taking some now before the work?"

"Wouldn't have shown it to you if I did, now would I?" Miriam quipped, hands on her hips.

Willow stepped closer, eyeing the nozzle. "How much can we take?"

"Enough to get your vehicle up here and whatever you need to keep moving," Miriam said. "As long as you make good on our deal."

Willow nodded, relieved. This was a far better outcome than they could have hoped for.

Guynn twisted the valve, letting fuel glug into their empty five-gallon can. The smell of gasoline filled the air as they worked.

"This should be enough to get the Suburban to the house," Guynn said.

Miriam gave a nod. "Then go get your friend. You can settle up with some hard work after."

Willow smiled. "Thank you."

Miriam waved her off with a faint smile. "Don't thank me yet, dear. We've got plenty of work waiting for you."

Willow and Guynn made their way back down the gravel drive, carrying the sloshing fuel cans. "Well, that went smoother than expected," Willow said.

"See? Not everyone is Leatherface." Guynn chuckled.

Willow rolled her eyes. "We'll see. We're not done yet."

They reached the Suburban, where Knox sat upright, watching them with half-lidded suspicion.

"What'd I miss?" he rasped.

"An elderly couple gave us gas, but now we owe them labor," Willow replied, handing Guynn the fuel can.

Knox blinked. "So … indentured servitude. Got it."

Guynn went straight to work and poured the fuel into the tank. "Just another day in paradise."

Willow climbed into the driver's seat. "Let's get up there before they change their minds."

With a turn of the key, the Suburban rumbled to life. They pulled away from the roadside, heading toward the farmhouse, the promise of a warm meal, honest work, and a full tank of gas waiting at the end of the long gravel drive. But Willow still couldn't shake the feeling that all this was too easy. She wasn't about to let her guard down. Not yet.

After settling Knox to rest on the couple's front porch, Willow and Guynn got to work. They drew water from the well, gathered firewood and placed it on the back porch. Next, they dug potatoes from the garden, and finally, it was time to milk the goat. When

Utter Devastation

Miriam led Willow to the small goat pen, Willow already knew she was going to hate this. The goat in question, a plump, smug-looking doe, was clearly just as nervous about Willow as she was of her. Her patchy gray and white coat was thick with dust. As Willow approached, she let out a long, judgmental bleat.

"Her name's Daisy," Miriam said.

"Of course it is."

Miriam sat on a low wooden stool and patted a second stool beside her.

Willow eyed the goat. "She's not gonna kick me, is she?"

Miriam smirked. "Only if she don't like you."

Great.

Willow sat down reluctantly, watching as Miriam demonstrated the technique.

"Start from the top, squeeze down. Don't pinch, just roll your fingers." She expertly coaxed a stream of milk into the metal pail.

Willow hesitated, then mimicked the motion.

Nothing.

Daisy huffed and stomped a hoof.

"She knows you don't got a clue what you're doing." Miriam chuckled.

Willow sighed through her nose and tried again. This time, a thin stream of milk hit the pail.

"There you go," Miriam said encouragingly.

Willow felt a brief, ridiculous moment of pride before Daisy kicked over the pail.

Watching the milk soaking into the dirt, Willow closed her eyes. "I hate this goat."

Miriam just laughed.

As Willow repositioned the pail and tried again, Miriam spoke softly, her voice laced with nostalgia.

"My husband and I built this farm from nothing. Cleared the land ourselves and lived without electricity or running water for nearly seven years until we could afford it."

Willow glanced at her, raising an eyebrow.

Miriam continued. "Raised our babies here. Buried some loved ones here, too. And one day, we'll go in the ground right beside them." She stroked Daisy's head as Willow finally got the rhythm of milking right. "Wouldn't change a damn thing about my life."

Willow paused. A faint pang of envy settled in her chest. She'd chased her career, buried herself in work, and let time slip away. She'd always thought there'd be time for marriage and family later—a life outside of the chaos of Washington. Maybe it wasn't too late. Maybe now she wanted more.

TWENTY-SIX

Willow

State Route 610
Montpelier, Virginia
Day Four

By the time the sun began to dip toward the horizon, Willow was bone-tired but ready to get back on the road.

"You sure you don't want any more help?" Guynn asked.

Virgil waved them off. "We got what we need."

Miriam wiped her hands on her apron. "You sure y'all don't want to stay the night?"

Willow shook her head. "Appreciate it, but we need to keep moving." As they approached the front porch, Willow nudged Guynn. "We still need to find a vehicle that won't burn through fuel so fast."

Miriam stopped, then glanced at her husband seated on the porch next to Knox.

"Well…" she began. "I might be able to help you with that, too." She led them around the side of the house, where a 2006 Jeep Grand Cherokee sat under a carport. Besides a thick layer of dust, it looked brand new. "That's my Jeep," she said, patting the hood. "Less than twenty-five thousand miles on her. Only drove it to church on Sundays. It's yours—if it'll start. Haven't been able to go anywhere much since Virgil broke his hip."

Willow exchanged a look with Guynn. She knew the newer model Jeep would get better mileage than the vintage Suburban due to its more fuel-efficient fuel injection, improved aerodynamics, and lighter weight. She couldn't read his expression. "What do you think, Colonel?"

"What's it get? About eighteen miles per gallon?"

"Twenty-two on the highway," Miriam said.

Guynn nodded. "Beats the hell out of eight."

"The keys are hanging on a hook in the kitchen." The woman gestured toward the house.

Willow nearly ran back to the house. She high-fived Knox on her way inside. "We've got a Jeep!" After locating the keys, Willow rushed back to the carport. She unlocked the SUV's door and climbed in, praying the Jeep would start. She turned the key. Nothing. Tried again. Nothing.

"The battery is probably dead if you haven't started it in a while. I'll get the Suburban and give it a jump," Guynn said.

A minute later, Guynn returned with Knox in the front passenger seat. As soon as they rolled to a stop, Knox tried to shove the door open and get out. Willow spun on him, hands on her hips.

"Don't even try it! You need to rest."

Knox scowled. "I can still—"

"Nope. Back in the seat. Doctor's orders."

Knox said something under his breath but slumped back against the seat, conceding defeat.

Guynn popped the hood of the Jeep, then attached the cables from the Suburban's battery to the Jeep's corroded terminals. They waited a few minutes, letting the charge build. Willow hopped into the driver's seat and crossed her fingers. She turned the key—still nothing.

Guynn sighed, rubbing his jaw. "Try again."

She did. Nothing but silence.

Knox, watching from the Suburban, grinned sleepily. "Well. Guess we live here now."

Willow shot him a glare before shoving open the Jeep's driver's door and getting out.

For three miserable, sweat-soaked hours, Willow and Guynn tinkered, troubleshooted, and cursed the damn Jeep as Knox sat in the front seat of the Suburban, napping. More than once, Willow flashed back to her youth, spent under the hood with her father.

"Did you check the starter relay?" Willow asked, shining the flashlight along the fuse box.

Guynn hesitated. He reached inside, removed the relay, and tapped it against the metal frame. "Feels loose inside."

"You think we can fix it?" Willow asked, trying to see what he was doing.

Guynn tossed the faulty relay onto the driver's seat. "Not unless you've got a new one in your pocket."

Willow rubbed her temples, glaring at the Jeep like she could will it to life. "Then we better figure it out because I am not spending the night here."

Knox appeared at the front of the Jeep. He rolled his eyes as Willow kicked the Jeep's front tire in frustration.

"All right, move over, Grandpa."

Guynn arched an eyebrow. "Grandpa? At least I can stand on my own two feet without falling over."

Knox cracked a lazy grin. "That's a low blow."

Guynn snorted but stepped aside, crossing his arms as Knox moved around the front of the Jeep, leaning on it for support.

"You shouldn't be up," Willow warned.

Knox ignored her, muttering under his breath as he leaned into the engine bay, hands braced against the Jeep's dust-covered fender.

"You got a starter relay in your pocket?" Guynn asked.

"No." Knox grinned, his eyes flicking toward the barn. "We improvise." With a flashlight clamped between his teeth, Knox shuffled through the old barn, poking around like a man on a mission.

Willow, arms crossed, leaned against an ancient, rusted tractor. "You know, this would go faster if you told us what you were looking for."

Knox mumbled something around the flashlight.

Guynn just watched, amused.

"Aha!" Knox grinned, already pulling a short length of wire from a worn leather tool bag. After returning to the Jeep, he pointed to the starter relay terminals. "See this? Normally, when you turn the key, this relay sends power to the starter. Ours is dead, so it's not completing the circuit. But..." He held up the wire. "If I bridge these two contacts, we bypass the relay. Give it juice straight from the battery."

"Colonel, hop in and turn the key to the On position," he said.

Guynn slid into the driver's seat and turned the key.

Knox grabbed the wire, poked it in the slot for the start relay, and jumped the terminals. A small spark flickered as the Jeep roared to life.

Willow let out a victorious whoop. "Hell, yes!"

Knox stepped back, tossing the wire onto the dashboard. "This'll work until we get a new relay."

"Looks like we got half a tank of gas," Guynn said, exiting the Jeep. He walked over and clapped Knox on the shoulder. "Not bad, kid."

Knox winced. "Ow. Watch the arm."

"Pansy."

Utter Devastation

"Easy for you to say. No one shot you."

"I've been shot. I didn't lie around and whine like you," he joked.

"You've been shot before?" Willow asked. "In war?"

"No. On my front lawn in a drive-by in St. Louis, Missouri. I left the state after that. Moved to rural Indiana."

"I guess it was safer."

"And quieter," Guynn said.

Knox sagged against the Jeep and yawned. His face was pale beneath the layer of dirt, and a fine sheen of sweat clung to his forehead. Still, he mustered a half-smug, half-weary grin. "We might survive the apocalypse after all." Then, his knees wobbled, and Willow stepped forward, ready to catch him if he went down.

"All right, MacGyver, let's get you off your feet before you pass out," she said, opening the Jeep's door.

Knox exhaled sharply, shaking his head as he slid into the seat with a wince. "Just need a damn nap," he grumbled, though he looked like he needed a hell of a lot more than that.

Willow lowered the Jeep's hood and was about to grab their gear from the Suburban when a voice called out from behind.

"Hold on now, you're not leavin' yet," Miriam said, stepping around the barn and wiping her hands on her apron. The old woman's expression was unreadable.

Willow tensed, expecting a new chore list. Anything but milking goats.

Guynn straightened. "Just about to. What's on your mind, ma'am?"

Miriam grinned and gestured for them to follow. "Virgil and I talked it over. That fuel tank behind the barn? Well, we won't be needin' what's left. Y'all might as well take the rest."

Willow blinked. "Wait ... what?"

Guynn arched a brow. "You sure? That's a generous offer."

Virgil shuffled up beside his wife, leaning on his walker, his voice gruff but steady. "Rather see it go to good use than sit there going bad."

It took a moment for the shock to wear off, but then they got to work. They searched the barn and a small shed out back, finding four five-gallon fuel cans and two three-gallon cans. It was more than they could have hoped for. They filled every last one, stacking them in the back of the Jeep with care. Once the last of the fuel from the five-gallon can was poured into the Jeep's tank, Guynn checked the gauge and gave a satisfied nod. "With the jerry cans, we have two full tanks of gas."

They could get at least seven hundred miles out of that if they were careful.

Miriam watched them load up, nodding in approval. "Should get you where you're goin'."

Once the Jeep was fueled and ready, Willow and Guynn worked to transfer all their gear from the Suburban. They filled the cargo area, making sure every supply was secure. The only thing they left behind was a box of canned goods, which they placed on the porch.

"You didn't have to do that," Miriam protested.

Willow smiled. "And you didn't have to give us all this fuel. Call it even."

Virgil grumbled something under his breath, but a ghost of a smile twitched at the corner of his lips.

Guynn clapped Virgil on the shoulder. "You folks just made our lives a hell of a lot easier. We won't forget it."

"We didn't know how we were gonna make it another day, really. Neither of us had the strength to carry water up from the well."

"Couldn't gather in the firewood either," Miriam added. "The nights get chilly this time of year. So, thank you."

"No. Thank you," Willow said. "We were stranded, and Knox can't walk. You two have renewed my faith in people."

Miriam patted her shoulder. "Oh, girl, you aren't wrong to be cautious. The world can be a dangerous place, especially in times like these."

Willow helped Knox into the back seat and then settled in the front across from Guynn, exhaling as she ran a hand over the dashboard. "Please don't break down on us, sweetheart."

Settling himself behind the wheel, Guynn adjusted the mirrors. "All right. Let's roll."

As they rolled down the drive, Willow was sore from the hard work but feeling encouraged. They had enough fuel to last them almost all the way to Arkansas. Means they'd only have to stop once to find more. With a final glance in the rearview mirror, Willow watched the farmhouse disappear into the distance.

Willow sat in the passenger seat, sucking on peppermint candy to ward off another wave of car sickness. The sky above them was an otherworldly spectacle—not the soft pastels of a typical sunset, but a chaotic, shimmering display of color. Faint bands of red and green streaked across the deepening twilight, flickering and undulating like something alive. Even this far south, the auroras still lingered, a reminder that the world had changed in ways most people couldn't begin to comprehend.

"Blimey," Knox said from his position behind Guynn in the back seat, staring up through the windshield. "It's still going."

Willow adjusted her grip on the passenger-side door handle, her gaze locked on the sky. "It's day four. Shouldn't it be dying down by now? It seems even more vibrant tonight."

Knox shook his head. "Not necessarily. The Carrington Event only lasted a couple of days, but this?" He gestured toward the sky. "This was bigger. Stronger. Might be weeks before it settles."

Guynn kept his eyes on the road but cast a glance at the horizon. "What's it doing to the atmosphere?"

"Supercharging it," Knox said. "We knew a storm this size would cause massive grid failure, but the sky's still flaring, which means the Earth's magnetosphere is still trying to recover from the initial blast. Until that happens, it's going to keep interacting with the residual charged particles."

Willow frowned. "Which means?"

"HF radio signals are gonna be a mess for a while." Knox ran a hand through his hair. "I don't think we'll be hearing from any of the ham operators until the ionosphere stabilizes."

"How long?" she asked. She knew next to nothing about how amateur radios worked.

Knox hesitated. "Could be days. Weeks." He exhaled heavily. "Hell, in some places, even months."

Guynn cursed under his breath. "And here I was, hoping we'd start hearing some good news."

Willow crossed her arms, staring at the blood-red streaks smearing the horizon. "Not today."

A beat of silence followed. The colors pulsed overhead, bleeding into the deepening blue of night. The Jeep rolled on, and soon, the sign for Interstate 64 came into view. They merged onto it, heading north, toward Charlottesville, Virginia. Willow's eyes scanned every stretch of pavement, every flicker of movement in the periphery. She wasn't thrilled about heading back into such a populated area, but the alternative was miles and miles of more winding roads that would burn through their fuel and upset her stomach more, making her weak and vulnerable.

Guynn's hands were steady on the wheel, but there was tension in his jaw as he focused on the road ahead. Fatigue etched his face. Knox slouched in the back seat. Every so often, he'd shift, trying to find a comfortable position to rest in the cramped back seat. He settled on sitting, facing the front with his head resting against the window.

Thirty minutes later, they neared Charlottesville. The exit ramps and on ramps were blocked, and the interstate was filled with abandoned cars choking every available lane. Makeshift refugee camps lined the interstate, people spilling out onto the road's shoulder, sleeping in tents constructed from tarp, plastic, and whatever scraps they could find.

It was pure chaos.

TWENTY-SEVEN

Willow

State Road 648
Montpelier, Virginia
Day Four

The interstate running through Charlottesville, Virginia was a mess. A group of ragged survivors huddled around a fire built in the shell of a burned-out car. Children sat on the guardrails.

"Dang," Willow whispered, taking in the scene and scanning the road for threats.

"Keep your eyes open," Guynn said.

As they slowed to navigate the congestion, headlights blinded them.

A car was coming at them in their lane at full speed—driving the wrong way.

"Shit!" Guynn barked, yanking the wheel.

The Jeep lurched into the left lane as they narrowly avoided a head-on collision.

Suddenly, a man stepped in front of their vehicle. Willow gasped and clutched the dashboard.

"Damn it!"

Guynn yanked the wheel hard to the right. The Jeep veered across the lane, metal complaining loudly as it clipped the guardrail. Willow slammed into the console, then flew back the other way as the SUV ricocheted off the barrier and spun out of control. The tires screeched against the asphalt, the force of the spin threatening to rip them off the road. The Jeep came to a shuddering stop in the middle of the road.

And then, silence.

Willow's pulse hammered in her ears. Her breath came in short bursts as she whipped around to check on Knox.

"I'm good," he grunted, rubbing his chest where the seatbelt had caught him. "Might need to change my drawers, but I'm good."

The Jeep sat idle in the middle of the highway. The man they had nearly hit came running toward them. Willow yanked her pistol free and snapped it up. The man skidded to a stop, hands flying into the air.

"Whoa! Easy! I just wanted to make sure you guys were okay!"

Willow held the gun steady as she studied him. He was young—maybe in his early thirties—clad in dirty cargo pants and a dark hoodie.

"I'm a paramedic," he added, breathless. He wiped a hand across his face. "You guys are lucky I didn't end up scraping you off the pavement."

"Lucky isn't the word I'd use," Willow said, lowering her pistol.

Guynn rolled down the driver's side window. "What the hell is going on here? Why is everyone sleeping on the interstate?"

The paramedic glanced north. "The city burned," he said grimly. "There were protests at City Hall after the lights went out. No one was telling them anything. People were scared. Then yesterday, with no news and the grocery store shelves empty, people started getting violent, trying to make their point loud enough to—"

A commotion up ahead near a cluster of makeshift tents interrupted him.

"He stole my diaper bag!" a young mother screamed.

Willow's head snapped in the direction of the noise just in time to see a ragged man sprinting away with a blue bag clutched to his chest. Behind him, a desperate-looking father lunged forward, chasing him down.

"I'm sorry! I got a kid!" the thief shouted over his shoulder.

The pursuer caught up and tackled him hard to the ground. They tumbled across the pavement, limbs flailing. The diaper bag flew from the thief's grip and skidded across the concrete. Then others joined in. A crowd swarmed him, fists flying. The man who had stolen the bag disappeared beneath a flurry of kicks and punches.

Willow's stomach twisted. Guynn swore under his breath.

"They're gonna kill him," Knox said from the back.

Willow instinctively reached for the door handle, but the colonel's voice stopped her.

"Not our fight."

She gritted her teeth. She hated it. Every instinct screamed to intervene. But this was reality now. The strong would survive. The desperate would turn violent. And no one was coming to stop it.

The paramedic continued speaking as if this were a normal occurrence. "Anyway, the fires spread," he continued. "We did what we could, but without water pressure, it was useless. As it raged throughout the city, everyone panicked, jumped in their cars, and tried to flee at once."

The scene he described sounded familiar. Willow had watched the same thing play out on the news in coverage of the wildfires out west. She glanced back at the melee as the paramedic continued.

"The roads were already clogged from the first wave of people trying to get out of town. Wrecks, cars running out of gas—" He gestured to the sea of vehicles. "There just aren't enough wrecker service trucks in town to keep them cleared. Nobody's going anywhere."

Willow exchanged a glance with Guynn. This was worse than she thought.

The paramedic jutted a thumb over his shoulder toward the beatdown. "People are more desperate now than before. I don't know how much longer we can hold out here." He glanced back at a young woman and child huddled on the side of the road. "Do you know what's happening anywhere else? Any word on FEMA? The state emergency response?"

Guynn shook his head. "No. Nothing."

Willow's throat tightened. "The solar storms knocked out power in DC. I was there. I'm not sure how long it will take for them to initiate some type of response and recovery…" Her voice trailed off. "I don't know how far south the damage extends, but I'd head that way if I were you."

Knox rolled down his window. "I agree. Her brother's a space weather prediction scientist at NOAA. He said this was a Carrington-level event."

The paramedic's face darkened.

Willow studied him. "You know what that means, don't you?"

He let out a bitter laugh and glanced at the burning remains of Charlottesville.

"Means we're screwed."

"Pretty much," Knox said.

A moment of silence stretched between them.

"You're a paramedic with the fire department?" Guynn asked. "You guys able to communicate by radio?"

The paramedic exhaled sharply. "We were using shortwave radios to communicate after the power went out. We'd get a signal for a few minutes, and then—nothing. Just static. It was getting clearer yesterday, but today, there was more interference. It's like the atmosphere is still fluctuating." The paramedic shook his head. "I don't think the storm is over. Might even be continuing."

Knox leaned forward from the back seat, his expression wary. "What do you mean? The CME has already hit. We're dealing with the aftermath."

The paramedic reached into his cargo vest, pulled out a small compass, and held it up.

Willow narrowed her eyes. At first, she thought the needle was pointing north, but then it twitched, wobbled, and began spinning in slow, uneven circles.

"That can't be good." Guynn frowned. "Is this ever gonna end?"

"If Earth's magnetic field is still unstable, that means another CME could be inbound," Knox said.

"Could that happen?" Willow's stomach knotted. "Another blast?"

Knox rubbed his jaw. "Yeah. CMEs often come in waves. The Carrington Event wasn't just one burst; it was a series of flares hitting back-to-back. If another hits, and the magnetosphere is still weak from the first impact..." He let out a slow breath.

Willow gazed upward. The auroras still streaked the sky, though they should have begun fading by now. Instead, the colors swirled, moving in a way that didn't feel natural. She swallowed hard. She hadn't noticed before, but now that she was paying attention, something felt off.

The paramedic glanced around, lowering his voice. "You hear that?"

Willow listened. She could make out the crackling of nearby campfires, the rustling of makeshift tarps in the wind, and the voices of the fight now breaking up. But something was missing. Her heart skipped a beat. "The night sounds," she murmured.

Knox leaned toward the window. "No insects. No frogs."

"There's no wildlife," Guynn said.

Willow had spent enough nights in the wilderness to know that silence was unnatural. At night, there were always crickets. Frogs. Owls. Something. But right now, it was as if the world was holding its breath.

"Animals sense things we don't," the paramedic said grimly. "They know when something big is coming."

Guynn exhaled slowly. "That's not a good sign."

The paramedic shifted from foot to foot.

"I don't know what's coming, son, but I do know this—you shouldn't just sit here waiting. Move now. Before people realize just how screwed we all are."

Willow locked eyes with the man.

He nodded once. "We're waiting to hook up with a group of fellow firefighters and police officers who stayed behind to gather their families." He nodded over his shoulder. "We don't stand a chance of making it without them."

"Well, I wouldn't wait too long," Guynn said, rolling up his window.

The paramedic took a step back.

"Good luck. You're gonna need it," Knox said as Guynn put the Jeep into gear and accelerated away from the chaotic scene.

Knox's soft snores filled the cabin of the Jeep as they traveled west on Interstate 64. Willow pushed the encounter from her mind —there was no point dwelling on it. Instead, she focused on the miles ahead and the uncertain days, weeks, and months that awaited them at their destination. Soon, they passed a sign marking their entry into the Shenandoah Valley Battlefields National Historic District, a reminder of another time when America had been torn apart. This national heritage area was meant to preserve and interpret the region's Civil War battlefields and historic sites. Now, as the world teetered on the edge of collapse once more, the echoes of past conflicts felt eerily close. Had it been daylight, she might have been able to appreciate the stunning natural beauty as they crossed the Blue Ridge Mountains—rugged peaks and deep valleys carved into the land like a testament to time. But at night, all she could see was the faint, ghostly glow of the aurora lingering above them, still pulsing in the sky.

Hours passed as Willow struggled to keep her eyes open. She glanced out the side window as the aurora shimmered over the Jackson River on their approach into Covington, Virginia. By the time they reached Alleghany, Virginia, exhaustion clawed at Willow's bones. She stifled another yawn, but Guynn caught it.

"I can't drive much farther," he admitted, rubbing a hand over his face.

Knox sat up in the back seat. "I can drive. I've had plenty of sleep."

Willow twisted around to glare at him. "You have one arm."

"I have two," Knox shot back. "One's just out of commission. I can drive one-handed."

"Nope," Willow said flatly. "Guynn and I have been up for over thirty hours—hell, I haven't really slept since the lights went out. I'm beat. We just need to stop for a few hours and get some rest."

Guynn didn't argue. Instead, he slowed the Jeep and made a U-turn, heading the wrong way up the Ogle Creek Road on-ramp. He pulled into the shadowed edge of a lumberyard parking lot behind two massive shipping containers.

Knox cracked open his door. "Okay. You guys get some shut-eye. I'll stand watch."

"I don't think it's a good idea for you to leave the vehicle," Willow said. "You're still unsteady on your feet. If you wander and pass out, we may never find you."

Knox huffed. "Fine. I'll lean against the Jeep."

"I'd feel better if you stayed inside as well," Guynn said.

"Okay, okay. Hand me your pistol, Willow."

She passed it back to him, grip first. He checked the magazine before setting it within reach.

Willow only just managed to get comfortable before sleep dragged her under.

TWENTY-EIGHT

Willow

Interstate 64
Albemarle County, Virginia
Day Five

After only a few hours of fitful rest, Guynn was ready to get back on the road. "What time is it?" Willow asked as she stretched.

The colonel pantomimed checking his watch. "It's a freckle past a hair."

"So funny," she said.

"You've been asleep maybe three or four hours."

"Did you sleep?"

"About as much as I usually do."

"I can take over driving now. I just need to pee first," she said as she opened the door.

Knox stirred. "I got your back."

She shot him a glare. "You better not watch my back."

Knox smirked but said nothing, gripping his pistol in both hands as he stepped out after her, scanning the area while she moved behind a thicket of trees.

The moment her boots hit the damp ground, the silence hit her again. Something wasn't right.

A branch snapped in the distance. Willow tensed, heart hammering. Then she saw it—a deer, standing in the tree line, frozen like a statue. Its ears twitched, but it didn't move. That wasn't normal. A strange, unsettled feeling crept over her skin. She finished quickly and hurried back to the Jeep. "Something's off," she said under her breath as she climbed inside.

Knox arched a brow. "What?"

"The animals." She shut the door. "They're acting weird."

"How so?" Guynn asked.

"They're too still. Too quiet. Might be nothing. But considering everything else that's gone sideways, I don't like it."

They decided not to linger. Breakfast was quick—cold canned soup and jerky, washed down with what little water they had left in their bottles. As they pulled back onto the road, Willow and Guynn started debating their route again.

"Are you sure we should keep going west through Kentucky?" Willow asked, adjusting the map in her lap. "Or cut south into Tennessee."

"I still want to stop in Owensboro," Guynn said, as they crossed into West Virginia. "My cousin's got a stash of guns. We could use the firepower."

"Think he's still there?" Knox asked.

Guynn shrugged. "If he had any sense, he'd have hunkered down. But if he's not there, he might've left behind something useful."

"I don't hate the idea," Knox said. "It's a good chance to get more weapons."

Willow folded the map. "Then Owensboro it is."

The Jeep moved steadily along the winding back roads west of Alleghany, Virginia. Willow sat in the passenger seat, chewing on a piece of peppermint candy to keep her nausea at bay. They helped some, but she still kept her window cracked for the fresh air. Knox was in the back, shifting restlessly, looking drained but unable to fully relax. The colonel, steady as ever, kept his eyes on the road, his posture rigid behind the wheel. They had decided earlier that morning to avoid major cities at all costs. What they'd seen in Charlottesville had been enough to drive that point home. The streets had been impassable, the exits clogged with dead cars, desperate and stranded people forming makeshift camps along the highways. The moment a city's infrastructure failed, it was only a matter of time before the worst of human nature took over. The back roads were slower, but safer—at least for now.

"Next stop, we should check for fuel," Knox rasped.

Guynn nodded, adjusting his grip on the wheel. "If we find a vehicle with enough left in the tank, we might not have to stop again before we get to Arkansas. I don't trust any place with a population over fifty right now."

Willow scanned the roadside, watching for any sign of movement. A handful of abandoned cars dotted the shoulders—some with doors flung open, others burned-out husks. Not worth stopping for. They passed a small, half-collapsed gas station, whose sign swung loosely in the wind. Someone had already stripped the place bare—no point in even slowing down.

Then, ahead, flashing lights got Willow's attention. Guynn slowed as they approached what looked like a makeshift checkpoint. Two Magoffin County sheriff's department vehicles were angle-parked across the road, their emergency lights still faintly pulsing in the early morning light.

A lone deputy stood in the middle of the road, raising a hand to flag them down.

Willow tensed.

"Problem?" Knox asked, sitting up straighter.

"Could be," Guynn said. "Keep your eyes open."

As they rolled to a stop, Willow noted the exhaustion on the deputy's face—the kind that came from too many sleepless nights and too much bad news. His uniform was dirty, his badge dull.

Guynn rolled down his window. "Everything all right, officer?"

"We're looking for two men," the deputy said in a central Appalachian drawl. "You folks seen two men in a white Toyota Camry out this way?"

Guynn's eyes narrowed. "Can't say that we have."

The deputy exhaled sharply. "Two escapees from the Magoffin County Detention Center stole it. Killed a family for their supplies. We got a few roadblocks up, but they're slippery sons of bitches."

Willow felt a chill run through her.

"How long ago?" she asked.

The deputy glanced at her, then back toward the road behind them. "Couple hours, maybe. We think they're heading west."

Guynn nodded, keeping his expression neutral. "We'll keep our eyes open."

The deputy waved them forward, already distracted by the next approaching vehicle. The moment they passed him, Willow let out a slow breath.

"That's unsettling," Knox said.

"No kidding. If they're heading west, we might cross paths."

"Let's hope not," Guynn said grimly.

There wasn't a single sign of life on the roads. Thirty minutes later, the Jeep had just rounded a bend when Willow spotted something on the shoulder up ahead. A lone car, a white Toyota, its hood open, emergency blinkers flashing. A man stood beside it. Willow's gut clenched as he raised a hand.

"Keep driving!" she said immediately, her face ashen.

Guynn didn't argue. He stayed in the right lane, moving past the stalled vehicle without slowing. The man didn't drop his arm. Then, as they passed, he darted toward them. Something slammed against the rear passenger door.

"Shit!" Knox shouted.

Willow twisted in her seat, catching a glimpse of a second figure emerging from the trees.

Utter Devastation

Guynn floored the gas. The Jeep lurched forward, throwing them back in their seats.

Through the side mirror, Willow saw two men sprinting after the vehicle, their faces twisted in frustration. One of them had something in his hand.

A gun.

A shot rang out, the sound sharp and violent in the night air.

"Go, go, go!" Knox barked.

Guynn kept the wheel steady, pushing the Jeep faster. Another shot. This one hit the rear bumper. Then—silence.

They kept driving. Finally, after another five minutes, Guynn eased off the gas slightly. "Everyone all right?"

"Yeah. If you don't count almost having a heart attack," Knox said.

Willow turned in her seat, watching the road behind them disappear. "That was them," she said, her voice tight. No one needed to ask who she meant. The escapees—the same ones who had slaughtered an innocent family.

TWENTY-NINE

Arthur

Carlisle Residence
Lakewood Heights
Dallas, Texas
Day Five

Arthur sat in the dim glow of the candlelight, his ears trained on the sounds outside. It had been quiet for hours, too quiet. But experience told him quiet didn't mean safe. His gut twisted as he checked the barricades one last time, running a hand along the plywood covering the windows in the garage. Then he heard it—a faint scraping sound. His pulse jumped. He moved carefully to the side window, staying low, keeping himself in the shadows. He pressed his ear to the wall, straining to hear.

"They nailed this one shut," a voice whispered.

Arthur narrowed his eyes.

Another voice, lower and hesitant, responded, "Maybe there's another way in."

There was shuffling, then the sound of fingers prying at the edges of the plywood. The wood groaned but held firm.

Utter Devastation

"Shit," the first voice said. "This isn't working."

Arthur shifted just enough to get a glimpse through the peepholes he drilled in the covering. Two figures crouched by the window, their faces half-lit by the faint glow of a flashlight. The taller one leaned in, frustration etched across his face.

"Forget it," he snapped. "We do it the other way."

"The other way?" the second voice asked nervously.

"Yeah. Let's get back to base. I have a plan. We burn 'em out."

Arthur's stomach turned to ice. "We don't have to go inside," he continued, voice lower. "We light up the porch and the windows. They'll have to come out. And when they do…"Arthur didn't need to hear the rest. He backed away, his mind racing. They weren't just trying to rob them—they were planning to destroy them. He turned and moved toward the back of the house, his thoughts already forming a plan. He needed to fight fire with fire, but with limited resources, every move had to count.

Katherine was waiting in the living room when Arthur walked in. One look at his face, and she stiffened. "What is it?"

Arthur filled her in on what he'd heard. "They're coming back," he said. "They couldn't get in, so now they're planning to firebomb the house."

Katherine's hand flew to her mouth. "Oh my God."

Arthur returned to the garage, throwing open the storage bins until he found what he was looking for—Carson's old water cannon. A sturdy, pump-action toy from years ago, still in decent shape. Katherine followed him, eyes darting to the toy in confusion.

"Arthur, what are you doing?"

He grabbed a bottle of rubbing alcohol from the bathroom and began unscrewing the lid. "Fighting fire with fire."

Katherine's brow furrowed. "You're going out there, aren't you?"

Arthur didn't look up as he poured the alcohol into the cannon's tank. "They'll expect us to come running out when the fire starts. I'd rather stop them before they can light the first match."

Katherine stepped forward, placing a hand on his arm. "Arthur, please. What if they catch you out there? What if they have guns?"

He sighed, rubbing his temple. "That's why I have to get the jump on them. If we wait inside, we're sitting ducks."

"But you have our pistol," Katherine said firmly. "Why can't we modify the window coverings? Create openings so we can see and shoot before they get close."

"There's no way to know what direction they'll come from, and we can't be at every window." Arthur gave a small, tired smile. "If there were more of us, that might work. But it's just you and me. If I'm outside, I can stop them before they ever get the chance to torch this place."

Katherine's face twisted with emotion. "I hate this. I hate all of this."

Arthur reached out and squeezed her hand. "I know." His voice was softer now, but still firm. "I don't want to waste our bullets. If I go out there and scare the hell out of them, maybe—just maybe—they won't come back."

She was silent for a long moment, her fingers tightening around his. "Promise me you'll be careful."

He nodded. "Always."

Out at the end of the driveway, Arthur crouched low in the bushes, his aching knees protesting with every second that passed. The humidity pressed against him, sweat dripping off his bushy brows. He gripped the water gun tightly, its plastic frame slick with sweat. The absurdity of it struck him. This same water cannon had once been part of wild summer battles in the backyard when Carson and Willow were just kids. He could still see them, laughing, shrieking as they darted across the lawn, soaked to the bone, the family's dog, Duke, on their heels. Carson had been relentless, always going for the sneak attack, while Willow had been the strategist, using the garden hose as her backup weapon. He had

Utter Devastation

chased them both, pretending to be the slow old man who couldn't keep up—until he turned the tables and drenched them with a water cannon when they least expected it.

Back then, the only war his children had known was over who got the last popsicle. He had kept the water cannon all these years —out of sentimentality, sure, but mostly because it made a damn good squirrel deterrent. Those little bastards were always after his bird feeders, and no amount of cursing or clapping scared them away. A few well-aimed blasts of water, though? That had done the trick. Now, he was using it for something else entirely.

A sick feeling settled in his gut. He couldn't imagine what was keeping Carson. His mind wanted to go to dark places—to picture his son lying in a ditch somewhere, his truck overturned or ambushed by looters on the road. But he pushed the thoughts aside. Carson and Willow were tough. They were smart. And if anyone could make it in this world, it was his two kids.

Arthur exhaled and glanced up. The aurora was still there. Brighter tonight than it had been the last few days. When the sky had first come alive in eerie green and violet streaks, it had been mesmerizing. Now, it felt like a bad omen. He shifted his grip on the water cannon and listened.

Just as he convinced himself they weren't coming back, he heard them -footsteps scraping against pavement and then their low voices. He held his breath and peered through the leaves. The group was larger than before, more confident, and moving with purpose. One of them, a lanky boy with shaggy blond hair, carried a dark bottle in his hand. Another, broader and nervous-looking, kept glancing around like he expected a trap. An older boy was in the middle, his expression set in a sneer. The others hung back slightly as if they'd just come for the show.

"They'll come out," the older one said. "They have to. Burn 'em out like rats."

Arthur's grip tightened on the water cannon. His heart thudded hard, a steady drumbeat in his ears. He watched as the blond kid pulled a lighter from his pocket and flicked it open, the small flame flaring to life. Before he could touch it to the wick stuck inside the bottle, Arthur moved. With a burst of effort, he shoved himself up from the bushes and sprayed. A fine mist of rubbing alcohol hit the boy's hand, arm, and shirt, and the bottle just as the flame sparked.

Whoosh!

Fire erupted. It leaped from the lighter to his soaked skin and clothing in an instant. The kid screamed—a guttural howl of torturous pain—before he dropped the bottle to the ground. It shattered at his feet, the liquid inside igniting in a burst of orange and blue flames. He stumbled backward, waving his arms wildly, his sleeve catching fire.

The broad kid yelped, stumbling away. "Holy shit! Holy shit! Tyler, do something!"

Tyler staggered back, his sneer vanishing as his eyes widened in shock. The kid on fire hit the ground, rolling, his friends scrambling to put him out. One of them, a girl who had been hanging back, hesitated for just a second before turning and running.

Arthur didn't move. He stood tall, aiming the water cannon at the others. "Next one of you who lights a match gets the same treatment," he growled.

The threat settled in, the tension thick as the boy on the ground moaned, his skin blistering from the flash burn.

Tyler clenched his jaw, his hands balling into fists. "You think this is over?" His voice was steady, but there was something unhinged behind it, a raw fury that sent a chill up Arthur's spine.

Arthur dropped the water gun and retrieved his pistol from its holster, leveling it at Tyler's chest. His hand didn't shake. "You come back here again, and you won't be walking away."

For the first time, doubt flickered across Tyler's face. He took a step back, then another. The others hesitated before dragging their burned friend to his feet, supporting him as they stumbled back into the darkness.

Arthur stood there, his breath ragged, his legs trembling, his

Utter Devastation

chest tight with exertion, watching as they disappeared into the night. He knew this wasn't over.

Tyler wouldn't let this go.

Arthur turned and limped back toward the house, every step a reminder that he wasn't the man he used to be. But he wasn't dead yet, either. They'd have to do a better job if they were going to take him out.

As the teens ran away, Arthur headed inside. "Katherine, it's me. Let me in," Arthur called from the front porch. It felt like an eternity as he waited for Katherine to open up. He stepped through the front door, closing it behind him with slow deliberation. He twisted the deadbolt, then reached for the two-by-four brace and slid it back into place. His hands were steady, but his chest ached from exertion. His breath still came in ragged pulls, and his knees burned from crouching too long in the bushes.

Katherine's face was tight with worry. "Did they—"

"They ran," Arthur said, lowering himself into his recliner with a groan. "But not because they're scared. They'll be back."

Katherine sank onto the couch, gripping the blanket draped over her shoulders. "Arthur, we can't do this again. Next time, it won't just be a couple of kids. Tyler's not going to let this go."

"Tyler—you know one of them?"

"Yes. Remember I told you about him. I reported him to the principal for making threats of violence against the school. They kicked him out."

Arthur didn't recall. "When was that?"

"Last year."

"Last year? And you think he's still upset about that?"

"He glares at me every time he picks up his girlfriend for school. He even threatened me once—well, not verbally. He dragged his finger across his throat. I took it as a threat. I reported it, but nothing happened to him. He was at the school pick-up line the day of the solar storms." Her eyes widened. "Do you think he followed us home?"

"I don't know—maybe." Arthur stared at the boarded-up windows, his jaw tightening. She was right. Tyler hadn't looked afraid—he'd looked angry. Humiliated. And nothing made a young man more dangerous than wounded pride.

"So this could be personal and not just them trying to rob us?"

"I think those kids are dangerous—Tyler and his girlfriend." Katherine exhaled slowly, her hands twisting in the fabric of the blanket. "You think they'll come with more people next time?"

Arthur nodded. "More people. More firepower if they can get it." He rubbed his temples, thinking. "We can't assume this was just a bunch of dumb kids."

"Something I didn't tell you." Katherine hesitated. "Tyler and that girl—the one that dresses in all black—they're believed to be involved with some kind of international cult."

"Who told you that?"

"The detective—after I reported him the first time."

"How does that work—the international cult?"

"It's mostly online—started by some guy in Germany. They have local chapters around the world."

Arthur shook his head. "Tyler is the leader of the local chapter of some cult? I mean. He and the girl seem weird, but lots of kids do these days."

"Not weird like these two."

"What kind of activities is this cult involved in?"

"The detective said they actively recruited other teens who felt alienated, pulling them into their local 'chapter'. New recruits had to perform escalating acts of rebellion—small acts of arson, vandalism, breaking into abandoned buildings, or even physically attacking authority figures like teachers or security guards. To prove their loyalty, members had to record their 'rites of passage' and share them with the international group. The more extreme the act, the more prestige they earned. Some local chapters were rumored to be involved in beatings, home invasions, or even sacrificing animals as part of their initiation."

"Well, there's one less of them to cause trouble. Maybe that will make them think twice about targeting us again," Arthur said. If not, Arthur was concerned about how they would hold them off until Carson arrived and they could leave Dallas.

Silence stretched between them.

Arthur leaned forward, elbows resting on his knees. "Carson should have been here by now."

Katherine swallowed hard. "You don't think—"

"I don't know what to think," Arthur admitted. He hated the doubt that gnawed at him, but the truth was, Carson was late. Too late.

Katherine shook her head, her voice small but firm. "Carson's coming. He's smart, like you said. He wouldn't stop unless something forced him to."

Arthur nodded. "He'll come, and then we'll load up and get away from all this chaos."

THIRTY

Bee

Wild Plum Lake Estates
Highland, Arkansas
Day Five

The next morning, as Bee set out down the street toward Audree's house, she was still struggling to understand why the girl had insisted on staying put. With Jimmy still out there—angry, reckless, and unpredictable—it didn't seem safe. Sure, a few of their neighbors had agreed to monitor her house, but what use would it be if Jimmy came back looking for trouble?

Bee had tried to convince her to stay at her place, but after what had happened there with Ezra and the baby being taken, Audree had remained firm.

"I appreciate it, Bee, really. But this is my home. My baby's home. If I leave now, I might never get it back."

And Bee understood that. Leaving meant giving up control, not knowing what might happen while she was gone, and letting someone else decide her fate. Audree had already lost so much—

her safety, her sense of security, and the trust she once had in Jimmy. The house was the only thing left. Bee had seen the fear in her eyes, but also the determination. Audree wasn't going to run unless it was necessary. So, Bee had backed off, promising to check on her every day.

Now, as she walked toward Audree's house, she saw the actual real sign of collapse. Greg's house had been ransacked. Someone had kicked in the door, trashed the inside, and taken all his food. Greg sat on the front steps, a rifle across his lap, his head in his hands. "They took everything, Bee. The last of my food, my ammo. Everything."

Bee crouched next to him. "When?"

"Must've been last night. I was out on patrol. Came back, and…" He gestured to the wreckage behind him. "Whoever did this, they knew what they were looking for because I'd hidden it well."

Bee's gut twisted. No outsider could have gotten past patrols without someone noticing, which meant it was someone from their own neighborhood. The realization made her stomach churn. "You think it was Jimmy?"

"No. We had the neighborhood locked down tight. He wouldn't have risked coming back with so many of us armed."

Bee wasn't as convinced. Jimmy was irrational, but Greg was right; they'd had at least ten people on patrol all night. "Did you tell anyone where you'd hidden your cache? Could someone have watched you?"

"No. But I bet it was Bob's people."

Bee exhaled sharply. She didn't trust Bob, but if this turned into open warfare inside their own neighborhood, everything would unravel faster than they could patch it up. She needed to get ahead of any trouble. She gathered the remaining members of the neighborhood's leadership group—Mark, Gretchen, Hank, and a few others—and called for a meeting on her patio.

"I know tensions are high," she said. "But if we turn on each other, we don't stand a chance. Someone stole from Greg last night. We need to find out who, and we need to deal with it before things get worse."

Bee sat at the worn wooden table on her back patio, her fingers tapping against the rough surface as the small group gathered. Mark, Gretchen, Hank, and a few others leaned in, their expressions grim. The air was thick with tension, the weight of the break-in pressing down on them all.

"We need to figure out who did this before Bob turns this into a witch hunt," Bee said. "We can't afford more division."

Mark nodded. "Agreed. But how do we narrow it down?"

Gretchen crossed her arms. "Who knew where Greg kept his stuff?"

"No one," Bee said. "At least, no one he told directly." Bee thought back to what Greg had said. 'They knew what they were looking for because I'd hidden it well.' That meant whoever it was either had inside knowledge… or they had been watching.

Hank rubbed his jaw, his face dark with frustration. "I was on patrol last night. Walked the damn perimeter all night. If anyone from outside got in, I'd have seen them. I didn't spot anyone suspicious."

Gretchen frowned. "I saw someone."

Everyone turned to her.

"I was coming back from checking on Audree and the baby," she said. "It was late, maybe two in the morning. I saw Amy out."

"Amy?" Bee's brow furrowed. "What was she doing?"

Gretchen shifted in her chair. "I asked her. She said she was looking for her cat."

Silence stretched between them for a moment before Hank snorted. "You believe her?"

Bee shrugged, crossing her arms. "I didn't even know she had a cat."

Gretchen's lips pressed into a thin line. "She doesn't. At least, I don't think she does. I thought she was allergic."

Mark tapped his fingers against the table. "That's suspicious but proves nothing."

Bee nodded. "That's what's bugging me. People don't just decide to wander around in the middle of the night with someone like Jimmy on the loose. And if she was looking for a pet, why didn't she ask someone on patrol if they'd seen it?"

"Amy was near Greg's house," Gretchen said, glancing at Bee. "I remember because I thought it was weird she was so close to his place. She was standing right at the edge of his yard when I saw her. She waved me off and said the cat ran off toward the other side of the block."

"That's a hell of a coincidence," Mark muttered.

"How would she know where Greg had hidden his food and ammo stash?" Hank asked.

Bee shrugged. She didn't want to ask Greg before talking to Amy. They didn't need him running over there and confronting her if she was innocent—and until proven otherwise, she was just that. Bee's mind worked through the pieces. Amy wasn't a known troublemaker, but neither was she particularly well-prepared. She and her husband, Jeremy, hadn't stocked up before the blackout. He was away on a business trip and still hadn't returned. Amy was taking care of her three kids on her own. Bee remembered her mentioning in passing that they were already running low on food before the lights went out.

Bee leaned back in her chair, pressing her fingertips together. "We can't just knock on her door and accuse her without evidence."

"So, what do we do?" Hank asked.

Bee thought for a long moment. "We talk to her. Tell her about the break-in and see if she'll confess. We don't accuse her outright, but we let her know we're looking into it. If she's lying, we'll know soon enough."

Mark folded his arms. "And if she did it, Bee?"

"Then we have to decide what happens next."

The words felt heavier than she wanted to admit. Exile? Punishment? They were stepping into dangerous territory, but they couldn't afford to ignore this.

A noise at the edge of the patio caused Bee to stiffen. The others turned just as a slow clap echoed through the air.

Bob stood just beyond the patio, arms crossed, his usual smirk replaced with something colder. "Well, well. I thought it was funny when half of you sneaked off for a little secret meeting," he drawled. "Now I see why."

Bee stiffened. "This is none of your business, Bob."

He stepped forward, resting one hand on the back of an empty chair but not sitting down. "Oh, but it is. You see, I have a vested interest in making sure our little community doesn't tear itself apart. And when people start holding secret meetings…" He leaned against the post, smirking. "Looks like you're in a quandary."

Bee's stomach clenched. *Damn it. How much did he hear?*

She held his gaze, refusing to back down. "We were talking about how to handle this without turning into a mob."

Bob chuckled. "Is that right? And what did you decide?"

No one spoke.

"So, what's the plan, Bee?"

She met his gaze, refusing to back down. "We're dealing with it."

"Sure." Bob's smirk widened. "But just remember—you let this slide, and it won't be the last time. One thief turns into two. Two turns into a mob. You either set an example now or you lose control."

Bee clenched her fists. "We'll handle it!"

"By all means, then. I'll just sit back and watch." Bob gave her a mock bow before turning and walking away. The message was clear: If they didn't deal with Amy, he would.

Bee looked at the others. "We need to move now. Before Bob does."

Silence settled over them. It was one thing to suspect Bob and his crew—people they already didn't trust. But to turn their suspicion inward and admit that one of their own had stolen from Greg, from all of them—that was harder to stomach.

THIRTY-ONE

Carson

Casterman's Feed Store
Ramah, Colorado
Day Five

After Casterman and Alicia left, Carson sat slumped in his restraints, slipping in and out of consciousness. He awoke hours later, unsure how much time had passed. No light filtered through the tiny window behind him. His ribs throbbed with every inhale. His wrists burned where the rope had cut into his skin, the fibers slick with sweat and blood. His head ached, his body was wrecked, but his mind was clear. Hannah had given him something. Hope. He couldn't sit here and wait for them to break Julie.

A guard sat slouched in the chair near the door, his boots kicked up on an overturned crate, arms crossed. Carson studied him through swollen eyes—big guy, heavyset, fidgeted constantly. He yawned and scratched his stubbled jaw before pulling a battered cigarette from his pocket. "Should be out there looking for that damn package," the man said to himself, shaking his head. "Not babysitting some half-dead idiot."

Carson tucked that away. They were still looking for Bruce's stash.

The guard grumbled again, shifting his weight, rubbing his temples like he had a headache. Carson caught the unmistakable whiff of whiskey. He was drunk.

Good.

His fingers flexed against the rope, feeling for the tiny scalpel Hannah had tucked into his bandages. The blade was no bigger than his thumbnail, but it was sharp—meant for slicing flesh with precision.

Come on. Come on.

He worked at the bindings, moving slowly, keeping his breathing even. The ropes were thick, but the blade bit into them, little by little.

The guard yawned again, said something under his breath, and leaned back against the chair.

Almost there.

A final stroke, and the rope gave. Carson forced himself to stay still, feigning exhaustion, waiting. Then, when the guard closed his eyes for just a second too long, Carson lunged.

The chair tipped over as the guard startled, but Carson was already on him, the scalpel flashing in the dim light. The guard's reflexes were faster than he expected. A thick, meaty hand shot up, catching Carson's wrist just as the blade hovered inches from his throat. Carson pushed down with every ounce of strength he had, muscles screaming in protest, but the man was bigger—stronger.

"Son of a—!" The guard grunted, his breath hot and reeking of whiskey. His fingers tightened around Carson's wrist like a vise, forcing the blade away from his exposed neck and back toward Carson's.

Carson growled through gritted teeth, shifting his weight to press down harder. His arms trembled, his entire body weak from the beating he'd taken earlier. But if he lost this fight, he and Julie were as good as dead.

I can't lose! I won't!

The guard's other hand shot up and slammed into Carson's ribs. Agony lanced through him, white-hot and paralyzing. Carson gasped, his grip loosening just enough for the guard to shove him back. Carson tumbled onto the floor, his vision blurring for half a second. The guard scrambled to his feet, towering over him, his face twisted with fury.

"You little piece of—"

Carson lunged before the man could finish. He drove forward with sheer desperation, wrapping his arm around the man's throat in a chokehold. The guard staggered but recovered in an instant. He twisted and slammed Carson's back into the wall. The impact sent fresh waves of agony through his body, but he didn't loosen his grip. The man thrashed and clawed at Carson's arm, trying to pry him loose. He was bigger and stronger, but Carson had adrenaline on his side. And something deeper—survival instinct.

He squeezed tighter, feeling the man's frantic gasps beneath his arm. The guard pounded his elbow against Carson's body, landing solid blows to his ribs. The pain was unbearable, but Carson didn't let go.

He couldn't.

His left hand scrambled against the floor, searching. Then he felt it. The scalpel. Small. Cold. Smooth handle. A sliver of steel honed to slice flesh with lethal precision. He gripped it and, with one last desperate surge, plunged it deep into the man's neck.

The guard's body convulsed, his hands clawing at Carson's arm as warm blood gushed from his wound onto Carson's shirt, soaking through the fabric. The man jerked once. Twice. And went limp. Carson held on for a second longer, making sure. His breath was ragged, his body screaming in exhaustion. Finally, he shoved the lifeless body off him and rolled onto his side, gasping for air. His head spun, nausea threatening to pull him under.

But he didn't have time to stop. Julie was still out there. Quickly, fearing that others might have heard, Carson grabbed the man's pistol from his waistband, retrieved the man's knife from his left pants pocket, and then retrieved an extra magazine from the other pocket. Using the chair for support, Carson forced himself to his feet. After confirming the weapon was fully loaded, he stuffed the ammo in his back left pocket.

Carson wiped the man's blood from his hands onto his already ruined shirt. He tucked the knife into his back pocket, and then, with the pistol gripped in both hands, he stepped toward the door. He eased it open with the toe of his boot. It creaked, and Carson tensed, holding his breath, waiting for the sound of footsteps. After not hearing any, he exhaled and stepped through the doorway. The hallway was dark. He listened for voices or movement. Carson crept along the creaking wooden floorboards, pressing himself against the wall as he neared the back rooms.

Muted voices filtered through a half-open door.

"—wasting time looking for something that might not even be here," a gruff voice said.

"Casterman thinks they know where it is."

A chair scraped. "And if they don't?"

A pause.

"Then they're dead either way."

"And so are we. Once Contreras gets here, we're all gonna die if we don't have his stuff."

"You still think it's gonna be business as usual? Look around. The shit has hit the fan."

"I don't know, but I don't want to be here when Contreras's crew shows up."

Carson's jaw clenched. They were running out of time.

He inched past the door, careful not to make noise, and moved deeper into the building. He checked every storage room. Every back office, but Julie wasn't there.

Nothing. They had to have moved her somewhere else.

A sinking feeling clawed at his gut.

What if they'd already—

No. Don't go there.

He needed help. Someone who knew this town. He needed to find the doc and Hannah.

Carson slipped through a back exit, the chilly night air like a slap against his battered skin. He ducked into the shadows, pressing against the weathered siding of the feed store.

The town was dead quiet. The streetlamps were dark, with the only light coming from the flickering glow of a fire down the road. Then—shouts.

"Hey! Back here!"

Carson didn't think. He ran.

His feet pounded against the cracked pavement, breath sharp in his lungs. The sound of boots thundered behind him—two, maybe three pursuers. He cut left, darting between abandoned vehicles, vaulted over a rusted dumpster, and slid into the narrow alley behind a row of shuttered businesses.

A gunshot cracked through the night.

The bullet ricocheted off a nearby metal trash bin, sending sparks flying.

Carson ducked into the shadows, heart hammering, concealing himself behind a stack of wooden pallets. His chest burned, his ribs screaming in protest, but he didn't dare move.

The voices grew closer.

"You see him?"

"Nah, but he ain't far. He's hurt."

"Flush him out." Flashlight beams bounced off buildings. "Damn it! We'll sweep the east side." Then, the boots pounded away—retreating.

Carson let out a trembling breath. Sweat dripped down his face as he waited until the silence stretched long and deep before easing out from his hiding place. He rose to step out, but a door creaked open nearby, sending him back into his hiding place. Carson barely breathed. He peered around the pile of pallets as a middle-aged woman in a stained restaurant uniform stepped out, muttering to herself. She wiped her hands on a rag, shaking her head as she walked down the alley.

At first, Carson thought she was drunk. But as she got closer, he heard her words.

"Bastards. Taking everything. Casterman and that witch of his … think they own the damn world. This town ain't theirs. Ain't never been." Her words were full of loathing.

Carson saw an opportunity. Could he risk it? What choice did he have? He didn't know the town, and Casterman's goons were looking for him. He stepped forward from the darkness.

The woman gasped, dropping the rag. "Jesus—!"

He raised his hands, one still sticky with blood. "I'm not with them."

Her eyes darted up and down the alley. "You're the one they're after."

Carson nodded. "I need help."

She hesitated. "You're gonna get me killed."

"I'm looking for a woman. Brown hair, mid-thirties. They took her earlier."

The woman frowned, thinking. "I saw them bring you people in. But I don't know where they took her. Could be anywhere. They control the whole damn town."

Carson's stomach sank.

Think!

"What about the doctor—veterinarian?"

She bit her lip, glancing down the road.

His pulse kicked up. "Where?"

She hesitated.

"Please," Carson said, his voice tight. "I don't have time."

She exhaled sharply. "Doc Reisser is at the hair salon; it's our acting clinic."

Carson gave a brisk nod. "Thank you."

She grabbed his wrist before he could go. "You need to run. If they catch you, they'll kill you slow."

Carson didn't need to be told twice. He moved fast, keeping low, staying in the shadows. The town stretched out, silent and lifeless. Buildings were boarded up, most long abandoned from the looks of them. Here and there, dim candlelight flickered behind curtains—either townsfolk huddled in fear or allies of Casterman. Every corner, every street was a risk. A truck rumbled by in the distance, its headlights cutting through the dark. Carson pressed himself into the doorway of a dilapidated house, heart hammering. Voices carried from somewhere ahead.

"She said he ran toward the post office."

"Won't get far. He's banged up bad."

Carson clenched his jaw. They were closing in.

The hair salon loomed ahead, just a block down. If he could make it to Hannah and Doc's place, maybe he had a shot at making it out of this alive and finding Julie.

He took a breath, steeled himself, and ran.

THIRTY-TWO

Carson

Ramah, Colorado
Day Five

Battered and barely standing, Carson moved through the shadows, his body screaming for rest. The only thing that kept him going was the desperate hope that Hannah and Doc could help him—and that somewhere, Julie was still alive. He kept close to the abandoned buildings, his breaths shallow, his movements careful. The town was quiet but not empty; danger lurked behind every darkened window and around every blind corner. He could feel eyes watching, hidden figures waiting to report his presence.

Ahead, the dilapidated salon-turned-clinic loomed, just as the waitress had said. Its wooden sign creaked in the biting wind, its windows covered with threadbare curtains that were doing a poor job of concealing the dim light within. He saw movement inside—Doc and Hannah likely tending to a patient. He prayed the door wasn't locked. Carson kept his body low as he circled to the back entrance. He turned the knob slowly and stepped inside. With careful, measured steps, Carson slipped deeper into the clinic.

Discarded beauty supplies cluttered the single hallway leading to the main room. In one corner were bloody rags, empty bottles, and a cracked IV stand leaning against the wall. He could hear indistinct murmurs from the room ahead—Doc and Hannah as they whispered over their patient. He crept closer and peered inside just enough to see.

One of Casterman's injured men lay on the treatment table. He groaned as Doc pressed a damp cloth against a gash on his forehead. Hannah checked his pulse and administered what little medicine they had. The man wasn't in fighting shape, but Carson knew he couldn't risk showing himself just yet. If Casterman's underling so much as twitched in his direction, it was over. He'd call out and alert the others.

Hannah turned, picked up a cloth bundle and headed toward the small supply room down the hall. Carson saw his chance. He darted forward and slipped inside just as she pulled the door open.

Before she could react, he grabbed her by the arm, pulling her inside, one hand pressing over her mouth. Her body went rigid, her breath sharp against his palm, but before she could struggle, he hissed, "It's me. Carson. The prisoner you treated."

Her wild eyes locked on to his, recognition flickering behind them.

"I'm not going to hurt you," he continued, his voice low, steady. "I need your help to find my friend. Can I trust you not to scream for help?"

A tense second passed. Then, she nodded.

Carson slowly removed his hand, stepping back just enough to give her space. Hannah swallowed hard and rubbed at her wrist where his grip had been. Her breath came fast, but her sharp gaze studied him, searching.

"You escaped!"

He nodded. "Thanks for the scalpel."

She glanced down at his shirt, and her expression darkened. "Did you kill one of them with it?"

Carson nodded. "They're looking for me."

She glanced toward the door, then back at him, hesitation flickering across her face.

"The kids? My cat?" he pressed. "Where are they? Are they safe?"

Hannah's expression softened. "They're with someone I trust," she said. "I can't tell you who. If they catch you again, they'll try to beat it out of you, and I won't put that person in danger."

Carson exhaled sharply. He hated it, but he understood.

"Julie," he said next. "Where do you think they moved her?"

Hannah hesitated, frustration tightening her features. "I don't know," she admitted. "Casterman keeps his prisoners moving so no one can track them."

Carson clenched his jaw. He couldn't afford to waste time searching blindly.

Hannah suddenly turned toward the door. "Wait here," she whispered. Then, louder, she called out to the doctor. "Grandpa? Can you help me find what you sent me in here for?"

A few seconds later, the doctor appeared, his face lined with exhaustion but his expression as sharp as ever. His brow furrowed when he saw Carson standing in the cramped closet.

Hannah stepped forward, keeping her voice low. "He needs help," she said. "He's looking for his friend."

Doc's jaw tensed. "Damn fool," he said. "You should've kept running."

"Not without her." Carson's voice cracked slightly with desperation. "Please, Doc. I need to find Julie. If you have any leads, any rumors … anything…"

Doc studied him for a long moment. Then, with a resigned sigh, he nodded. "Stay here."

Carson waited in the suffocating quiet of the hallway as Doc returned to the injured enforcer. The man stirred slightly as Doc checked his pulse, then reached into his pocket, pulling out a small vial.

"Let's make sure he sleeps through the night," Doc said, measuring out just enough medicine to knock the man out cold.

The enforcer mumbled something incoherent before his body sagged against the cot. A few minutes later, Doc returned to the hall.

"All right, he's out for the count." Doc rubbed a tired hand over his face. "Let's figure out how to get your friend back."

THIRTY-THREE

Carson

Winner Hair Salon
Ramah, Colorado
Day Five

"We don't have much time. It'll be light soon. We need to alert the sheriff at the substation in Falcon." Hannah's eyes burned with determination as she spoke. "It's our best shot at getting Julie out safe and rescuing this town from Casterman and his men."

Doc shook his head. "Casterman's men are everywhere. There's no way to get a vehicle. They've either disabled them all or have them locked up in the warehouse."

"I have to get my horse from the ranch," Hannah said. "It's the only ride that can outrun those enforcers. I can cross the farms and avoid the roads."

Carson's heart pounded at her words—hope mingled with dread. "I can't let you do this alone. I'll make sure you get to your ranch."

Carson and Hannah moved like ghosts through the streets of Ramah, their bodies low, pressed against the crumbling facades of long-abandoned buildings. The town was a graveyard of broken dreams, its narrow alleys littered with debris—shattered glass from storefronts looted long ago, discarded cans rusted from exposure. They kept their movements careful and measured—every step deliberate, every sound controlled. Carson's battered body screamed for rest, but he pushed forward, driven by something stronger than pain.

Hannah moved ahead of him, light on her feet, her every movement practiced and fluid. As a local, she knew these alleyways well. She had learned to survive in this town under Casterman's rule—to slip between the cracks, to exist where his men weren't looking.

A muffled cough sounded from a darkened doorway. Carson tensed, his hand reaching for his pistol. He lowered it as a frail figure emerged from the shadows—an elderly woman, her face deeply lined with hardship. She motioned them forward, then pointed toward a narrow corridor between two buildings.

Hannah hesitated. "Mrs. Gordon?"

The elderly woman nodded, her sunken eyes flicking past them toward the street, where the distant voices of Casterman's enforcers carried on the wind. "Go now," she whispered. "Before they come this way."

Carson met her gaze, searching for some sign of hesitation, but all he found was a resolute certainty—an unspoken defiance against the men who had turned this town into a prison.

"Thank you," Hannah murmured.

Mrs. Gordon faded back into the darkness as swiftly as she had appeared.

They pressed on.

Farther down, another figure appeared—a wiry man in his fifties, his face gaunt but his eyes sharp with recognition. He lifted a hand in a silent greeting, then stepped back into the doorway of a boarded-up auto shop, his body blocking the dim lantern glow from inside. Carson didn't know him, but the man gave Hannah a small, quick nod.

"You didn't see us," she whispered.

The man dipped his chin in silent acknowledgment.

The town was waking up—not with noise, not with open defiance, but in these quiet, careful moments of rebellion. People who had once been too afraid to act now slipped from the cracks, offering small acts of resistance—an open doorway, a concealed escape route, a nod that meant keep going. Carson and Hannah moved faster now, threading through the maze of narrow corridors, rusted fences, and the skeletal remains of buildings that had once been homes and businesses. They darted through a collapsed storefront, past the shattered display cases of what had once been a bakery.

The voices of the enforcers grew louder behind them.

They were running out of time. Hannah pulled Carson toward an alley that emptied out near the town's edge, where the first hints of the open road and the tree line beyond beckoned them to freedom. The escape was so close. A flashlight beam sliced through the darkness, catching Hannah's shoulder for the briefest moment before she jerked away.

"Hey! Over there!" A shout rang out.

And the chase began.

Hannah's eyes widened with terror, but she didn't hesitate. "Carson, run!" she screamed, grabbing his arm and pulling him forward. Behind them, enforcers—brutal, relentless men—spilled out of the shadows. Their shouts blended with the cacophony of gunfire.

Carson's heart hammered in his chest as he dove behind a crumbling wall, the fall sending a shock wave of pain through his battered body. He could see Hannah breaking into a sprint towards the tree line, her silhouette framed by the flickering lights of the aurora. "Go!" she urged, glancing back over her shoulder. "Get out of sight! Get back to the clinic!"

The gunfire intensified. Carson's instincts took over as he returned fire, emptying the weapon into the dark. Only seven rounds left. He had to conserve them and save the last one for Casterman. From the ground, he picked up a length of steel pipe and hurled it toward the far side of the barn, hoping to draw their attention. The clang echoed through the night in sharp contrast to the rapid bursts of gunfire.

Every second counted.

At the edge of the property, a dilapidated barn loomed ahead—his only hope for cover. Adrenaline surged through Carson's veins as he scrambled toward it, using the remnants of a crumbling stone wall to shield his movements. A bullet whizzed past, slicing through the air near his ear. Another struck the edge of his shoulder—not a direct hit, but close enough to burn like fire. He gritted his teeth and pressed on, clutching his side as he reached the barn's entrance.

Two henchmen closed in fast. One fired wildly, the muzzle flashes lighting up the darkness, while the other moved more carefully, scanning the shadows. They were hunting him.

Carson ducked behind the splintered frame of the doorway. He had to keep them occupied and buy Hannah more time. He tightened his grip on the pistol he'd taken off the guard, running his thumb along the slide to remind himself how many rounds he had left. Not enough.

Outside, the two men whispered, hesitant to storm the barn blind. So far, they hadn't realized Hannah was already gone. Carson moved toward the back and pressed his body against the wall as he peered through a gap in the rotted boards. Hannah rode away. The rhythmic pounding of hooves was barely audible over the wind. He needed to cover the sound before the henchmen caught on. His eyes landed on a shovel propped against the wall. Grabbing it, he banged it hard against the side of the barn, the metallic clash ringing through the night. The reaction was instant.

Carson's chest tightened. She was free. Soon, help would arrive. He prayed they were in time.

"Inside!" one of the enforcers barked.

Carson had mere seconds to move before the first man lunged through the front door.

Gunfire erupted.

A bullet struck a rusted tractor near him, sending shards of metal and debris flying. A jagged edge tore into Carson's side, drawing a sharp grunt, but he pushed forward, using the hulking machinery as cover. His vision tunneled, and every sound magnified. The crunch of boots on dirt. The whisper of shifting hay. His own ragged breath. The silhouette of the first man came into view. Carson fired.

Boom!

Boom!

The enforcer staggered, a sharp gasp escaping before he collapsed. The second man, bigger and faster, charged from the opposite side, a hunting knife gleaming in his hand. Carson barely got his pistol up before the man knocked it aside, sending it skidding across the dirt.

The fight turned brutal.

The enforcer grabbed Carson by the arm, wrenching him forward with sheer brute strength. Carson stumbled but managed to drive his knee into the man's ribs. The enforcer grunted, shook it off, then slammed Carson into the tractor. White-hot pain exploded in Carson's ribs. His body screamed in protest, but he couldn't stop now.

The enforcer grabbed for his throat. Carson snatched the stolen knife from his belt. With all the strength he had left, he drove the blade deep into the man's side. The enforcer let out a strangled cry. His eyes went wide as he stumbled back. Blood soaked through his shirt, but still, he fought. He grabbed Carson's head and banged it repeatedly against the tractor, causing the knife to tumble from his grip. He had seconds—maybe less—before he passed out. His right hand searched for anything he could use to save himself and landed on the cold steel handle of a torque wrench. Carson swung it, pounding the guy in the head over and over until he let go.

He staggered, choking on blood before he collapsed to the ground.

Silence.

Carson swayed where he stood, vision swimming. His breaths came fast and ragged, and his limbs felt like lead. He pressed a shaking hand to his side, which came away sticky with blood.

Somewhere in the distance, Hannah was still riding. She was safe. He'd stopped them from following her.

THIRTY-FOUR

Carson

Doc Reisser's Ranch
Ramah, Colorado
Day Five

Carson retrieved the first henchman's pistol and then patted the man's pockets for spare magazines but found nothing. A fresh wave of frustration coursed through him. *I'm running out of options.* The pistol's weight was solid in his palm, but in the pitch-black room he couldn't see a thing. He ejected the magazine briefly, feeling the tension of the spring, but the thick darkness inside the barn made it impossible to count the rounds. Could be full. Could be almost empty. Either way, it would have to be enough. His own gun was gone, buried somewhere in the thick straw that muffled every movement beneath his boots. He crouched for a second, feeling blindly through the mess, but it was useless. The darkness swallowed everything beyond a few feet, and he didn't dare flick on a flashlight—not with the risk of giving away his position. Time pressed in, slipping through his fingers.

Gritting his teeth, he abandoned the search and turned toward the open door. Carson blinked away the sting of sweat and blood dripping into his eyes. He wiped his forearm across his face, his breath coming fast, heart hammering. Beyond the doorway, the night stretched into a fading shimmer of green and violet—the last fragile traces of an aurora dissolving into the deep blue haze of early morning, just before dawn. Somewhere out there, more of Casterman's men were hunting him. He had to move. Now.

Before he even made it back to the road, headlights lit up the road. Carson scanned the area for an escape route. His eyes landed on a narrow creek bed, barely visible beneath tangled brush and debris. With no time to waste, he bolted toward it. Behind him, the sounds of pursuit intensified—car doors opened, boots pounded, voices shouted commands—and he knew that if he didn't vanish into the shadows, they would soon find him.

Carson moved along the dry creek bed, the faint pre-dawn light casting the world in blurred shades of blue and gray. The uneven terrain offered a fragile kind of cover—just enough to stay hidden, but not enough to move easily. He stumbled over loose rocks and wove around scrubby juniper, each step a jolt of pain that reminded him just how broken he was.

Soon, he reached a point where the enforcers' voices began to fade. Hidden beneath a low-hanging branch, Carson paused, gasping for breath. The adrenaline slowly ebbed from his body to reveal the full extent of his exhaustion and pain. Every muscle ached. His vision blurred, but he forced himself to stand. Every moment he lingered meant more danger for Hannah, Julie, and the kids. Carson struggled back toward town. He clutched his side, wincing as each step sent waves of pain through his battered form. Carson made his way through the alleys, each step calculated for silence. Relief washed over him as the clinic door came into view. As he stumbled inside, he was met by the doctor.

"Carson!" Doc called out as he rushed to his side. "Did she make it?"

Utter Devastation

Carson managed a weak nod. "Hannah ... she got out. I saw her riding toward the tree line."

Doc's eyes softened. "Thank God she's safe. That means we have a chance." He helped Carson toward the deserted house next door. "Now listen. I've been talking to a few folks. There's chatter about Julie's location. We have several potential leads. After I patch you up, I have a plan to find her."

In the muted light of the abandoned house, a few brave souls of Ramah gathered, offering Carson a glimmer of hope amid the chaos. He knew his escape had come at a high cost, but every scar and every bruise was a testament to his resolve. He would keep fighting if it meant saving Julie and ensuring the safety of the children, whose fate now hung in the balance.

The whispers from the townsfolk grew louder as word spread. Julie had been seen in various locations: a dilapidated warehouse near the main square, an abandoned farmhouse on the town's edge, even a former community center that Castleman had repurposed as a makeshift detention facility.

"Carson," Doc said quietly, leaning in, "we need to organize a search. I'm rallying every willing soul, but they're still too frightened to go up against Casterman's crew."

"That's okay, Doc. Just point me in the right direction," Carson said.

Doc handed him a hand-drawn map with several locations marked. Carson dropped the magazine of his stolen pistol and counted the remaining rounds. *Five—they'll have to do.* Before he left, a battered but hopeful young woman—one of the town's many quiet resistors—stepped forward.

"I overheard something," she whispered. "They say the enforcers are moving Julie to an old residence near the fire station. It's your best lead."

Carson gripped her arm, a mix of gratitude and desperation in his eyes. "Thank you. I'll check it out." With a last nod to Doc and a promise to return with news, Carson slipped out into the dangerous streets once more. The stakes had never been higher, and the clock was ticking. He kept moving, his instincts screaming that every second counted, but his body protested. He stopped for a moment to catch his breath.

The distant rumble of the wind against broken shutters, the occasional scrape of a boot against gravel—it was all background noise to Carson's sharp, focused mind. His body ached, but the urgency of his mission drowned out the pain. His footsteps were quiet against the cracked pavement as he moved toward the fire station. He stayed in the shadows. He used the maze of abandoned vehicles and derelict buildings for cover. Carson spotted movement ahead. He froze and pressed himself against the doorway of an old gas station as a pair of Casterman's goons walked the street, speaking in hushed voices.

"Boss wants her moved by morning," one said.

"She's more trouble than she's worth," the other grumbled. "Damn woman put up a fight. Nearly took Derrick's eye out."

Julie!

Carson's hands tightened into fists. He had to act now. Carson trailed the guards from a distance, sticking to the darkest corners. He followed them to the house near the fire station—a two-story residence that had once been a family home, now twisted into something sinister. A single oil lamp flickered in the window. Carson circled the property, scanning for an entry point. The front door was too risky—guarded. The side windows were boarded up. But the back door, half off its hinges, was an invitation. Carson slipped inside, his breathing controlled, his movements slow. The house smelled of something putrid, like raw sewage. The floor creaked beneath his weight, and he stilled, listening. Above him— a muffled sound. He recognized the voice.

Utter Devastation

Julie.

He'd found her. A surge of adrenaline coursed through his body.

Then, another voice drifted down the stairs.

Alicia.

THIRTY-FIVE

Bee

Wild Plum Lake Estates
Highland, Arkansas
Day Five

Bee, Mark, Gretchen, and Hank walked toward Amy's house, their steps slow and heavy. They had to handle the issue before Bob got involved.

Bee knocked, then stepped back with her arms crossed. The curtain twitched, and a few seconds later, Amy cracked the door open just enough to peer out. Her eyes flicked between them, her lips pressed tight.

"We need to talk," Bee said evenly.

Amy hesitated, then pulled the door open wider and stepped aside.

The stench hit them immediately—unflushed urine mixed with the thick, putrid rot of waste. Bee swallowed against the burn in her throat. Obviously, Amy hadn't taken Bob's warning about not using the toilets.

Inside, Amy's three children huddled on the worn couch, their

Utter Devastation

wide eyes darting between the adults. Amy stood rigid, arms folded, her jaw set. She knew why they were here.

Bee didn't ease into it. "We need to talk about a break-in that happened in the neighborhood last night."

Amy's eyes flicked toward Gretchen, then back to Bee. "Okay."

Bee kept her voice calm. "Someone broke into Greg's house. Took some of his belongings." She eased herself onto a chair across from Amy. "Gretchen saw you out near there late last night."

Amy's lips tightened. "And you think that was me?"

"No one's accusing you of anything," Bee said. "We're just talking."

Amy exhaled, then turned to her children. "Go to your rooms, boys."

The three boys, ranging in age from four to ten, hesitated before scurrying down the hall. The moment their doors clicked shut, Amy sagged against the cushion and shook her head. "Guess I should've known you'd figure it out."

Bee kept her expression neutral. "Why?"

"Why?" Amy's eyes flashed. Her voice rose, sharp with resentment. "Because Greg's hoarding while my kids go hungry. Because we're supposed to be in this together, but some of us are running out of food while others sit on stockpiles."

Bee's stomach tightened. She understood the fear of running out, the desperation that clawed at a person when their children were hungry. However, Amy's defiance, the way she wore her anger like armor, wasn't going to win her any sympathy from the others.

"You should have come to us," Bee said. "We would've helped."

"Help? You mean charity? Amy let out another harsh laugh. My husband wouldn't allow it."

Gretchen scoffed. "So, let me get this straight. He's not okay with charity, but you think he'd be fine with stealing?"

Amy's face darkened. "I didn't think anyone would ever suspect me. I would've gotten away with it if Gretchen had kept her mouth shut."

Bee's gut twisted. This wasn't guilt. This wasn't regret. Amy didn't see what she'd done as wrong—just unfortunate that she'd gotten caught.

Gretchen's face reddened. "So, now it's my fault you're in trouble?" She stepped closer, her voice tight with frustration. "You didn't even try to make this right. You just took what you wanted and let the rest of us tear each other apart over it."

Amy lifted her chin. "I did what I had to do."

Gretchen let out a breath of disgust. "Girl, you deserve whatever punishment the others decide to give you." She spun on her heel and stalked out, slamming the door behind her.

Bee followed, her stomach knotting. The second she stepped onto the porch, she spotted Bob leaning against the railing, arms crossed.

"You want me to handle it now?" he drawled.

Bee stiffened. Mark and Hank flanked her as they stepped outside, leaving Amy inside with her kids.

"So? What's your plan, Bee?" Bob smirked. "A trial? A slap on the wrist?" He tilted his head. "Or do we actually enforce some consequences?"

Bee met his stare, unwavering. "Like what? Execution?"

Bob's silence was answer enough.

"We're not killing people over food," Bee said, her voice steady. "But there needs to be a punishment."

Hank, normally quiet, spoke up. "What about exile?"

Bee hesitated. It was a harsh solution, but it was better than the alternative. "We need to think this through. Talk to the others."

"Not much to think about, sweetheart," Bob said. "Either we make an example of her, or we invite more of this. More theft.

More people thinking they can do whatever they want without consequences." He leaned in slightly. "You know I'm right."

She clenched her jaw. She hated that Bob had a point. If they let Amy off too easily, it wouldn't stop with her. But if they let Bob handle it … it wouldn't be justice. It would be revenge. And that was a road Bee wasn't ready to walk.

THIRTY-SIX

Willow

Interstate 64
Fayette County, Kentucky
Day Five

The miles stretched interminably through the rolling Kentucky hills. By now, the adrenaline had worn off, but tension still coiled in Willow's stomach like a wound spring. She forced herself to relax and lean against the window, but her mind wouldn't quiet. She imagined Carson out in Boulder, her brilliant, stubborn, pain-in-the-ass brother, probably buried in data, scrambling to analyze the biggest geomagnetic storm in history while the world around him crumbled. What was it like out there now? Was the NOAA still standing? Had he made it home to his wilderness retreat? Was he even alive? She clenched her jaw and pushed the thought away. No sense in spiraling.

They drove in silence for a while, skirting the outskirts of Lexington, Kentucky, to avoid what had once been a sprawling city. In the distance, the skyline loomed, the once-bustling streets now deserted. Willow was glad they'd chosen to stay off the main roads. They didn't need another Charlottesville.

After passing the city, Guynn merged them back onto Interstate 64, hoping to make better time now that the worst of the urban sprawl was behind them. The heaviness of the moment eased, giving way to something softer, lighter—trivia.

"So," Knox said from the back seat, shifting. "Kentucky. Known for bluegrass music, right?"

Guynn nodded. "And horse racing."

"Makes sense," Knox said. "Saw a sign for Keeneland back there before we turned off."

"World-famous racetrack," Guynn said. "The Derby is up in Louisville, but Keeneland's where the real horsemen go."

Willow scoffed. "Let me guess—you're a racetrack guy, Colonel?"

"Not so much anymore." He chuckled. "Can't afford it."

Knox smirked. "I appreciate a good bourbon."

"Well, you're in the right state for it," Guynn said. "Kentucky's famous for bourbon and tobacco. Not much tobacco's grown here now, though." He shook his head. "Used to be fields of the stuff as far as the eye could see. Now, it's all soybeans and corn."

Knox frowned. "Tobacco? Who the hell gets nostalgic over lung cancer?"

"I'm not saying it was good for you."

Knox stretched, rolling his shoulder. "Yeah, but neither is fried chicken. That's what Kentucky's really known for."

Willow shook her head. "Well, one good thing might come out of all this—no more processed fast food."

Guynn groaned dramatically. "Yeah, but what a way to go. Imagine a world with no more biscuits and gravy."

"Somehow, I think we'll manage." Knox grinned. "Our food will still be fast, though."

"How do you figure?" Willow asked.

Knox leaned forward, resting his good arm on the back of the driver's seat. "Deer can run thirty-five miles per hour. Rabbits? Forty-five miles per hour. If we're eating, it's gonna be something fast."

Willow laughed, shaking her head. "That's ... um ... not wrong."

Guynn patted his stomach. "Well, maybe I could stand to drop a few pounds."

The mood grew quieter after that. The silence settled in again, but it wasn't tense anymore—just thoughtful. Then, after a long stretch of road, Knox broke the quiet.

"Colonel," he asked, his voice casual. "Have you ever grown a garden?"

"Nope. Never had to. How hard can it be, though? You dig up the soil, plop a seed in the ground, pour some water on it, and voilà. Food!"

"You'd be surprised," Willow said. She leaned back against her seat. "I tried once. A tomato plant on my balcony."

"What happened?" Knox asked.

She deadpanned. "It died."

Guynn laughed, shaking his head. "Sounds about right."

"Well, if we're gonna survive the apocalypse, we better learn," Knox said. "Because the new 'fast food' is likely to run out real quick."

"Overhunting?"

"Exactly. We won't be the only ones getting our meat from the woods," Knox said.

"What about livestock? We can get us some cows, maybe a goat or two, and chicken for eggs and meat."

"Where are you gonna raise livestock? My mom's yard is less than a quarter acre?"

"Arkansas is pretty wooded, right—lots of forest area?" Guynn asked. "Might have to knock down some trees."

"I think you've got an oversimplified image of farm life," Knox said.

Utter Devastation

"I know. I was just bullshitting you. Some of my family farm, and I know how hard they work. Actually, I don't know how folks like us will survive without farmers to teach us."

"I don't mind adding more vegetables to my diet. Just don't expect me to be a farmer," Willow said.

Guynn tapped the steering wheel. "Gotta start somewhere."

"You think… you think most people aren't gonna make it?" Willow asked.

Guynn didn't answer right away. Finally, he said, "A lot of people aren't prepared for something like this."

Knox exhaled sharply. "Yeah. I keep thinking about—" He hesitated, glancing out the window. "My family. My little sister. She's got two kids. They lived in a damn apartment in Tampa. No land. No backup food. Just … there. In the middle of a city that's probably gone to hell by now."

"I keep thinking about Carson." Willow stared at the dashboard, her throat tight. "Wondering if he's okay."

"He's probably on his way to Arkansas as well," Knox said.

"In a way, I hope he isn't. Look at everything we've been through, and this place is rather more rural than his trip would be."

Willow watched the interstate stretch out before them. For the first time in days, she let herself think about what came next. What happened when they made it to her mom's? Would it be safe? How long before the world settled into whatever the hell this new normal was? Would they just plant a garden, raise some chickens, and try to pretend life hadn't completely fallen apart? Could they even get that lucky? She didn't know. They just had to make it there first.

Knox leaned forward, a devilish grin spreading across his face. "All right, since we're heading to Arkansas, I figured I'd brush up on some local culture. Y'all ready for some Arkansas trivia?"

Willow groaned. "Oh no."

"Boy, don't go there," Guynn said.

Knox ignored them both, clearing his throat. "Why do the Arkansas Razorbacks eat cereal straight from the box?"

Willow pinched the bridge of her nose. "Please, don't."

"Because they choke when they get near a bowl."

Guynn chuckled despite himself.

Knox continued, unfazed by Willow's groan. "What's the best thing to ever come out of Arkansas?"

"I feel like I don't wanna know," Guynn said.

"Interstate 40."

Willow rolled her eyes, but she couldn't fight the small smile tugging at her lips.

"Okay, okay, last one," Knox promised, holding up his hands in mock surrender. "Why did the Arkansas farmer bring a ladder to the bar?"

Guynn huffed, but he played along. "Why?"

"Because he heard the drinks were on the house!" Knox beamed.

The Jeep filled with groans and reluctant laughter.

"Knox, if my mom hears you talking like that, she'll make you drink a gallon of sweet tea and listen to bluegrass until your ears bleed," Willow warned.

Knox sighed dramatically. "Fine. I'll behave. But only because I value my life and access to home-cooked meals."

The colonel glanced in the rearview at Knox, just for a split second. "I got one for you. Why did the Arkansas football team go to the bank?"

"I don't know. Why?"

"To get their quarterback."

Willow laughed. For a moment, things felt normal.

At Elizabethtown, Kentucky, they took the Western Kentucky Parkway west, and the miles passed in a blur, conversation easing the tension for a time, but reality always crept back in. Just past Leitchfield, Kentucky, the road curved to the right. As they crested a small hill, a wrecked bus came into view. Or at least, what had once been a bus. The charred skeleton of a prison transport vehicle sat jackknifed across the road, its exterior blackened, windows shattered. The heat had warped the metal, curling parts of the frame like wilted leaves. It had peeled away the paint, but faint remnants of blocky white lettering were still visible through the soot—the barely legible insignia of the Kentucky Department of Corrections.

Willow swallowed hard as the burned corpses came into focus. Some still buckled into their seats, their forms reduced to grotesque, blackened husks. Others had tried to crawl away, their last moments etched into the scorched pavement. A few had collapsed just beyond the bus, curled into unnatural shapes as if they had been reaching for freedom that never came. Handcuffs still hung from melted seat frames. Some of the dead had shackles fused to their bones.

Knox let out a low whistle from the back seat. "Damn. That's some nightmare fuel."

Guynn slowed the Jeep and scanned the wreckage. "Doesn't look recent. Fire's out. Could have happened the day of the solar storm."

Willow tore her gaze from the bodies and checked out the surrounding area. The road was too quiet. There were no onlookers, scavengers, or birds picking through the charred remains—just silence.

"Probably for the best," Guynn said.

Willow's head snapped toward him. "What?"

He didn't flinch, his expression unreadable as he stared at the wreckage. "This new world doesn't need people like that."

"You don't know that. Not all of them deserved to die like this."

Guynn exhaled, rubbing a hand over his face. "Some, maybe. But you think they were transporting first-time shoplifters? These weren't jaywalkers, Willow. That was a maximum-security transport. You don't send someone to a facility like that unless they've done something really bad." He nodded toward the melted shackles still clinging to blackened bones. "The world's already dangerous enough without releasing a pack of wolves into it."

Willow bristled. "You're saying they all deserved to burn?"

"No. I ain't saying that."

Knox spoke up from the back. "But you are saying the world's better off without them."

Guynn didn't deny it.

Willow crossed her arms. "You don't know their stories. Not all of them were murderers or rapists. Some of them could've been wrongfully convicted. Maybe some were just in the wrong place at the wrong time."

Guynn let out a slow breath. "You're right. Maybe there were a few in there who didn't deserve it." He turned to her, his voice softer but firm. "But what do you think happens when you throw a bunch of killers and career criminals into a lawless world? You think they're gonna get rehabilitated just because society crumbled? Hell, no. They're gonna do what they always did. Take. Kill. Survive at the expense of everyone else."

Willow wanted to argue, but the words stuck in her throat. Because deep down, she knew he wasn't wrong on that point. She'd already seen what desperation did to people. And those were civilians—parents, neighbors, everyday folks who once had stable lives. If those people were already turning violent, what would hardened criminals do? Still, the finality of the thought made her uneasy. "We're not judge, jury, and executioner," she said.

"The world's already handing out sentences," Guynn said, his voice calm, almost resigned.

Willow pressed her lips together, unsettled by the finality of it.

Without another word, Guynn eased off the brake and hit the gas. The Jeep rumbled forward, rolling past the blackened wreckage and back onto the open road. Twenty minutes later, the highway stretched ahead of them, the only sound the steady hum of the tires against the asphalt. Then, up ahead—a vehicle, sitting dead in the middle of the road.

"Trouble?" Knox said from the back.

Without hesitation, Guynn swerved into the left-hand lane to go around it. "Don't like the looks of it."

Willow turned her head as they passed, catching a glimpse of the abandoned car. The driver's side door hung open. No bodies. No movement. Something about it didn't sit right. And then—

BOOM!

Their tires exploded. The Jeep lurched, metal screaming as the steering wheel ripped sideways in Guynn's hands. Willow's stomach slammed into the seatbelt, her ears ringing from the gut-wrenching impact. The tires shrieked.

"Shit!" Guynn barked, wrenching the wheel.

Willow's stomach slammed into her seatbelt as the Jeep fishtailed, almost spinning out. She gritted her teeth and braced herself on the door handle.

The vehicle veered toward the shoulder, Guynn fighting to keep control.

Then—silence.

THIRTY-SEVEN

Carson

Witch's Roost
Ramah, Colorado
Day Five

Alicia's voice was sharp, taunting. "You're lucky he still wants you alive," she sneered.

Carson moved cautiously, clearing the lower rooms before he made his way up the staircase. The closer he got, the more he could hear. He placed his foot on the first tread and then another. It creaked against his weight. Carefully, he moved up step by step, determined to be as silent as possible, prepared for Casterman's henchmen to rush in and find him before he could rescue Julie.

Julie's defiant tone followed. "Casterman doesn't want me alive. You do."

Carson flinched at the sound of a slap and then a grunt of pain. His blood ignited. Moving fast, he reached the top of the stairs and peered into the dimly lit room. Julie sat bound to a chair, blood smeared along her cheek. Across from her, Alicia paced, twirling a knife in her fingers. Against the wall to his right leaned one of the

Utter Devastation

guards. Carson had one chance to do this right. He acted on instinct.

Stealth was his only advantage. If he started shooting, the echo would carry through the streets and alert every enforcer to his position before he could even reload. That left him with one option: his knife. The attack would be up close. Silent. And with luck—deadly.

He sprang into the room and lunged. The blade sank deep into the guard's side. Carson felt the resistance of flesh and muscle momentarily slowing the thrust. A gurgled cry escaped the man's lips as his body jerked in shock. Carson wrenched the knife free, twisting as he did, and let the body crumble to the floor.

Julie's eyes widened, her breath ragged.

However, Alicia just grinned. "You should've stayed gone," she muttered. Then she pounced.

Carson barely dodged in time, her blade slicing through the fabric of his sleeve, nicking his skin. He countered by swinging at her with his knife, but Alicia was fast.

Too fast.

She sidestepped his strike, delivering a sharp kick to his right knee. Carson stumbled, but he didn't go down. He couldn't.

Julie struggled against her bindings, her rage-filled cries mixing with the sounds of combat.

Alicia went for another strike, this time aiming for his throat. Carson caught her wrist and twisted hard. She yelped, but instead of pulling away, she used the momentum to slam her knee into his stomach. Pain exploded through his ribs. Carson gritted his teeth and fought through it. He swung again, catching Alicia across the jaw. She staggered, her breath hitching as blood dripped from the fresh split in her lip, but she didn't wipe it away. Instead, she smiled again. Not in pain. Not in fear. In amusement.

Carson's pulse pounded in his ears. He knew that look—it was the kind a predator gave right before the kill.

She dropped her shoulder and lunged, her speed startling

despite the injuries she'd taken. Carson saw a blur of movement, then pain. He had mere seconds to react before her head slammed into his ribs, a strike that sent a fresh jolt of agony through his battered body. He gritted his teeth, refusing to go down.

She came at him again, but this time he was ready.

He shifted his weight, twisted, and then drove his elbow hard into the base of her spine.

Alicia let out a strangled gasp, her body seizing from the impact before she collapsed onto the floor in a heap of tangled limbs and ragged breath.

Carson didn't wait to see if she'd get back up. His gaze snapped to Julie. She was struggling against her bindings, her wrists raw from where she'd tried to fight free. Her breathing was shallow, her face pale, but her eyes burned with defiance. He grabbed the fallen knife, the handle slick with blood, and dropped to his knees beside her. "Hold still," he rasped, his hands moving fast as he sawed through the thick rope. The blade bit through the fibers, fraying them and loosening them. With a final snarl of effort, the bindings snapped.

Julie lurched forward, sucking in a sharp breath as she yanked her arms free. Her fingers trembled, but she was already pushing herself upright, her body tense and ready. She stood beside him, her wrists raw and bruised from the ropes he had just cut. Julie flexed her fingers, shaking out the pain, but her focus was elsewhere—her wide, searching eyes scanning the room.

She turned to him, voice hoarse. "Where are the kids?"

Carson smiled. "They're safe. Hannah found someone to hide them. They're being kept out of sight until we can get them out of this town."

Julie's shoulders sagged in relief, but only for a moment. "Who is Hannah?"

"An ally—Casterman brought Hannah and her grandfather in to patch me up so they could continue torturing me. She's gone to Falcon to get the sheriff."

Utter Devastation

Julie let out a shaky breath, nodding. Hope flickered in her expression—momentary, but real.

Carson locked eyes with her. "Can you run?"

She nodded once.

That was all he needed to know. He grabbed her hand and turned toward the door. Suddenly, a thundering sound echoed through the house. Downstairs, a door exploded inward, the wood splintering with a deafening crack as it blew open. The impact rattled the entire house, shaking peeling paint from the ceiling above them.

Heavy boots thundered against the floorboards, and urgent voices barked orders.

More enforcers.

Carson's stomach knotted. His body reacted before his mind could process, instinct screaming—*move, fight, survive.*

They were coming, and this time, there was no way out. He met Julie's gaze, a silent command passing between them: *Run. Fight.* Carson grabbed a chair. "The window! I'm going to throw this chair, and when I do, break the window and jump out."

Julie stared back at him for a moment and then spun toward it. He didn't wait for her to jump before he stepped into the hall and hurled the chair toward the bedroom at the end. The wood splintered with a deafening crash, the echo bouncing through the narrow halls.

"He's in here!" a voice barked from the top of the stairs.

Carson bolted across the hallway, leading them away from where Julie was escaping.

The guard stormed in after him, pistol raised. Carson was already moving toward him. Before the enforcer could fire, Carson drove his shoulder into his chest, slamming him against a rickety bookshelf. The wood cracked and splintered, sending books and debris tumbling around them. The guard was at least two hundred and fifty pounds of muscle and rage. Carson narrowly managed to react before a fist the size of a cinder block crashed into his back.

The impact sent him sprawling against the wall, his breath escaping in a sharp gasp.

"You're dead," the enforcer growled, cracking his knuckles.

Carson didn't wait. He lunged, grabbing a broken table leg and swinging it hard. The wood struck the guard's temple with a dull thud, staggering him. But not for long. The man recovered fast, charging like a bull, slamming into Carson with full force. They crashed through a side table, the legs snapping beneath their weight. Carson fought dirty. He threw an elbow into the man's throat, clawed for the knife on his belt, and drove his knee into his gut. The guard grunted but didn't go down. Instead, he grabbed Carson by the throat and slammed him against the wall. The room spun. Carson's vision blurred at the edges.

Move, damn it!

His fingers scrabbled at his belt, his lungs burning. His hand found the handle of the stolen knife. With one last burst of strength, he drove the blade up under the enforcer's ribs. The man let out a guttural, wet gasp, his eyes widening in shock. His grip weakened and faltered. Carson wrenched the knife free, twisting as he did. The guard staggered once, breath hitching—then collapsed to the floor, unmoving.

Silence.

Trembling, Carson sagged against the wall. Every inch of him screamed in pain, but there was no time to stop. He had to make sure Julie was safe.

THIRTY-EIGHT

Bee

Wild Plum Lake Estates
Highland, Arkansas
Day Five

The news about Amy's theft spread like wildfire through the neighborhood. Bee was less than halfway to Greg's to inform him what she'd learned about the theft at his house when she started hearing people discussing it. Some were furious Amy had stolen, demanding swift punishment. Others were just as angry that Greg had been hoarding while families like Amy's struggled to feed their kids. Bee kept her pace steady, pushing aside the tension coiling in her stomach.

Greg was out front, pacing near the steps of his porch. His shotgun rested against the railing, a deep scowl etched across his face. He looked up as Bee approached, his expression still tight with frustration. "You here to tell me I should just let this go?" he asked, crossing his arms.

Bee exhaled. "No. I just want to talk."

Greg gestured toward a pair of chairs on the porch, and Bee followed him, sitting down while he leaned against the railing.

"I get why you're upset," Bee started. "I'd be mad too."

"Mad doesn't even cover it," Greg muttered, shaking his head. "If Amy had come to me—if she'd just asked—I would have given her food. Hell, I would've helped her. Better yet, I would've shown her boys how to hunt, fish, and gather so they wouldn't have to depend on people like me." He let out a heavy sigh. "Stealing's not survival. Learning how to provide for yourself? That's survival."

Bee sat forward. "Are you still willing to do that?"

Greg frowned slightly. "Do what?"

"Teach," Bee said. "Not just Amy's boys—anyone in the neighborhood who wants to learn."

Greg blinked, then straightened. "You really think they'd be interested?"

Bee nodded. "I do. People are scared, Greg. They don't want to be in this position again, and you have the knowledge to help make sure they don't have to be."

Slowly, a smile broke across Greg's face. "Now that is something I can get behind." He rubbed his jaw thoughtfully. "Everyone should learn how to provide for themselves. We've grown so dependent on grocery stores and restaurants that we can walk right by potential food and never recognize it. Our ancestors survived for thousands of years by living off the land, but today? A lot of people are going to die because that skill is gone."

Bee nodded. "But this group doesn't have to—if they're willing to learn from you."

Greg's eyes lit up with purpose. "I can teach them how to make snares, how to fish without fancy gear, what plants are safe to eat, how to make fire the right way. Hell, I can even show them how to butcher an animal properly. If they're willing to listen, I'll teach."

For the first time in days, Bee felt something close to hope. "Then let's get started. I'll get a group together. Can you meet me at my house, say around midday?"

"I'll make myself available any time you want."

Bee strode toward home, hopeful for the first time all day that the neighborhood could still come together for the good of all. As she walked, she mentally mapped out a list of people who might be willing to learn from Greg—those with families to feed, those who had already begun to worry about what came next.

She stopped by Mark and Gretchen's first, eager to share the idea. They listened, nodding along, their expressions shifting from exhaustion to something that almost looked like hope.

"This could be exactly what people need," Gretchen said.

Mark agreed. "If we're going to make it, we need skills—not just supplies."

Without hesitation, they sent their two teenage daughters out to spread the word, knocking on doors and delivering the invitation to those Bee had listed—including Amy and her boys. It wasn't a solution to everything, but it was a start.

Greg arrived early and set up a demonstration at the picnic tables near Wild Plum Lake. He stood beside Bee on her front lawn as they greeted his first students, but quickly, the tension in the neighborhood reached its boiling point. A crowd gathered in front of Bee's house, and voices rose in frustration.

"We should've been pooling resources from the start!" a woman named Karen shouted. "How many more of you are sitting on food while the rest of us starve?"

Greg, still fuming over his loss, squared his shoulders. "It's not hoarding when I worked my ass off to prepare. Maybe you should've done the same."

That set off an explosion of voices, accusations flying back and forth.

"We were supposed to work together, not keep secrets!"

"And what? Let you people take from my family when I worked so hard to provide for them? I planned ahead—you didn't. That's not my problem."

Then someone shoved Greg. He shoved back. In an instant, it erupted into a full-blown brawl.

Bee barely had time to react before fists were flying. People tackled each other to the ground, kicking, punching, and screaming. A man yanked another off his porch and slammed him into the dirt. A woman grabbed a wooden plank and swung it wildly, barely missing her target.

Pressing Penelope close, Bee stepped aside just as a scuffle tumbled past. "Stop! This isn't helping!"

A punch caught Mark in the ribs, sending him stumbling. Gretchen yanked her daughters back from the chaos. Then a gunshot rang out.

Everyone froze.

Bob stood on Bee's porch, rifle raised, his face twisted with impatience. "Enough!" he barked.

Silence settled over the street.

Bob lowered the rifle. "This neighborhood has two options. Either we come together under real leadership, or we let this place turn into a war zone." He swept his gaze over the crowd. "You all know which choice makes sense."

Bee's stomach twisted. This was precisely what he wanted—a power grab. And the worst part? People were listening.

The fight outside her house had ended, but the battle for control had just begun.

In the hours that followed, the neighborhood's uneasy truce crumbled. Conversations turned into arguments. Accusations flew like sparks, igniting the fear and resentment already simmering beneath the surface. Bob and his men wasted no time fanning the flames, twisting the chaos to their advantage.

"We can't afford selfishness," Bob declared as he stood in the center of the street, his voice carrying over the murmuring crowd. "No more hoarding, no more secrets. We survive together or not at all."

Some people nodded, muttering in agreement. Others looked

uncertain, glancing at one another with wary eyes. But no one spoke up against him.

Bee saw it happening in real time—the shift. The way Bob's presence grew heavier, his authority solidifying with every nod of reluctant agreement. Almost immediately, doors began banging open. The first door was Mr. Langford's, an older widower who had been quiet since the world went dark. A group of men—some of Bob's, some just desperate—pounded on his door. "Langford, we know you've got food in there!" one of them shouted.

Bee rushed over, weaving through the growing crowd, hands raised in an attempt to de-escalate. "Hold on! There's no need for this—let's talk."

The old man cracked the door open, his wrinkled face lined with fear. "I don't have much, just a little rice and—"

A boot crashed against the door, sending Langford stumbling back. The men pushed their way inside, shoving past him like wolves descending on a kill.

Bee clenched her fists and started forward, but Mark caught her arm.

"There's too many," he said under his breath.

Bee's stomach turned as she heard the shouts from inside—demands, accusations, the sound of glass shattering. When the men finally came out, one of them had a sack slung over his shoulder, stuffed full of Langford's food. The old man stood in the doorway, arms hanging limp at his sides, looking smaller than ever. And then it spread. House after house, group after group, Bob's men stormed in, taking not just food but every gun and piece of ammunition they could find. The sound of splintering wood and shouts of protest echoed through the neighborhood as once-secure homes were stripped bare.

Bee's worry deepened as they headed for Greg's house. He wouldn't give up his weapons without a fight. She lingered in the shadows as Bob and his men left, their expressions smug, their arms burdened with supplies. But Greg was nowhere in sight.

Something was wrong. Concerned, Bee slipped into his backyard, crept up the steps, and knocked several times. "Greg? Marcy? It's me, Bee Carlisle. I just want to know you're okay."

Silence.

She tried the doorknob but found it locked. A cold unease crawled up her spine. She spun at a thump that came from the side yard. Cautiously, Bee stepped around the corner of the house, nearly holding her breath. But before she could call out again, movement next door caught her eye. Bob and his men were already at the Ramirez home. Mrs. Ramirez stood in the doorway, arms outstretched, and blocked the entrance. "No. You're not coming in. My kids are here," Mrs. Ramiez cried.

A man grabbed her by the shoulders and yanked her aside. She fell hard against the porch steps as the group forced their way in.

At another house, Bee saw a teenage boy get struck across the face as he tried to stop them from taking what little his family had left. He fell to the pavement, clutching his cheek. His mother screamed but was powerless to stop it.

Bee, Mark, and Gretchen ran from house to house, trying to stop the madness.

"Listen to yourselves!" Bee shouted as a crowd gathered around another home. "You think this is survival? Beating your own neighbors? Stealing from the people you'll need to rely on in the weeks ahead?"

One of the men turned on her, his face red with anger. "What do you expect us to do, Bee? Starve? Sit back while people like Greg hoard what they've got? How do we know that he didn't steal all that stuff?"

"This isn't how you fix it," Mark snapped, stepping between them. "You think taking from others is going to make things better?"

A woman Bee had known for years, Mrs. Dobbins, pointed a shaking finger at her. "You're just saying that because you still have food."

Bee's breath caught. "That's not true."

"Isn't it?" someone else sneered. "We've all seen you and your little group sticking together. Bet you've got a stash hidden away somewhere."

The murmur spread, turning suspicious eyes on her, on Mark, on Gretchen. Bee's pulse pounded. She knew where this was heading. Then came the real breaking point—the crowd turned on Amy.

THIRTY-NINE

Carson

Witch's Roost
Ramah, Colorado
Day Five

Carson's breath was shallow, his muscles screaming in protest as he stumbled back into the main room, gripping his ribs. He stopped short, stunned to see Julie still there, clutching her arm, blood running down her sleeve. But she was alive.

Across from her, Alica stood with a smirk on her battered face. Blood matted her blonde hair, which clung in dark streaks to her temple, but she was still standing. Still grinning. Her knife was still slick with Julie's blood. "You look like hell, Carson," she purred, tilting her head.

Carson's fingers curled into a fist. "I have the package."

Alicia's smirk flickered, just for a second. Was it doubt? Hope? "Liar."

"Think about it," Carson said, keeping his voice steady. "Casterman would kill you if he knew you lost it. I can take you to it, but only if you let her go."

For a moment, something flickered behind Alicia's cold eyes. Then, she laughed. "You're so full of shit. Think I'd fall for that?"

"You can be the hero and return the package to your boss," Carson pressed.

Alicia let out a sharp chuckle. "Boss?" She wiped the blood from her lip, shaking her head. "I know you don't have the package because Bruce didn't take it. I did. I wanted our boss to show up and discover it missing on Casterman's watch. Then, he'll take him and his crew out and get me the hell out of this backwater town. I'm going back to Venezuela with them. They won't stick around and suffer waiting for the lights to come back on."

Julie shifted slightly, positioning herself between Alicia and the door.

Alicia's eyes narrowed. Then, without warning, she lashed out and sliced a deep gash into Julie's other arm.

Julie hissed in pain, stumbling.

"Stop!" Carson barked.

Alicia pressed the blade against Julie's throat. "You think you can play me, Carson?" she murmured. "That I don't know a desperate man when I see one?"

His hand twitched toward his gun.

Alicia pressed harder. "Drop it," she ordered.

Carson's pulse thundered in his ears. Julie's gaze met his, her expression unreadable. Carson took a slow breath. He had no choice. "Fine." He set the gun down, watching everything as if in slow motion.

Alicia's smirk widened, and her mouth opened to say something but was cut short when Julie took off toward the door. Alicia lunged after her. Carson moved on instinct. He launched himself forward, catching Alicia's arm and shoving the blade aside.

Alicia snarled like a cornered animal. Pivoting, Julie whirled, fists raised, rage flashing across her face. They clashed. The fight was fast, brutal. They slammed into walls, overturned furniture, and grabbed anything they could to use as weapons.

Carson tried to jump in but took an elbow to the nose as Julie reared back to punch Alicia. He stumbled back, grasping his bloody nose. As he recovered, Julie was knocked to the floor. Alicia threw herself on top of her. A second later, the female enforcer groaned and went limp. Julie rolled Alicia off her and scrambled to her feet with a knife in her hand. Alicia lay motionless, clutching her chest for a moment, and then closed her eyes and took her last breath.

Carson pressed a hand to Julie's back, urging her toward the door. "Run! "

Julie's eyes widened. "What about you?"

"More are coming for us." Carson checked his ammo. "You go. I'll hold them off."

"No. I'm not leaving you. We stick together."

Carson hesitated, listening. Again, he heard heavy footsteps on the stairs—more this time. He shoved Julie toward the window. Carson's breath came hard and fast. "Go, Julie!"

Julie hesitated for a split second, obviously torn between escape and staying.

Another gunshot shattered the air, splintering the wooden frame of the doorway. Carson spun toward the sound. The enforcers were closing in. They had seconds. Julie made the choice for him.

"Come on!" she urged, moving toward the window.

Carson backed away toward her, his stolen pistol trained on the door. His fingers tightened on the grip.

Downstairs, the commotion grew. "Police! Drop your weapons!"

There was a long pause.

"Last chance!" a gravelly voice roared. "Drop your weapons, or we drop you!"

Carson exchanged a glance with Julie. The cavalry had arrived.

A shout of defiance erupted from below, followed by a barrage of gunfire and then screams. The unmistakable thud of bodies hitting the floor.

Then, silence again.

Carson swallowed hard. He had no idea who had won that fight, but he wasn't about to wait and find out. Julie had already thrown one leg over the window ledge. Carson turned to follow, keeping one ear trained on the door.

There was a creak on the stairs. Then another.

More enforcers? Or was it the sheriff's deputies? He couldn't risk it. He needed to buy Julie time. Easing the door shut, he stood to one side of it with his back pressed against the wall.

"Go!" Carson hissed. "I'll be right behind you."

Julie hesitated, her blue eyes locking on his. "Don't be an idiot, Carson."

Another voice—closer this time.

He lifted his gun.

Too late.

The door exploded inward, slamming against the wall and a man charged through. "Hands up! Drop your weapons!" the deputy barked.

Carson dropped the pistol just as Hannah pushed her way into the room, her rifle raised, eyes sweeping for threats. "That's Carson!" she yelled. Her gaze dropped to the floor where Alicia and the guard lay. "Where's Julie?"

Carson gestured toward the window. "Outside now."

Hannah followed him to the window. Below, Julie stood in the street with the other deputies. Enforcers lay strewn in the streets—some dead, some groaning, hands clutched to bleeding wounds. Others were surrendering and dropping their weapons as deputies forced them to their knees.

Around them, the people of Ramah were rising. One man swung a shovel at one of Casterman's thugs. Another, his face bloodied, tackled a second enforcer and wrenched a rifle from his grasp. A middle-aged woman in an apron smashed a wooden crate over a third enforcer's head.

The town had turned.

Carson caught Hannah's eye.

"You made it," he said in a rush.

"I did." Hannah glanced down at Alicia. "So did you."

The town of Ramah lay quiet beneath the weight of the past few days. The gunshots had faded, and the bodies had been cleared from the streets. The people—shaken but free—stood among the ruins of Casterman's rule, picking up the broken pieces of their lives.

Hannah led Carson down the stairs, stepping over bodies on their way down and out into the street to join Julie.

One of the deputies strode toward them, his badge flashing under the light of the aurora. He held out a hand. "Deputy Mick Jensen."

Carson shook his hand. "Carson Carlisle."

"Casterman's pinned down at the feed store. We've got him cornered. We want to take him alive. We need to know who he is working with," Deputy Jensen said.

Carson clenched his jaw. "A Venezuelan gang."

"We know that. But we need his contact."

Julie shifted beside him, clutching her wounded arm. "We make sure the kids are safe."

Jensen nodded. "Already handled. Bruce's wife is caring for them."

Carson felt a lump rise in his throat. He turned to Julie. "I thought she was dead." He should have known not to believe anything Casterman said.

Half an hour later, Carson stood at the threshold of the makeshift clinic door, his body battered, his ribs aching with every breath. Julie leaned against the doorframe beside him, her own injuries bandaged but fresh. They had survived, but the wounds ran deeper than skin.

In the town square, Jensen's deputies had Casterman and his remaining enforcers in custody. Their wrists were bound, their faces bruised from the brawl that had finally taken them down. Casterman sat slumped against the steps, his once-proud sneer replaced with empty resignation. He didn't speak as Jensen turned to his deputies.

"Lock them up," Jensen ordered. "We'll decide what to do with them when the time comes."

Casterman didn't protest. The fight was over. He had lost.

FORTY

Willow

Western Kentucky Parkway
Caneyville, Kentucky
Day Five

The Jeep shuddered to a stop, tilting slightly forward. Heart pounding, Willow unclipped her seatbelt and turned to Guynn. "What the hell was that?"

Knox groaned, rubbing his head. "Did we hit something?"

"No," Guynn said as he opened his car door and stepped out.

Willow followed, and the moment she saw the front two tires, her stomach dropped. Both were completely shredded, jagged rubber curling away from the steel rims. Knox climbed out of the back seat, whistling low.

"Damn. That's bad."

Willow squatted down, running her fingers over the torn rubber. Something sharp had hit them. It wasn't just bad luck. "What could do that?"

Guynn turned, scanning the darkened road. His eyes were hard and calculating. "That," he said quietly.

Utter Devastation

She followed his gaze to the long stretch of highway ahead, and what she saw there caused the hair on the back of her neck to stand on end. One hundred yards from the disabled Jeep, Guynn crouched and ran a calloused hand over the spike strip stretched across the road—thick metal spikes welded into a heavy frame, designed to puncture tires instantly.

"You think the cops left these here following a police chase?" Knox asked, scanning the darkness beyond the tree line.

Willow swallowed hard, exchanging a look with him. "Who else would have these?"

"It's strange they'd leave them here," he said.

"Something must have happened for them to abandon them on the roadway," Guynn said, as he straightened.

Willow scanned the surrounding area. The woods on either side of the road were thick and dense with shadows. Too many places for someone to hide. Too many places for an ambush. "What do we do now?"

Guynn was already on the move back toward the Jeep. "I need to find a new vehicle."

Willow pivoted, glancing around. "How? We're in the middle of nowhere."

"In the next town," he said flatly.

"That's too dangerous. We don't have anything left to trade for one."

"We can't walk all the way to Arkansas. What other choice do we have?"

Willow and Knox followed Guynn as he walked to the back of the Jeep.

"You're not planning on going alone?" Willow asked as he opened the back hatch.

"You guys need to stay with the Jeep and our gear."

Willow glanced west down the interstate. She wasn't looking forward to going blindly into some town to steal a car, but staying put might be just as dangerous.

"You can't do this alone. Someone has to watch your back."

"Willow's right," Knox said. "We should all go."

Willow hesitated, looking between Knox and Guynn. He was recovering from a gunshot wound and excessive blood loss. He was in no shape for a hike.

"I can make it," he said, as if reading her mind.

The Jeep wasn't going anywhere without new tires. But after all they'd seen so far, leaving it—and Knox—unguarded was a risk.

Willow crossed her arms. "What if you collapse halfway there?"

"We'll roll him into a ditch and say a few words," Guynn quipped.

Knox let out a chuckle. "At least make it sound heartfelt."

"Can we be serious for just one minute?" Willow snapped. "We don't know how far we'll have to go to find a new ride. And once we find it, who knows what we'll have to do to get it."

Knox waved a dismissive hand. "We'll cross that bridge when we come to it. First, we have to find one."

"What about all our supplies and gear?" Willow asked.

"We hide them," Guynn said. "You guys in or out?"

"In," Knox said.

"I don't know about this."

"It's walk into town and find a new vehicle or hoof it all the way to Arkansas," Knox said.

"Maybe I should go, and you two stay with our gear?"

Guynn shook his head before she even finished. "No. You're not going in there alone."

She opened her mouth to protest, but he cut her off with a look.

"I know you're capable," he said. "That's not the issue. But towns like that right now? They're full of people running on fear and hunger. You need someone watching your back. We go in together. Always."

Willow hesitated, then gave a small nod.

Knox grunted. "So what's the plan?"

"First, we get the Jeep off the road and hidden. Then we figure out where we're going and how we're getting in and out without drawing attention."

With that, they got to work. Together, Willow and Guynn, with Knox inside steering, pushed the Jeep off the road and hid it behind a thick stand of trees. They grabbed the essentials—the shotgun, a med kit, and water. Knox moved slowly but resolutely, his stubbornness overriding his obvious fatigue.

Willow sighed. "This is a bad idea."

"Yeah, well," Knox said, adjusting his grip on his pistol. "So was confronting those guys back at the gas station."

Willow gave him the side-eye but didn't argue. He had his view of things, and she had hers. And with that, they set off west down the interstate toward the tiny town of Caneyville, Kentucky, just a mile ahead. At first glance, it seemed … intact. Too intact. No wrecked cars clogged the streets. No smashed windows or signs of looting. Just an eerie, unnatural stillness.

Willow's gut tightened. "Where is everyone?"

Guynn nodded, keeping his shotgun snug to his shoulder. "Feels like a ghost town."

They walked cautiously, their boots scuffing against the cracked pavement. An automotive shop loomed on the corner, its overhead doors down and its parking lot empty. Willow scanned the side of the building. She gasped, and her hand came up to cover her mouth at the sight of the dark red drag marks smeared across the pavement.

"What's that?"

"Trouble." Guynn stepped into the street and moved away from it.

Willow followed the trail around the side of the building, making sure to avoid the dried substance as well. She stopped in her tracks as a body came into view, crumpled against the wall. The almost unrecognizable man was dressed in a sheriff's department uniform, covered in dried blood, his chest riddled with bullet holes. His badge was still pinned to his chest.

Behind her, Knox let out a low whistle. "That's not a good sign."

"No, it's not," Guynn said, coming alongside them.

A soft shuffle of movement startled Willow. She turned sharply just as a group of men stepped out from the alley dressed in filthy, torn, bloodstained prison jumpsuits. Then it clicked. The burned-out prison bus. All those bodies inside. The inmates. Her pulse spiked. These men had been on that bus.

At the center of the group of men was a tall, broad-shouldered man with hard, dark eyes. A shotgun rested against his shoulder like he had all the time in the world.

"Knox!" she cried out. She stepped back and grabbed his arm.

He and Guynn turned around.

"Didn't mean to interrupt," one of the prisoners drawled. His voice was smooth, almost amused. "But you folks are a little too well-armed to be wandering through my town."

Willow scarcely had time to react before the first shot rang out. She hit the ground hard, rolling around the corner of the building as bullets slammed into its concrete blocks, sending debris flying. Guynn ducked behind a rusty dumpster and returned fire. Knox dropped to the ground and grunted as he dragged himself behind a car.

Gunfire cracked through the deserted streets.

"Move!" Guynn barked, waving her toward the alleyway.

Willow didn't hesitate. She pushed off the ground and sprinted, her boots pounding against the pavement. Bullets whizzed past, splintering wood and shattering glass. She ran, zigzagging to make herself a harder target. Her lungs burned, heart hammering against her ribs. The colonel and Knox were still pinned down, forced to take cover behind an overturned truck. They wouldn't last much longer out there. She veered left, catching sight of a church up ahead. Its doors hung open. She turned, raising her pistol, and fired down the street to cover her retreat—one, two, three.

A figure staggered back, cursing, as it ducked for cover.

Just get inside, she willed her legs. Willow reached the church steps, taking them two at a time, and threw her shoulder against the door. It didn't budge. Panic surged. She pounded her fist against the wood. "Please!" she yelled. "I'm in trouble. Let me in!"

No answer.

Guynn fired from his position, forcing their attackers to scatter. She turned and searched the street. Knox and Guynn were moving from vehicle to vehicle, working their way toward her. She had to buy them time. A shadow shifted near a parked car. Someone was repositioning. She raised her pistol and fired, forcing them back behind cover. She turned her attention back to the church and yanked on the door handle again.

It was locked tight.

Inside, something shifted. A shuffle. A whisper. Someone was in there. Watching. She slammed her palm against the wood. "Please!" A shadow appeared behind the stained-glass window. Then a voice—shaky, afraid.

"We can't."

Willow's breath hitched. "What?"

"They'll kill us," the voice said. "If we open the door. They don't know we're here. We can't help you."

"Please!" she cried, pressing her back against the door as another gunshot cracked the air. "If you don't, I'm as good as dead."

Silence.

Then, a new voice sounded from behind the church door—firm, unyielding. "Move!"

There was the sound of shuffling, hesitant footsteps, and then the door swung open. A man in his early twenties stood in the dim light—lean, sharp-boned, with crude tattoos snaking up his arms. Dark hair, hard eyes, and a shotgun held loosely at his side. He stepped back. Just as Willow stepped across the threshold, Guynn and Knox pushed inside, moving fast, weapons still raised as they scanned the dim interior.

Knox's gaze landed on her as they moved down the center aisle. "You all right?"

She nodded. "Yeah."

Guynn's expression was grim. "We lost 'em for now, but that won't last. We need a plan."

The man with the shotgun shut the door again and threw the lock.

Willow dragged in a sharp breath, scanning the room. Terrified townspeople huddled behind overturned pews, eyes wide, bodies tense. Fear thickened the air, clinging to the walls like the scent of old incense and dust.

The man turned from her, his expression hardening. "You need to get out of here." He swept his gaze over the cowering people. "This town ain't safe. Not with Quinnell running it." His voice was even, but something behind his eyes burned with urgency.

Willow felt a cold weight settle in her gut. "Is he one of the escaped prisoners?"

The man's jaw clenched slightly. "Yes."

"We need a plan," Guynn said, moving toward the rear of the church.

"You need more than that," the young man said. "You need to get out of here." His gaze flicked to Willow again, then to Guynn. "Because Q won't stop until every single one of you is dead."

FORTY-ONE

Willow

Caneyville Friendship Church
Caneyville, Kentucky
Day Five

The young man's words hung in the air like a warning bell as they moved toward the back of the church. Willow felt their weight settle deep in her gut.

Guynn's gaze swept the room. "You guys are living here?"

Their pastor stepped forward, wringing his hands. "In the basement. It's where we've been hiding."

"How have they not broken in yet?" Willow asked.

"They didn't know we're here—until you showed up and Miguel let you in," one of the men said.

Guynn turned to him. "Is there somewhere I can get eyes on the street?"

Miguel spoke up. "The attic. It overlooks the street and the alleyway. That's where I've been staying."

Guynn's expression hardened. "Show me."

Knox gestured to the pastor. "I'm going to check out that basement—see if it's secure."

Guynn nodded.

Miguel motioned for them to follow. Willow hesitated only a moment before falling in step. The pastor led Knox down the narrow steps toward the basement, while Miguel guided Willow and Guynn up the attic staircase. The steps groaned under their weight, each creak loud in the stillness. At the top, Miguel pushed open a wooden hatch to reveal a vast, open attic space. Sunlight streamed through tall, arched windows at each end of the gables, casting long slants of light across the dust-covered floor.

The attic was nothing like Willow expected—not the cramped, suffocating space she had imagined. Instead, it stretched the length of the church, high-ceilinged and open, with wooden beams arching above like the ribcage of a sleeping giant. The air up here was stale but not stifling, carrying the faint scent of aged wood and time-worn hymn books stacked along one wall.

Miguel moved easily through the space, stepping over crates and a broken rocking chair. This is where I've been staying," he said. "I'd rather be up here where I can see what's coming. The basement feels like a damn tomb."

Willow's gaze flicked past him, sweeping over the attic. The room was sparse, the wooden planks beneath their feet scuffed and warped with age. She stepped farther into the space. Dust swirled in the dim light filtering through the gable windows, illuminating a makeshift cot in the corner and a neat pile of folded clothes at its foot. But it wasn't the cot that caught her attention. A leather-bound journal lay open atop a crumpled blanket. The ink was fresh; someone had written in it recently. Something about the journal tugged at her, an unshakable pull she couldn't ignore. Before doubt could take hold, Willow stepped forward, her gaze drifting to the curled edges of its worn pages. The ink stood stark against the yellowed paper, the words seeming to leap off the page, demanding to be read.

Utter Devastation

If you're reading this, don't bother returning it. I'm dead.

Her breath caught. He had written his own eulogy. Quiet resignation bled through every word. He was a man who had already decided how his story would end.

How hopeless, she thought. *I'm not like him. I refuse to be.* Willow had no intention of dying in this cursed town. They were getting out. No matter what it took.

Guynn moved to one of the gabled windows, his broad frame silhouetted against the dim glow of moonlight filtering through the rippled glass. He studied the street below, his eyes sharp and unreadable.

"Good view," he said, his voice low and calculating.

Willow moved to the opposite end of the attic, looking through the north-facing window. From here, she had a clear view of the street below and beyond—the abandoned storefronts, the rusting cars, the too-quiet town that felt more like a trap than a refuge.

Miguel stepped beside her, pointing. "They've got two lookouts up there." He gestured toward the old drugstore rooftop a block away. "And another two near city hall. They rotate shifts, but they're always watching."

"How many of them are there?" Knox asked.

"There were twelve that escaped the prison bus."

Guynn's gaze hardened as he studied the layout. "And this Q?"

Miguel exhaled, shaking his head. "He doesn't come out much. Sends his guys to do his dirty work."

Willow swallowed hard. They were outnumbered, outgunned —and it seemed—out of options.

"This will do," Guynn murmured, his tone shifting. He turned to Willow, a look of resolve in his eyes. "We're gonna need this vantage point."

Miguel frowned. "For what?"

Guynn glanced back at the street. "Because we need to be ready."

Willow, Guynn, and Miguel navigated down the narrow staircase behind the pulpit. The door creaked as they pushed it open, revealing a damp, low-ceilinged space lined with stone walls. The scent of old wood and moist earth filled her nose.

She ran her fingers along the rough stonework. "This looks very old."

The pastor approached. "The church has stood here since 1842. This basement was a hiding place for prominent citizens during the Civil War. There's a tunnel that was built to connect the different buildings in town, but most of those have collapsed."

"Are you sure they've all collapsed?" Willow asked. "Those tunnels could be a lifeline."

The pastor's lips pressed into a thin line. "We don't know for sure. No one's gone down there in years."

"If we're lucky, this particular tunnel might still be our way out," Guynn said.

Knox gestured toward the staircase. "We should check it out and see."

"No need," Miguel said. "There's still one that's open."

"You've been in it?" Guynn asked.

"Yeah. It leads to an old school building."

"Show me?"

Willow stepped around him, taking Knox's hand. "Show us too."

Miguel hesitated for only a moment before nodding. He led them through the dimly lit basement, past stacks of old hymn books and dusty wooden pews shoved against the walls. At the farthest corner of the basement, behind an old wooden shelf cluttered with half-burned candles and dusty boxes, was a heavy wooden door. Pastor Whitmore's fingers trailed along the warped edges. "It's been here as long as I can remember," he murmured, voice hushed as if speaking too loud might wake something long forgotten. Miguel gripped the iron handle and yanked the door open. A gust of cool, stale air rushed upward, carrying the scent of wet stone and decay. A steep set of narrow, crumbling steps led down into the darkness.

Willow tightened her grip on her pistol. "Great. A tunnel that smells like a tomb. That's reassuring."

Knox smirked. "Ladies first?"

She shot him a glare as she holstered her weapon and stepped onto the first rung of the ladder attached to the side wall, descending cautiously. The air grew thicker and colder as she dropped into the underground passage. Her boots landed on solid dirt, the ground uneven beneath her feet. Miguel followed, then Guynn and Knox brought up the rear. Willow worried he was doing too much but knew there was no way Knox would hang back for this.

The tunnel stretched forward in a long, curving path, its ceiling a patchwork of wooden beams and stone reinforcements. The walls were lined with rotting wooden planks, some still bearing faint markings—old carvings, names etched into the surface, forgotten messages left behind by those who had once hidden here.

Knox traced a set of initials with his fingers. "History lesson aside, does this thing actually hold up?"

Miguel pressed forward, stepping carefully over loose stones. "Holds up enough."

The further they went, the narrower the passage became, forcing them into single file. The tunnel twisted and turned, dipping lower, the air growing cooler and heavier. Water dripped somewhere in the distance, echoing like a whisper. They walked in silence for several minutes before a faint sliver of light glowed ahead. Miguel slowed and motioned for them to keep quiet as they neared the tunnel's exit. The end of the tunnel opened into a basement—larger than the church's, with remnants of old school desks and discarded books scattered across the floor. A rusted boiler sat in the corner, its pipes stretching along the ceiling like skeletal fingers.

Miguel placed a hand on Guynn's arm. "Careful. Some of Q's guys are upstairs—top floor."

Willow tensed. "How many?"

Miguel's jaw tightened. "Two usually. And they're not alone."

Knox's expression darkened. "What do you mean?"

"They've got a couple of girls—ones they took from town."

A heavy silence fell between them.

Guynn's voice was grim. "So, this escape route isn't an option unless we clear them out first."

Willow clenched her fists. They had two problems now—escaping and saving those women.

Knox glanced back toward the tunnel. "We head back?"

Guynn nodded. "Yeah. We plan first. Then we act."

With one last glance toward the school basement, Willow turned and followed them back into the tunnel. As they moved swiftly through the dark passage, her mind raced. They'd come to town to steal a car but now found themselves trapped in the town's nightmare.

Once they were back at the church, Guynn motioned for Miguel and Willow to help him secure the entrance. They pushed an old wooden bookshelf over the basement door and stacked crates and pew benches.

"Not perfect," Guynn said, dusting off his hands. "But it'll slow them down."

Willow eyed the barricade, an uneasy knot forming in her gut. It would slow them down, sure. But if Q's men came looking for them, they'd find a way through, eventually.

She swallowed hard, glancing toward the others. She hoped it wouldn't become their Alamo.

FORTY-TWO

Willow

Caneyville Friendship Church
Caneyville, Kentucky
Day Five

Willow and the others moved back into the dimly lit basement, where the fear remained thick. A single lantern flickered on the battered wooden table. She took a seat on an overturned crate, still reeling from the firefight outside. She was alive—but barely. Willow studied the faces of the frightened people.

Knox pulled up a metal chair and folded his arms, watching Miguel with a calculating gaze. "You seem to know an awful lot about this Quinnell and his men," he said. His voice was casual, but there was an edge to it.

Miguel's jaw tightened. He didn't look at Knox. Instead, he stared at the barricaded tunnel entrance as if weighing his words. Then, with a slow nod, he turned back to them.

"Because I was one of them," he admitted.

Silence fell over the basement. Even the frightened townspeople, huddled in the dim light, stopped murmuring. Willow's stomach clenched, and Guynn's expression darkened.

Knox scoffed. "Of course you were."

"I was on that transport. One of the prisoners."

Willow studied him, searching for some tell, some crack in his composure. "Then why aren't you with them now?"

"Because I don't want to be."

Knox let out a dry laugh. "That's convenient."

Miguel's gaze flicked to him, but he didn't rise to the bait. Instead, he inhaled, slow and measured, and spoke in a voice that carried the weight of something long buried. "I was a different man before." He ran a hand over his face, rubbing his eyes with the back of his hand. "I was young. Stupid. Thought I was proving something—earning my place." He hesitated. "I was involved in a drive-by. I was the driver. It was supposed to be a hit on a rival—a gangbanger like me—instead a woman and her kid died."

The words dropped like stones, sending a ripple through the room.

Willow sucked in a breath. Knox's fingers twitched toward his pistol. The colonel didn't move or speak—just stared at Miguel with an unreadable expression.

Miguel continued, his voice quieter now. "I was prepared to do my time. Jail ... it changes you. You either become worse, or you start seeing the truth about who you are." He exhaled. "I took responsibility for my actions. I stopped making excuses. Not that it fixes anything or brings them back." His throat worked as he swallowed hard. "But I wasn't like Q and his crew. I never was."

"Yeah, right," Knox said. "And yet you were on a bus with them."

Miguel's eyes met his. "I was on my way to prison—where I belong. I pleaded guilty and was ready to face my fate—on death row."

Willow's mind raced. He was a convicted murderer. A gang member. But he was also the man who had pulled her into the church and saved her life. The man who had been living in the attic, away from the others, choosing solitude over dominance. She wanted to believe him.

Knox, though, didn't look convinced. "So what, you just decided to sit here and play hero?"

Miguel's eyes flashed. "I decided not to be a monster."

Guynn finally spoke, his voice low and cold. "That's real easy to say when you've already done the damage."

"You think I don't know that, sir?" He took a slow breath, his fists clenching at his sides. "You think I don't see their faces every time I close my eyes?"

Willow watched him, trying to decide if she saw guilt or just another mask.

"Their blood is on my hands," Miguel admitted. "Nothing will ever change that. But I had a choice when that bus flipped. I could have run with them. Could've taken what I wanted, done what they did. No one would have stopped me."

Knox crossed his arms. "And yet, here you are."

"Here I am."

The silence stretched, thick and suffocating. Willow could feel the weight of the decision pressing on them all.

She wanted to trust him.

Knox didn't.

And the colonel? He was already walking away.

Willow remained.

She watched them disappear into the shadows before shifting her gaze back to Miguel. He stood there, jaw tight, shoulders squared against a weight she couldn't see.

"They won't trust you," she said plainly.

Miguel huffed a humorless laugh. "No reason they should."

Willow studied him, searching for cracks in his composure for anything that would give her a reason to walk away like they had. But he didn't flinch or look away.

"You could've run with them," she said. "Quinnell and the others."

"Could've," he admitted. "Would've been easier."

"But you didn't."

"No."

She tilted her head. "Why?"

"Because I've already done enough damage."

Willow crossed her arms, watching him closely. "Why didn't you move on? Why didn't they? Tell me why you all stayed here in this town?"

"The county sheriff must have learned we stole a box van and were heading this way," he said, jaw tightening. "He and a deputy set spike strips on the interstate to stop us, but the driver managed to get around them—just barely. We ended up in a ditch." His voice darkened. "Q and his crew piled out with more firepower than the sheriff and his deputy could withstand."

Willow's stomach twisted. "Where did they get all those weapons?"

"The box van." His voice was heavy. "It was packed with food, water, supplies, weapons, and ammo. The owners—a husband, wife, and two young kids—were bugging out. But they weren't prepared for what they ran into." His expression hardened. "Cold, hard killers. They overwhelmed them when they stopped to refuel."

Willow inhaled sharply. "We didn't see a box van out on the interstate."

"With all of us pushing, we got it back on the road. But we didn't make it far. Something was messed up with the engine. It started rolling smoke from under the hood. We came here to get a new ride."

She frowned. "Then why stay?"

Miguel hesitated again. "Because at the time, the military was crawling all over the area—up and down the interstate. We thought they were looking for us. Figured lying low here was the safest bet."

"And the box van?"

"Q has one of his guys working on it, last I knew. Not sure if it's fixable."

Willow's pulse quickened. A box van. Big enough to transport supplies. Big enough to transport people. Big enough to get these folks out of here. She let the thought settle, the pieces snapping into place. They had come to town looking for a vehicle—well, here it was. And if they could steal it, they could do more than just escape—they could help save lives. Her mind whirled, already forming a strategy. "Where is it?" she asked.

Miguel hesitated, studying her. "In an old maintenance garage, north end of town."

Willow pushed to her feet. "We didn't come here to play hero. But we can't just leave these people to die."

"And what exactly are you proposing?"

She met his gaze, her decision firm. "We hit them where it hurts. We create a diversion; something that forces them to shift their focus. Then we take the van."

Miguel exhaled sharply. "You're serious."

"Dead serious."

A slow grin spread across his face. "Damn. I think I love you."

Willow ignored him, already turning toward Guynn and Knox. "Let's get to work."

FORTY-THREE

Willow
───────

Caneyville Friendship Church
Caneyville, Kentucky
Day Five

Willow's mind raced as she stepped back from Miguel, her pulse thrumming with urgency. The box van—it was their way out, but not just for them. If they could get it running, it could mean freedom for the townspeople trapped under Quinnell's rule. She turned, scanning the dimly lit basement. The townspeople still sat huddled against the walls, whispering, too scared to act. Knox sat in a metal folding chair, arms crossed, while Guynn cleaned his pistol with steady, practiced motions. Willow took a deep breath, squared her shoulders, and strode toward the table at the center of the room.

"We have a way out," she announced, her voice cutting through the murmurs.

Knox lifted a brow. "Care to share with the class?"

"We came here for a vehicle," she said. "And I found one. A

box van," she said. "It's big enough to get us out of here—and get these people to safety."

"How do you know this?" Knox asked.

"Miguel." She waited for him to say something.

"Are you going to tell us where it is?"

"The prisoners have it." She paused. "It's in a shop across town getting fixed."

Guynn stopped cleaning his gun, watching her now with sharp, assessing eyes. "You're suggesting we steal it."

Willow met his gaze head-on. "I'm suggesting we take it. But we can't just walk up and drive off. We need a plan."

Guynn set his gun down and pushed himself to his feet, nodding. "Then let's make one."

"You're going to take that murderer's word for it?" Knox spat. "He could be a plant. He could still be working with them for all we know."

Miguel hesitated before stepping forward. "I'm not. I've protected this group…" He looked away. "I tried anyway."

The pastor stepped forward. "He's telling the truth. He's put himself in danger to rescue people and go for food and water. We wouldn't be alive if it weren't for Miguel."

Willow studied Knox's face. He still wasn't convinced. She could tell by the deep furrows above his brow.

Miguel cleared his throat. "If you're serious about this, you need to know exactly what you're up against."

"Then let's start talking," Willow said.

Knox motioned toward the center of the room. "And we'll need a damn map."

A few minutes later, Willow leaned over an oversized town map spread across a makeshift table, tracing a finger along the worn edges of Caneyville's layout. Now, it was time to plan their attack.

"It won't be easy," Miguel said. "Q's got a grip on this town, and he's not the type to just let us walk away."

Guynn studied him. "Tell me about their setup."

Miguel leaned forward, jabbing a finger at a cluster of buildings on the map. "They're holed up at the old police station—reinforced, lots of cover. The sniper post is here, on top of the old drugstore. They've got a damn good view of the entire block. If you make a move, they'll see you coming."

Knox cursed under his breath. "So, we're basically sitting ducks."

"Not necessarily," Guynn said, his voice measured. He turned to Miguel, eyes sharp. "You've been here long enough. What do you know about their habits? Their routines? Anything we can predict?"

Miguel exhaled, rubbing a hand over his jaw. "They've got a bar near the east side of town. Only place left with booze. They keep it guarded, but they're complacent now. Lazy. If it goes up in flames, they'll panic."

Knox let out a low whistle. "Take out their liquor, and they'll be too busy putting out the fire to worry about much else."

The colonel dragged a finger across the makeshift map, his gaze calculating. "We can't just sneak out. We'll need time to get to the van, make sure it runs, drive back here, load everyone up, and roll out. That means keeping them distracted and busy."

Willow studied the map, her mind racing through the pieces falling into place.

"The fire pulls them east," she said. "They scramble to put it out. In the chaos, we take out the sniper post so they don't have eyes on the street." Her stomach clenched. "And we get those girls out of that school."

Miguel nodded. "Q's got at least two men keeping watch there, but if the bar goes up, they'll be called to help."

Knox cracked his knuckles. "Sounds like the perfect time to clean house."

"We don't have to kill them all." Guynn straightened. "We just need enough breathing room to get the hell out."

Utter Devastation

Willow met his gaze. "Then we make every shot count."

The plan was simple. Brutal. But it was their best shot.

"First, we set fire to the bar and force Quinnell's men into chaos. Second, use the distraction to take out the sniper post and rescue the girls. Third, we steal the box van, load up everyone, and get the hell out of this town." Guynn looked at each of them, his face grim. "We only get one chance at this. No screw-ups."

Willow nodded, gripping the edge of the table. "Let's make it count."

"You hit them, and they'll come hard," Miguel warned.

Willow didn't flinch. "Then we hit them harder!" She took a steadying breath as she stood at the front of the church basement, facing the terrified, weary townspeople.

The dim lantern light cast flickering shadows across their faces —faces lined with fear, exhaustion, and hopelessness. Some held on to their loved ones; others sat hunched over, arms wrapped around their knees. Every single one of them had suffered since Quinnell's men took over, and it showed. She had to make them see this wasn't just about her, Guynn, Knox, or Miguel. It was their fight, too.

"We have a plan," Willow said, her voice firm. "A real shot at getting out of here. But we can't do it alone."

A murmur rippled through the crowd. The pastor folded his arms, brows drawn together in concern. A few of the younger men, who had been quiet until now, leaned forward, listening.

"We're going to hit them where it hurts," she continued. "The bar is their biggest comfort, and we're going to take it away. That fire will force them to react and give us the distraction we need. While they're scrambling, we take out their sniper post so they won't see us coming when we move. And most importantly..." She met their eyes, her voice hardening. "We rescue the girls they took."

A few gasps. A few horrified looks. They hadn't known. Willow's gut twisted.

"These bastards don't stop. They take what they want and kill anyone who gets in their way." She gestured around the room. "You think staying here is safer? How long until they decide to come for this church? For your daughters and your wives?"

There were more murmurs. Some of the townspeople exchanged glances.

Guynn stepped forward. "We're not asking you to charge in with guns blazing," he said. "But we need your help. We need hands to clear a path and move supplies. If you can shoot, we need you covering us when we make our move."

Knox crossed his arms. "Or you can sit here and wait for Quinnell to come knocking. Up to you."

A heavy silence followed. Finally, a younger man—maybe in his early twenties, tall and wiry, with dark circles under his eyes—stood. "I'll help," he said. "I'm done hiding."

That small crack in their fear was all it took. Another man stood. Then a woman.

The pastor exhaled, rubbing his chin. "I can help get everyone into the van when you get here. We'll keep them hidden while you do what you need to do."

Willow nodded. It was something.

Not everyone was standing. Some still sat frozen in fear. Some would never move or fight back. But it didn't matter. They had enough backup now.

She looked at Knox, at Guynn, then at Miguel. "Let's get to work."

One man in particular had been quiet the entire time. He stood by his wife and two kids, arms crossed, his face pale and drawn. "My wife and I need to talk about this," he said.

Guynn nodded. "Make it quick."

The man never came back. Willow barely noticed, too deep in the logistics of ensuring every moving piece of their plan fit into place. Guynn ran over escape routes with Miguel, while Knox studied the map, muttering under his breath. They needed to move fast, hit hard, and be gone before Quinnell's men figured out what was happening.

FORTY-FOUR

Bee

Wild Plum Lake Estates
Highland, Arkansas
Day Five

Bee had known Bob wasn't going to let Amy's theft slide, but she wasn't expecting what came next. He and his men had dragged the young woman into the center of the street and forced her onto her knees. Her children sobbed nearby, held back by Bob's men.

"That's enough, Bob!" Bee snapped as she fought through the crowd.

Bob didn't look at her. He stood over Amy, gripping his rifle like a judge passing sentence. "She stole from all of us. That can't go unpunished."

Amy spat blood onto the pavement, holding her cheek where one of them had struck her. "Greg had plenty," she muttered. "My kids were hungry."

"So were a lot of people," Bob said as he towered over her. "But they didn't steal."

Utter Devastation

Bee stepped forward, her heart pounding, her voice sharp with fury. "Oh, so now it's not stealing because you're the one taking?"

"Call it what you want, but it's providing for the entire group," Bob said. "Not selfish hoarding. Not stockpiling for just one person or family."

"That's a lie, and you know it." Bee clenched her fists. "You're not providing for everyone; it's just a way of controlling them. You decide who eats, who suffers, who gets punished."

Bob's smirk faltered. His jaw tightened. "Someone's got to take charge, Bee. If I don't, people like Amy will think they can do whatever they want, take whatever they want, and this whole place will fall apart."

"Fall apart? Look around you, Bob! That's happening right here, and you're the reason why!"

Bob stepped closer, jabbing a finger in her face. "I warned you. Your bleeding heart, your waste of resources—this is the result. You didn't mind handing out food to a few of your favorites, letting the rest struggle. Now you want to stand there and tell them that keeping food back is suddenly okay?" He turned to the crowd, feeding their anger. "She's the hypocrite, not me."

Bee saw the shifting expressions of the people watching: uncertainty in some, blind loyalty in others. But the worst was the desperation—the fear that had made them willing to trade morality for survival.

"There's a difference between willingly sharing and breaking down doors to take what you want."

Bob chuckled. "That's old-world thinking. Now? It's survival of the fittest." Then he flicked his wrist, signaling to his men.

Amy screamed as they yanked her forward.

Bee lunged. "No!"

Mark caught her by the arm. "Bee, don't."

Bee struggled against his grip. "She has kids, Mark! They'll kill her!"

"If you step in now, they'll kill you, too. I'm not letting go, Bee."

Amy thrashed against the hands holding her. "Please!" she sobbed. "Just let my boys go—please!"

Bob turned to his men, his expression cold. "Strip her supplies. Every last thing."

"No," Bee whispered as they ripped the bag from Amy's shoulder, pried her wedding ring from her trembling fingers, and pulled the shoes off her feet.

"She and her kids get nothing," Bob said, "until they learn how to contribute."

Amy gasped as someone yanked her to her knees. Her boys screamed, arms reaching for their mother, held back by Bob's men.

Mark let go of Bee just as he stepped in front of Bob. "That's enough!" His voice boomed through the crowd, drawing startled looks. "You want to take her supplies? Fine. But you're not going to beat a mother in front of her kids."

Bob tilted his head, almost amused. "You think you can stop this?"

Mark squared his shoulders. "I won't let you do this."

The crowd went silent, waiting. Bob sighed and then gave another flick of his wrist. One of his men lunged forward and yanked Mark's rifle from his hands. Two men seized him from behind and wrenched his arms back. Mark struggled to break free, but a third man drove a fist into his stomach. Mark doubled over, coughing; his knees buckled as they held him in place. Bee screamed his name, but before she could reach him, one of Bob's supporters struck him across the face. Mark collapsed to the ground. Blood trickled from the corner of his mouth. Gretchen and her daughters rushed to his side as Bob turned back to Amy.

Bee clenched her fists so hard that her nails dug into her palms. Mark groaned, barely lifting his head off the pavement. Bee crouched beside him. She glanced back as Bob's men descended on Amy. There was nothing they could do. She looked away. Her voice trembled. "We have to go. Now."

"Go where?" Mark asked.

"Away from here, before they turn on us next."

"I agree," Gretchen said. "Girls, help me get him up."

As they did, Bob raised a hand, and his men stepped back. Amy collapsed onto the street, barely breathing. Bee stared at Amy's motionless body. The brutality. The indifference. This wasn't a community anymore. It was a regime.

Bee turned to Mark, her voice like ice. "We don't have a choice. Unless you want your daughters to watch them do that to you or Gretchen."

"Okay." Mark ran a hand through his hair. "Okay. We leave."

As Mark and Gretchen loaded their van to flee, Bee knew she had to try to convince Audree to leave with them.

Audree stood in the doorway to her house, arms crossed tightly over her chest. Bee knew immediately that something was wrong when she didn't invite her inside.

"It's not safe here anymore," Bee pleaded. "You know where this is headed."

Audree glanced toward the street and the chaos that had just unfolded. "And where do we go, Bee?" she asked, her voice weary. "Where is safe? Do you really think there's a place that isn't just like this?"

"No, I can't promise that. But we have to try. We have to find somewhere better."

"No, I don't think that exists anymore." Audree shifted from foot to foot. "But I do know one thing—Jimmy won't come back here while Bob's in charge."

Bee's heart clenched. "Audree—"

"Sorry, Bee." Audree met her gaze. "I appreciate everything you, Mark, and Gretchen have done for me and Josiah, but I can't leave without knowing that where we're going is safe from Jimmy. I can't risk him taking Josiah again."

Bee swallowed hard, fighting against the lump in her throat. She wanted to argue, to make her see reason, but she saw the fear beneath Audree's resolve.

"Just promise me you'll be careful. Don't trust Bob and his people. They aren't on your side."

"I know. I'm very familiar with people like him."

Bee turned and walked away, not looking back.

Mark's van was already packed when she returned. He stood by the driver's door, jaw tight, eyes scanning the street as if expecting Bob's men to appear at any moment. Gretchen's daughters scrambled into the van, their faces pale and wide-eyed. Bee slid into the back passenger seat behind Gretchen, clutching Penelope against her chest. The little dog trembled so hard that Bee could feel it through her jacket. She didn't know where they were going—only that staying wasn't an option anymore. One thing she knew for sure: she wasn't going to let Bob get away with this. Somehow, some way, she would stop him.

Gretchen exhaled sharply. "I think we should go to the police." Her voice wavered, but her frustration was evident. "This isn't right. We shouldn't have to abandon our home like this."

Mark let out a low scoff as he turned the key in the ignition. "And what do you think they'll do? Send a squad car to talk to Bob?"

"I don't know, but we can't just let him bust down doors and beat people in the middle of the street like that and get away with it."

Bee leaned forward. "We can try, Gretchen, but I have a feeling they already have their hands full with situations just like this."

Mark nodded grimly. "If we even find anyone at the police station to tell."

Silence settled over the van as the reality sank in. There was no one coming to help. No one to hold Bob accountable. They were on their own.

Bee stared out the window as they pulled away from the curb, her mind racing. "What about Ezra's place? He's in the hospital... the house is empty, and it's not far."

Gretchen glanced over her shoulder. "It's a good idea, but we should probably ask his permission first."

Bee nodded. "We'll swing by the hospital. If he's awake, I'll ask him."

Mark slowed as they neared the intersection to leave the subdivision. "What if—" He whipped his head to his left just as one of Bob's men stepped into view, rifle raised.

"Stop right there," the man shouted.

"Get down!" Mark shouted as he stomped on the gas.

FORTY-FIVE

Willow

Caneyville Friendship Church
Caneyville, Kentucky
Day Five

As midnight rolled around, they laid out their plan to hit Quinnell and his crew of inmates.

"We'll need a way to start the fire," Miguel said, glancing around the basement.

Knox smirked. "Lucky for you, I've got just the thing."

Guynn arched a brow. "That supposed to reassure me?"

Knox ignored him and rifled through one of the supply crates stacked in the corner. He pulled out a glass bottle, held it up to the lantern light, and grinned. "Ever made a Molotov cocktail?"

"You can't be serious?" Willow said.

Knox's grin widened. "Worked like a charm when I ran into a roadblock back near the Maryland state line. They had cars lined up, checking everyone who passed through. Didn't have enough firepower to shoot my way out, so I gave them a different problem to deal with." He shrugged. "Trust me, it'll work."

Utter Devastation

Miguel leaned forward. "What happened?"

"Let's just say they were too busy putting out fires to notice me slipping through the trees."

Miguel nodded. "We just need gasoline, cloth for wicks, and something to light them."

"We've got a vat of old cooking oil from the church pancake breakfast," the pastor said. "It's flammable."

Guynn nodded. "Get to it."

Knox turned to Willow. "I'm guessing you want me handling the van?"

She hesitated. The thought of splitting up gnawed at her, but the plan wouldn't work otherwise. They needed the van ready the moment they set the fire—there was no time for scrambling once things went loud.

"Help us take out the snipers at the school, and then take one of the locals with you to get the van," she said. "Someone who knows the back streets and alleyways. Stay low, stay fast. If we're not back in twenty minutes, don't wait."

Knox gave her a lazy salute. "Yeah, not gonna happen."

"You have to get these people out of here. We can handle ourselves. We'll meet you…" She grabbed the map. "Here," she said, pointing to a spot on the map. "The restaurant we passed on the way here. By the Save a Dollar store."

Knox stared back at her with his mouth open.

"Let's move," Guynn said. "We don't have much time."

"You're down with this plan?"

"It's as good as any. Just park the van behind the restaurant and wait," Guynn said.

The plan was straightforward. The execution? Not so much.

Jacob and Sam, two of the townspeople who had volunteered to help, joined them as they moved swiftly through the tunnel, their footsteps muffled by damp earth and old brick. Miguel led the way, his flashlight flickering against the rough stone ceiling. The passage stretched beneath the town, a relic of another era, but tonight, it was their way out.

"You guys watch the stairway," Willow said. "I'll set the girls free and get them to start yelling to draw out Quinnell's men on the roof." She knew that getting them alone and doing this quietly was their only option. Any loud noise—gunfire, shouting, a struggle—could alert Quinnell's men and ruin their escape plan.

They moved through the abandoned school, crept up the old stairwell, and paused at the last landing before the rooftop exit. Through the cracked doorway, they could see the two men, their shadows stretching long in the sunlight. One sat on the ledge, lazily scanning the town below with a rifle across his lap. The other stood near the access door, stretching his arms with a bored yawn. Miguel leaned in close, his voice barely above a whisper.

"The one on the left is Flint. He's one of Q's favorites. The other guy … I don't know his name, but he's just as mean."

Guynn's jaw tightened. "We take them both out fast. No time for hesitation."

"Where are they holding the young women?"

"In there." He pointed across the hall to a closed door.

Willow stepped out toward it, but Knox grabbed her arm.

"How do you know there's only two of them? They could have someone watching the girls?" he whispered.

"That's all that is ever here—same two guys."

Willow slipped across the hallway, turned the knob, and eased it open.

The door creaked slightly as Willow pushed it open, revealing a dimly lit room with a single flickering battery-powered lantern in the corner. Old, broken desks lined the walls, their surfaces layered with dust and grime. Two young women sat on the floor against the far wall, their hands bound to the legs of a desk with strips of cloth. Their faces were smudged with dirt, their eyes wide with exhaustion and terror. One looked barely out of her teens, her dark hair matted, dressed only in a torn T-shirt. The other, slightly older, was totally nude. She had bruises along her jaw and arms, as if she had fought back at some point and paid the price. They stiffened at the sight of Willow, their gazes darting between her and the doorway.

Willow held up a hand, speaking low and steady. "I'm here to get you out."

The younger girl shook her head frantically. "They'll kill you. They'll kill all of us."

Willow crouched beside them and pulled a knife from her belt. "Not if we kill them first."

The older girl swallowed hard, her voice barely above a whisper. "How?"

"I'm not alone. I brought help." Willow glanced toward the doorway. "We need to lure them down here. Make them come to us."

The girls exchanged a wary glance.

"They expect you to be quiet and compliant," Willow continued. "But if you start shouting—nothing alarming, just annoying—they'll come down here to shut you up."

The younger girl licked her split lips. "What do we say?"

Willow smirked. "Anything that'll piss them off but not set off any alarms."

The older girl nodded. "Like… hey, guys! We have to pee. Something like that?"

"Exactly," Willow confirmed. "They'll come to shut you up. And when they do, we'll be waiting."

The two girls hesitated, fear flickering in their eyes.

"You want out of here, right?" Willow pressed.

The younger girl's expression hardened. "Yeah."

Willow nodded, cutting through their bindings. "Then let's make some noise."

The girls moved toward the windows and positioned themselves where their voices would carry up to the roof.

"Hey! Guys!" the older one called. Her voice wavered at first, but she steadied herself.

The younger girl joined in. "Come on! We need to go real bad!"

"I'm going to shit on the floor again," the other yelled. Their voices echoed through the old schoolhouse, bouncing off the decayed walls.

Willow eased back into the hallway, her grip tightening on her knife as she slipped toward the stairwell where Knox, Miguel, and Guynn waited, crouched in the darkened hallway near the bottom of the stairwell. She heard footfalls on the treads above. She met Guynn's gaze and gave a small nod.

One of the lookouts groaned. "Shit," a gruff voice said. "What now?"

"They won't shut the hell up," his partner answered.

The first man growled. "Go see what their damn problem is."

Boots thudded down the metal stairwell, slow and heavy, the man descending just enough to peek his head around the corner.

Knox tensed. "Here he comes."

They all pressed against the wall, knives ready.

It was time to finish this.

The man bounded further down the stairs, cursing the girls and his fate in life. Willow moved first. She lunged, driving her knife deep into the soft space between his ribs. His breath hitched as Knox clamped a hand over his mouth and yanked him down the stairs. The man struggled, but the colonel stepped in, twisting the blade and silencing him for good. They eased him down onto the floor, his body slumping against the cold concrete.

Knox exhaled sharply. "One down."

Willow stepped back into the room with the girls. "Great job. It's working. One down. One to go. Keep going."

The girls started taunting the second guard, calling him by name and saying he was missing the party. Willow ran back to the stairs, where Guynn and Knox were helping Sam drag the first guard's body out of sight into a side room. They had just enough time to wipe the blood from their hands before the second lookout cursed above them.

"What the hell's takin' so long?"

Willow motioned for the girls to keep screaming. The voices rose in pitch, frantic, selling the panic.

The second man sighed. "Damn idiot can't handle anything by himself!"

Willow tensed as she heard boots on metal. As soon as his foot hit the bottom step, Miguel struck him in the throat. As he pitched forward, Jacob grabbed the man's rifle, wrenching it to the side to allow Guynn to drive his knife into the lookout's gut. He barely let out a grunt before Knox slashed the blade across his throat, silencing him.

Blood spilled onto the floor.

Willow exhaled. "That's two."

They stripped the bodies of weapons, gathering extra magazines, pistols, and knives. Miguel slung a rifle over his shoulder. With the lookouts down, the rooftop was theirs. One of the townspeople took a position there, covering them with the second rifle as they left the old school building. While Sam led the girls out back through the tunnel to the church, Knox, Jacob, and Miguel would set out to steal the van.

Willow and Knox hugged. He kissed her lips and then whispered in her ear. "I love you. Please be careful."

"I love you, too," she said. "I'll see you at the restaurant."

FORTY-SIX

Willow

Gary's Bar
Caneyville, Kentucky
Day Five

The bar sat on the outskirts of town, a two-story dive that had seen better days long before the world ended. Now, it was little more than a lawless den for Quinnell's men—a place where they drank, fought, and celebrated their newfound reign of terror. Bottles, crushed beer cans, and cigarette butts littered the parking lot. A rusted-out truck sat abandoned near the entrance, its tires slashed and its doors hanging open.

Guynn took a slow breath, gripping a metal pipe in his hand. "Okay. We do this quiet."

Willow nodded. "Or as quiet as setting a building on fire can be."

She and Guynn sped along the side of the building, sticking to the shadows until they were close enough to see the stubble on the guards' faces. The first leaned against the doorframe, dragging on a cigarette, while the other scuffed a boot through the gravel, an expression of boredom on his face.

Willow and Guyn waited. Minutes passed before the first guard turned and went inside. As soon as he shut the door, Guynn bent down, picked up a rock from the ground, and hurled it against the rusty pickup. It caught the remaining guard's attention, and he came to investigate. The colonel moved first. He gripped the metal pipe hard, waiting for the guard to pass their position. When he had, Guynn crept up behind him and swung.

CRACK!

The guard went down like a sack of bricks, the cigarette tumbling from his lips.

Willow sprinted toward the bar, her heart hammering as she pressed her back against the side of the bar beside the door. Through the grimy window, she caught a glimpse of the interior. It was a mess. There were broken chairs and a shattered pool table. A crack ran down the center of the mirror behind the bar like a spiderweb. Dark stains smeared the floor, and the bar itself was missing most of its bottles. It looked like Q and his men had already had a major brawl in there. The other guard was the only one left inside. Willow gave Guynn a thumbs-up, and he tossed a discarded beer bottle against the side of the building. The second guard took the bait.

"What the hell?" His boots pounded against the wooden floor as he raced toward the door. It flung open with force, and he stepped out. As he did, Willow hooked her foot around his ankle and swept his legs out from under him. He hit the ground hard, eyes wide, but before he could cry out, Willow drove her knee into his ribs and slammed the heel of her hand into his temple. Lights out.

Guynn grinned. "Nice work." He finished the job with a slice of his knife to the man's throat.

Willow smirked, brushing off her hands. "Not bad yourself."

They high-fived, a quick slap of mutual respect, before turning back toward the bar. Time to light the match. She grabbed one of the bottles from her pack, stuffed a rag inside, and soaked it in waste cooking oil. Guynn struck a match. The flame flared to life, small but hungry.

"No turning back now," he said, holding it out.

Willow didn't hesitate. She touched the match to the rag, which lit immediately. She reared back and tossed it against the back door of the bar. The bottle shattered against the wooden beams of the doorway, flames licking up the frame like they'd been waiting for this moment. Guynn threw another. Spreading fast, the fire devoured the dry, neglected interior. Willow and Guynn wasted no time in getting away from there. They stopped at the corner and looked back, watching the flames grow. Then, the first explosion rocked the night. A fireball erupted from inside, blasting out the front windows. Smoke billowed into the sky, thick and black, blotting out the sun. Willow and Guynn exchanged a glance.

"That'll get their attention," Guynn said.

They waited in the shadows for Quinnell and his men to take the bait. But then, gunfire rang out. Not from the police station where they were staying. From the direction of the church.

Willow spun toward the sound, her stomach dropping. Something had gone wrong.

Guynn swore under his breath. "Move! Now!"

He was huffing and puffing as they ran toward the church, weapons drawn, their boots pounding against the pavement. Willow wasn't sure he'd even make it there. The gunfire intensified, echoing off the surrounding buildings. Her throat constricted at the shouts of the prisoners over the screams of the town's residents. Guynn slowed as they neared the church's side entrance.

"Wait," he said, bending at the waist to catch his breath. "We can—" He sucked in a short breath. "Can't run in without a plan."

Miguel skidded to a stop beside her, chest heaving. "Terry sold us out," he growled. "He made a deal with them to get his family out of town."

Utter Devastation

"Who the hell is Terry?" Willow asked.

"One of the guys from the church. Q's crew was waiting for us at the garage—hiding to ambush us, but we saw them first and got away." Miguel tried again to catch his breath.

Knox's voice rang through the chaos, sharp and desperate. "We're pinned down in here! They're coming in through the back!"

Guynn didn't hesitate. He kicked the side entrance open, and they surged inside.

Willow ran into the sanctuary. Inside, the church was a war zone, filled with the deafening crack of gunfire and the desperate shouts of townspeople trying to survive. Knox was crouched behind the large wooden pulpit, firing methodically at the invaders. At the same time, the townspeople were scattered throughout the sanctuary, some seeking cover behind the pews, others clashing with the outlaws in a brutal, close-quarters fight.

Quinnell spun around to face her. His eyes locked onto Willow, a cruel smile twisting his scarred face. He raised his pistol, and a shot rang out.

Boom!

But she was already moving. She threw herself sideways, barely dodging the bullet as it tore through the wood inches from where her head had been. Splinters exploded outward, cutting into her cheek, but she wasn't aware of the pain. She hit the ground hard, rolling behind an overturned pew. Her ears were ringing from the blast.

Quinnell was already shifting, his movements unnervingly fast. He ducked behind another pew, using it as cover.

Willow's breathing came in sharp bursts as she gripped her pistol. She had to be smarter.

There was a sudden flash of movement.

She fired—two quick shots.

CRACK. CRACK.

The bullets slammed into the wooden pew where Quinnell had

been, sending more debris flying. But he had already disappeared into the shadows.

Miguel's voice rang out, sharp and urgent. "Willow!"

A chill shot through her. Willow spun around, eyes locking on Quinnell as he rose from his cover, pistol aimed at her.

Time slowed. Her muscles tensed, instinct screaming at her to move.

Miguel lunged in her direction, and simultaneously, a shot rang out.

Boom!

Miguel gasped as blood sprayed across the pew. A split second later, his body crashed into Willow, knocking her off balance before he crumpled to the floor.

Willow's world tilted. *No!*

Her mind went blank as she scrambled toward him, hands already reaching. Miguel clutched his chest, blood seeping between his fingers, dark and slick. Quinnell smirked, stepping back toward the door, his pistol still raised. "This," he sneered, "is why you should've stayed the hell out of my town."

Willow's grip on her gun tightened. Her anger boiled into something white-hot. She wouldn't let this bastard walk away.

Quinnell raised his gun to finish her.

But Willow was faster.

Boom!

Her bullet hit his shoulder and spun him sideways. Quinnell staggered, cursing through gritted teeth.

Boom!

The second shot buried itself in his chest.

Quinnell gasped, stumbling backward. Shock widened his eyes. He clutched his wound, swaying—but he was already dead on his feet. His legs buckled, and he collapsed. His pistol slipped from his grip and clattered onto the stone floor.

Willow spun, scanning the battlefield. Knox and the colonel

fought side by side, taking down the last of Quinnell's men with brutal efficiency.

A scream tore through the air. One of the girls from the school, her face smeared with dirt and fury, plunged a blade into the gut of one of Q's crew. He gasped, blood trickling from his lips before he crumpled. The other girl stood beside her, wielding a pistol taken from one of the dead prisoners. Their revenge was swift. Deserved.

Willow watched as the last prisoner fell. The church descended into silence. The fight was over.

"Miguel!" She spun around and dropped to her knees beside him. His breathing was shallow and uneven. His skin had already begun to pale. "No, no, no," she whispered, pressing her hands against the wound. "Stay with me, Miguel."

He gave a weak, lopsided smirk. "Didn't think I'd go out like this." He coughed, blood staining his lips. "Was supposed to rot in my cell. It's what I deserve."

"You don't deserve this," Willow snapped. "You saved me. You took a bullet meant for me. That makes you a hero."

"I'm—" He coughed blood. "I'm no hero."

Grim-faced, Knox crouched beside them. "Hold on, we'll get you patched up."

Miguel's grip tightened on Willow's wrist. His voice was weaker now. "Listen to me."

She leaned closer, her breath catching.

He exhaled. "In the attic. My journal." He swallowed hard. "Send it … to my mom. The address … in it."

Willow's throat tightened. She knew it might be months or years even before mail was running again, and the likelihood that his mother would still be at the same address was slim. But she nodded, fighting the burn in her eyes. "I promise."

His fingers relaxed. His chest rose—fell—and didn't rise again.

Willow swallowed the lump in her throat and looked at Guynn.

He met her gaze, nodding once. "At least he died on the right side of justice."

Willow shook her head. "The world needs people like him in times like these."

"I agree," Guynn said.

"Well, hell," Knox said, running a hand through his hair. "That didn't exactly go as planned."

"No, but we adapted, overcame, and accomplished the mission anyway."

The townspeople slowly emerged from their hiding places. Some whispered prayers. Some sobbed. Some just stared at the bodies of the men who had tormented them. One by one, they began moving the bodies out of their sanctuary. It was over. Caneyville was free. But Willow knew better than to believe in peace.

She stood, Miguel's blood still on her hands, and looked toward the attic. She had a promise to keep. Guynn stopped her just short of the attic stairs.

"You did good today, kid. You're a warrior."

She smiled and nodded. Willow placed her foot on the first tread and repeated the word in her head.

Warrior?

Was that what she'd become? A wide grin spread across her face. "Hell, yeah! I'm a warrior!"

FORTY-SEVEN

Willow

Caneyville Friendship Church
Caneyville, Kentucky
Day Five

The town of Caneyville was still in the bloody aftermath. As the smoke settled and the last remnants of gunfire faded into memory, the townspeople began to stir, their shock giving way to quiet determination. A few moved toward the smoldering remains of the battle to retrieve what they could, salvaging weapons, supplies, and anything useful. Others gathered near the church steps, murmuring amongst themselves and exchanging glances as if trying to put words to the impossible.

The bodies of the prison inmates lay stacked up outside the church. Once a sanctuary, it now bore the scars of war—bullet-riddled pews, shattered stained-glass windows, and dark patches of blood staining the wooden floor. Miguel was gone. Willow wiped her face as she stepped back from where he lay. Knox and Guynn stood a few feet away, silent, watching as the surviving townspeople comforted one another.

The pastor approached, his face haggard but relieved. "We can't ever repay you," he said, his voice hoarse from the smoke. "But I hope you know what you did here … it mattered."

Willow glanced at Miguel's body. "Not all of us made it."

"No." The pastor's gaze softened. "But he made a choice. He found his way back before the end. That's more than most ever do."

Willow nodded, swallowing the lump in her throat, still clutching his journal.

Somewhere down the street, a deep rumbling filled the air. Heads turned as a box van emerged from the alley, its engine coughing at first, then settling into a steady growl. A familiar face leaned out from the driver's seat—one of the townspeople, a wiry man in grease-streaked coveralls. He pulled the truck to a stop in front of the church and hopped down, wiping his hands on a rag.

"Here you go," he said, nodding toward Willow, Guynn, and Knox. "Quinnell's men were halfway through putting this thing back together when all hell broke loose. A few of us finished the job."

Guynn eyed the vehicle. "It runs?"

"Like a damn dream," the mechanic said with a tired grin. "Got a full tank, too. Least we could do for what you did here."

Willow exchanged a glance with Knox, then looked back at the truck. She didn't have words for the lump rising in her throat, so she just nodded.

The pastor placed a hand on the mechanic's shoulder. "They gave us a chance to start over. It's only right we do the same for them."

Knox wore a wide grin as he stepped over to the van and ran a hand along the reinforced metal siding. "Hell of a parting gift."

"Much appreciated," Guynn said, shaking the mechanic's hand.

The man nodded. "Take care of it. And take care of each other."

With that, the final goodbyes began. The townspeople gathered, some with tears, others too stunned to process everything that had just happened. One of the young girls they'd rescued from the school, now clothed in a donated oversized hoodie and jeans, broke from the crowd and ran to Willow. She threw her arms around her neck, clinging tightly.

"Thank you. If you hadn't rescued us today, I was going to kill myself."

That hit Willow hard. She stiffened for a moment, caught off guard by the raw confession. Then, slowly, she wrapped her arms around the girl and held on tight.

"You don't have to think that way anymore," she said, her voice thick with emotion. "You survived. And you're free."

She pulled back just enough to meet the girl's eyes, her grip firm on her shoulders. "No one gets to take that from you now. Promise me!"

The girl nodded, tears brimming. Willow gave her a small, reassuring squeeze before letting go.

"Be strong," Willow said softly. "For yourself. For the others. You've got a second chance—don't waste it."

Willow cast one last look at Miguel's journal in her hands, then at the town itself—still scarred and battered, but standing. Maybe, just maybe, they had given these people a fighting chance. Guynn took the driver's seat, Willow sliding in beside him in the middle, while Knox settled into the passenger-side seat. With a final wave to the people on the church steps, Guynn started the vehicle, and it rumbled forward, rolling out of town and toward the empty highway where they'd hidden the Jeep. Willow was relieved to find it just as they had left it.

Guynn and Knox took turns siphoning the last of the Jeep's gas and transferring their belongings to the box van. Willow lingered for a moment, staring at the Jeep. She remembered when it had been their only hope. Now, it was just another vehicle they had been forced to leave behind—another reminder that nothing was permanent anymore.

Twenty minutes later, Guynn eased the box van up the on-ramp onto Interstate 165 toward Owensboro, Kentucky. The road stretched endlessly before them, miles a mere blur. Willow sat with Miguel's journal open on her lap. His words pulled her in, raw and unfiltered. She picked it up, running her fingers over the worn cover.

If you're reading this, don't bother returning it. I'm dead.

The words hit differently now. He had started out as a kid with no hope and no choices, born into violence and surrounded by it until it consumed him. He hadn't believed in redemption, not truly. But in the end, he had fought for something bigger than himself.

She turned a page, reading his confession.

I have blood on my hands. I don't know if God forgives people like me. Sometimes, I wonder if he's even listening.

Willow closed the journal with a quiet snap. She stared out at the empty road ahead, her mind drifting through the countless battles she'd fought since the lights went out and the lives she had taken. Her mind replayed the first life she had taken. The man's face, contorted in pain, was burned into her memory—the shock in his eyes, the way his blood pooled across the pavement, dark and final. How many lives had she taken now? Two? Three? More? Somewhere along the way, she'd stopped counting—maybe because keeping track would make it all too real. Perhaps because it didn't matter. The dead were dead. Nothing would change that.

It wasn't an easy thing to take a life—even when it was necessary. Even when the man on the other end of the barrel deserved it. Quinnell had. That wasn't in question. But killing wasn't something Willow could just shrug off. It left a mark. A deep, invisible wound that didn't heal—not really. The first time had been the hardest, but it never got easier. The weight of it all pressed down on her, settling in her bones, making her question how much more she could take before she cracked.

War did that to people. She had read about soldiers in the past, how some had returned home as shadows of themselves, haunted by the things they'd done, the things they'd seen. The difference was that their wars had ended. Hers hadn't. This wasn't over. And as long as she was still in the fight, she couldn't afford to go to those dark places, couldn't let herself get lost in the faces of the dead. She had to remain battle-ready. There was no space for doubt, no room for hesitation. Not if she wanted to survive. Not if she wanted the people she fought for to survive. But the question lingered in the back of her mind, a quiet whisper she couldn't shake. How much more violence lay ahead? How much more was she capable of? And when this was finally over—if it ever was—would there be enough of her left to put the pieces back together and live with what she'd done?

A warm touch pulled her from her dark thoughts. Knox's hand found hers, their fingers weaving gently together. His thumb traced slow, soothing circles against her skin. She glanced at him. Neither spoke. They were both too spent—physically and mentally—for words. She shifted and leaned her head against Knox's shoulder. He winced, and she straightened immediately.

"I'm sorry. I didn't mean to hurt you."

"You didn't," he said. He pressed his hand against her cheek. "Please. Just rest."

She hesitated, then leaned back against him, closing her eyes.

"Rest now, sweetheart. I've got you," he whispered in her ear.

Three words had never felt so comforting. Her father had said them to her when she was young, when she was afraid to try something new and when she fell from a horse or scraped her knees climbing too high. She had never needed to hear them more than she did now. As independent and self-reliant as she was, Willow knew they all needed one another, and no one survived this life alone. She didn't know what she would have done had Knox not made it. Willow let the rumble of the truck lull her into sleep, exhaustion pulling her under as the miles slipped away. She woke to a nudge.

"Willow," Knox's voice was soft. "Wake up."

She blinked, rubbing the sleep from her eyes.

A rusty pipe gate blocked the road ahead. A long, winding driveway led into the property beyond. There was a farmhouse barely visible in the distance. The land stretched out in rolling hills. A man leaned against the gate, wearing a plaid shirt, jeans, and boots. A baseball cap featuring the Kentucky Wildcats sat low over his brow. He squinted as he stepped closer, shifting his rifle from one shoulder to the other.

"Didn't expect to see you, Byron," he said, a slow grin spreading across his face. "Come on up. Momma's got biscuits in the oven."

Guynn grinned, shaking his head. "Damn, I sure could use a real meal."

He pulled the truck forward. The gate creaked as the man shut it after they'd passed through. Willow sat up straighter, looking ahead. This was just another stop in a world that refused to settle. She wasn't the same person she had been before the lights went out. And she wasn't sure how much further she'd change before the journey was over. But, for the first time in days, she let herself breathe and believe that, maybe, they had a shot at something better.

Willow glanced down at Miguel's journal. Her fingers traced his name. She didn't know what came next, but one thing was certain—she would keep fighting. With a quiet exhale, she closed the book and lifted her gaze toward the rolling pastures. A thin mist curled over the fields. It clung to the wooden fence posts and the sleek coats of grazing horses. The sight stole her breath. A rooster crowed in the distance. From the barn, a horse let out a low, contented whinny. The sound blended with the faint laughter of children somewhere near the house. After everything—the destruction, the gunfights, the death—this place felt untouched, as if it had been waiting for them. The world had fallen apart, but here, life remained. It lifted something inside her, something she hadn't realized had been sinking under the weight of all they had endured.

Hope.

Not the naive kind that believed everything would return to what it once was. That world was gone. But standing there, surrounded by the quiet beauty of the land, she realized that even in a world turned dangerous and unpredictable, joy could still exist. Laughter could still ring out. Life could still go on. She let out a slow breath, allowing herself, just for a moment, to believe in that.

Above them, the aurora had begun to fade, its colors bleeding into the dawn—a lingering reminder of the CME that had upended everything. But for the first time in a long time, Willow wasn't staring at the sky in fear. She was looking ahead—at what life could become.

With one last glance at Miguel's journal, she tucked it away, squeezed Knox's hand, and turned her gaze toward the ranch. The golden light of morning stretched over the land, the rolling hills and sturdy wooden fences almost too perfect against the backdrop of a broken world.

"This place looks like something out of a travel magazine," Willow said.

Knox smiled. "Yeah, I can see the headline now: 'Come for the end of civilization, stay for the pretty lights.'"

Willow snorted.

Knox shot her a sideways grin. "Not your style? Fine. How about, 'Welcome to the apocalypse—now featuring mood lighting'?"

Willow tried not to laugh as they exited the box van and fell in behind the colonel, drawn forward by the comforting scent of bacon drifting through the farmhouse's window.

FORTY-EIGHT

Carson

Witch's Roost
Ramah, Colorado
Day Six

The morning after the battle, the town carried the weight of both relief and grief. The gunfire had stopped, the immediate danger had passed, but the scars of the fight remained—some visible, some buried deep. Smoke still lingered in the air while the wounded lay in makeshift recovery rooms under Doc's watchful eye.

Carson barely remembered being pulled from the battlefield, his body numb with exhaustion and pain. Doc had been relentless, forcing both him and Julie to rest. Carson had fought it at first—there was too much to do, too many people to account for—but in the end, his battered body had won. He and Julie had collapsed into an uneasy sleep, haunted by everything they'd seen, everything they'd lost.

Now, as he stepped into the town square, a strange stillness hung over the place that had been a war zone just hours ago.

Utter Devastation

People moved cautiously, speaking in hushed voices, as if afraid too much noise might shatter the fragile peace. Survivors gathered in small clusters, assessing damage, tending to the wounded, or simply standing in stunned silence, trying to process the new reality.

Across the square, Evelyn Corinton, Bruce's wife, stood on the steps of an old boarding house, holding Henry in her arms. The baby rested peacefully against her, his tiny fingers curled into the fabric of her worn sweater. Raelynn stood, clasping her leg, her small face still weary from all she'd endured. The moment Evelyn's eyes met Carson's, he knew she had something to say.

He pushed off the doorframe and crossed the street. Julie fell into step beside him. Evelyn watched them approach, her expression unreadable at first. Then, she took a slow breath and spoke.

"I know why Bruce came back," she said softly.

Carson stilled. The name—Bruce—hung between them like an unspoken ghost.

Julie touched her bandaged arm. "Why?"

Evelyn's eyes glossed with memories. "We had just found each other again." She shifted the baby in her arms, looking down at the little one as if the child had belonged to her all along.

"After … after the crash that took our kids, Bruce left. He couldn't face it. Couldn't face me. He ran. I hated him for a long time. Then, one day, he came back, and none of that mattered anymore. He came to me, thinking maybe—just maybe—I'd take him back." She let out a breath that shook with something deeper than sorrow. "And I did. I forgave him, and we were going to give it one more try—even talked about having more children."

Carson felt a weight press against his chest. He had seen plenty of people break under the weight of grief, but Bruce had tried. He had come back.

"He never stole from Casterman," Evelyn continued. "That was Alicia."

Julie's fingers tightened into a fist. "Alicia admitted it to us."

Evelyn nodded. "Bruce told Casterman he didn't take his drugs, but the man wouldn't hear it. Bruce tried to get me out before they could kill him, but he was already being hunted. He fled to Aurora to make a deal with one of Casterman's rivals—offered up information about this place in exchange for a way out for us both."

Carson's jaw clenched. "But he never got the chance."

"No." Evelyn let out a heavy sigh.

Silence stretched between them, the wind whistling through the shattered remnants of a town that had seen too much death. Evelyn looked up, her expression stronger now. Determined. She gazed down at Raelynn and Henry, still sleeping in her arms. "I think he brought them here for me…"

Julie's throat bobbed with emotion.

Carson studied the children—the way Henry clung to Evelyn's sweater, the way Raelynn shifted, nervous but hopeful, holding her hand.

"Their parents would have wanted them to have a home," Evelyn whispered. "And I want to give them one."

Jensen stepped up behind them, arms crossed. "There's no Child Protective Services out here," he admitted. "No social workers. If these kids have family somewhere, we don't know how to find them." He looked at Evelyn, his expression softening. "But if you're willing to take them in until we do?"

"I don't know if anyone's coming for them," Evelyn said. "But until we know for sure, I can be there. They deserve a home. A warm bed. A mother."

Her eyes met Carson's. "If Bruce had any good left to give, let it be this. Please."

Carson didn't know what to say.

Raelynn took a small step forward. She hesitated for only a second before she threw her arms around Evelyn's waist. Evelyn froze, her breath catching. Then, she knelt and wrapped her free arm around the little girl.

Carson exhaled, blinking against the emotion threatening to claw its way out.

Julie touched his arm. "It's a happy ending," she whispered.

Carson watched as Evelyn kissed the top of Raelynn's head, whispering something neither of them could hear.

He nodded. "Yeah. It is."

Carson swallowed against the lump in his throat as he stepped toward Raelynn. He glanced down at Henry. The little boy was just a baby, barely a few months old. He'd never remember his birth parents. Evelyn would be the only mother he'd know. Raelynn, however... She stood a little apart, her big brown eyes searching Carson's face.

Julie knelt in front of the girl, brushing a few strands of tangled hair behind her ear. "You're going to be okay," she said gently. "Evelyn will take good care of you. You don't have to be afraid anymore."

Raelynn didn't speak right away. She glanced up at Evelyn, studying her as if looking for some kind of reassurance. Then—slowly—she nodded. A tentative smile tugged at the corners of her lips.

Julie smiled back. "You're really brave, you know that?"

Raelynn nodded again, a little firmer this time.

Julie reached out, squeezing her tiny hand. "I'm so proud of you."

Raelynn hesitated, then threw her arms around Julie's neck, holding on tight. Julie let out a breath, her own arms wrapping protectively around the small girl.

"You don't have to worry about us," Julie whispered. "We'll be okay, too."

Henry let out a tiny sigh, completely at peace despite everything that had happened. Carson reached out one finger and brushed it against the baby's hand. Henry stirred, his tiny fingers curling instinctively around Carson's.

Carson's throat went tight.

Evelyn watched the exchange, her expression soft but knowing. She rested a gentle hand on Raelynn's shoulder and looked Carson in the eye. "I'll keep them safe. I promise."

Carson smiled and nodded. "Thank you."

∽

Later that morning, Carson and Julie stood at the edge of town, their supplies packed, their weapons secured, and Sophie tucked inside her carrier in the back.

Hannah's grandfather walked up, arms folded. "You sure you're heading out? You've got a place here, if you want it."

Carson shook his head. "Thank you, but we have somewhere to be, sir."

Hannah approached. "So soon?"

"We're anxious to get going. We need to check on our families," Julie said.

The doctor sighed, then stuck out a hand. "You ever need a safe place to come back to ... Ramah's yours."

Carson shook it, gripping the doctor's hand firmly. "Thanks, Doc."

He turned to Hannah. She gave him a knowing smile. "Be careful out there," she said.

"We'll try."

With one last glance at the town, Carson, Julie, and Sophie set off down the road. The journey wasn't over. Carson still had to get Julie to her family's ranch and then navigate through Dallas to convince his dad and stepmother to follow him to Arkansas. That might prove to be his toughest battle yet.

∽

Thank you for reading ***Utter Devastation***, the second installment of the heart-pounding *Black Sky Event* series. Click here or go to

Amazon.com to continue the journey in Utter Despair, book three of the series, coming in June.

Don't forget to sign up for my spam-free newsletter today to receive a FREE ebook copy of This We'll Defend: A Desperate Age Novella and be the first to know about new releases, giveaways, and special offers.

If you enjoyed *Utter Devastation*, I'd love to hear from you. Please consider leaving a review on Amazon. Doing so helps me find new readers who might enjoy the book.

Also by T. L. Payne

Black Sky Event Series

Utter Darkness

Utter Devastation

Utter Despair

Utter Decimation

Days of Want Series

Turbulent

Hunted

Turmoil

Uprising

Upheaval

Mayhem

Defiance

Sudden Chaos: A Post Apocalyptic EMP Survival Story

(Newsletter signup required)

Fall of Houston Series

A Days of Want Companion Series

No Way Out

No Other Choice

No Turning Back

No Surrender

No Man's Land

Gateway to Chaos Series

Seeking Safety

Seeking Refuge

Seeking Justice

Seeking Hope

Survive the Collapse Series

Brink of Darkness

Brink of Chaos

Brink of Panic

Brink of Collapse

Brink of Destruction: A FREE Novelette

Desperate Age Series

Panic in the Rockies

Getting Out of Dodge

Surviving Freedom

Trouble in Tulsa

Defending Camp

This We'll Defend: A Desperate Age Novella

(Newsletter signup required)

Reign of Darkness Series

Endure the Dark

Escape the Destruction

Evade the Ruthless

Engage the Enemy

Last Light: A Reign of Darkness Novella

(Newsletter signup required)

Conquer the Dark Series

A Reign of Darkness Companion Series

Collapse

Ruin

Carnage

Desolation

Resistance

Recompense (Coming Soon!)

About the Author

T. L. Payne is the author of over thirty-five bestselling post-apocalyptic series. T. L. lives and writes in the Osage Hills region of Oklahoma and enjoys many outdoor activities, including kayaking, rockhounding, metal detecting, and fishing in the many lakes and rivers of the area.

Don't forget to sign up for T. L.'s VIP Readers Club at www.tlpayne.com to be the first to know of new releases, giveaways, and special offers.

T. L. loves to hear from readers. You may email T. L. at contact@tlpayne.com or join the Facebook reader group at https://www.facebook.com/groups/tlpaynereadergroup

Join TL on Social Media

[Facebook Author Page](#)
[Facebook Reader Group](#)
[Instagram](#)
[Follow me on Amazon.com](#)
Website: https://tlpayne.com
Email: contact@tlpayne.com

Printed in Dunstable, United Kingdom

68142701R00173